The
REAL
DEAL

AMELIA HALL

The Real Deal

Copyright © 2024 by Amelia Hall

All rights reserved.

The characters and events portrayed in this book are fictitious. Any similarity to real persons, living or dead, is coincidental and not intended by the author.

No part of this book may be reproduced, or stored in a retrieval system, or transmitted in any form or by any means, electronic, mechanical, photocopying, recording, or otherwise, without express written permission of the publisher.

ISBN 978-1-7382562-1-1

Cover design and formatting by: Alt 19 Creative

Printed in the United States of America

Published by:
Invisible String Press

For Dallas

CHAPTER ONE

"I KNOW THAT IT doesn't look like much from the outside, but I really think this might be the perfect house for you," I say as I lead my clients, Ben and Jia, past the scraggly, overgrown lawn and up the sagging porch steps of the yellow Victorian that just hit the market this morning.

I bend down to enter the code into the lock box hanging from the front door. The house is a lot more rundown than it looked in the listing photos, but I'm still optimistic that this could be Ben and Jia's dream home. I hope so, anyway. Over the past few months, I've shown them nearly twenty properties all across Vancouver—mostly condos, all of them new or newly renovated—and they haven't liked a single one of them, for one reason or another. I figured that taking them in a totally different direction, showing them a fixer-upper, something they can put their own stamp on, might actually be the answer.

I pull out the key, then turn around and give them my peppiest smile, but when neither of them smiles back at me I start to worry that I've made a grave mistake. What if they blame me for wasting their time and fire me? I cannot afford to lose any clients—it's been months since I last sold anything and if I don't close a deal soon I'm fairly certain that I'm going to be living on instant noodles and boxed macaroni and cheese forever.

"You did say you'd be open to renovations," I remind them, hoping they don't hear the desperate edge to my voice.

"*Some* renovations, yes," Jia says, frowning at the broken porch railing, the peeling black paint on the door and, finally, at me. "But Piper this place looks like it's going to need a whole lot of work."

My heart sinks but I smile even harder at them. "It's definitely going to need some updating but if you can just keep an open mind then I'm sure that you'll see its potential." I could tell from the listing photos that the house has great bones—with a little love and care, it could easily be brought back to life. And a charming older home is so much better than a boring, cookie-cutter condo. Surely they will see that. "This is a great neighborhood," I add. "Houses don't come up on this street very often."

And this one is priced very well, practically a bargain—as much as anything can be a bargain in Vancouver, one of the most expensive cities in the world. Even factoring in the cost of renovations, this house is a great investment.

Jia shakes her head. "It's a lot further out than we'd like to be."

"East Vancouver isn't exactly the boonies," Ben says and I feel a spark of hope—maybe he's coming over to my side.

"It's not downtown, either," Jia replies.

And this, right here, is the problem, the main reason why the two of them haven't settled on a property yet: they can't seem to agree on where they want to live. It's hard for me to help them when I can't figure out what they really want.

"You know, if you buy a house then you won't have to deal with condo fees," I say. One of their complaints about the buildings I've shown them is the high monthly cost for amenities they don't think they'd ever use, like an indoor pool and a gym.

Ben scratches his chin, considering. "I guess we could always rip the whole thing down. Build something new."

My chest tightens. Everyone is always so quick to want to tear down older houses instead of putting the time and effort into restoring them. As a result, all the history is starting to disappear from the city. Not to mention that the mishmash of different housing styles make for weird, disjointed neighborhoods.

But while it pains me to think of this house being razed—the house deserves better than that—if that's what they want then I'll do my best to make it happen for them, even if it kills me a little. I'm certainly not in any position to be righteous—there are ten thousand other realtors in Vancouver. Ben and Jia can take their pick.

Jia sighs. "I guess we might as well take a look at it since we're already here," she says.

I slide the key into the lock and throw open the door before they can change their minds, then stand back to let them inside.

The house is bare of furniture, which is not usually a good thing—a vacant house makes it harder for buyers to visualize living there. If it had been my listing I would have talked the sellers into having it professionally staged. Still, empty is better than outdated or loud décor—either of which I know would immediately send Ben and Jia running for the hills.

As we wander into the living room, I fill them in on the basic details: built in the early 1940's, three bedrooms, three bathrooms, seventeen hundred square feet. No garage but finding street parking is usually not a problem. Walking distance to Commercial Drive, a vibrant, eclectic street lined with cool cafes and bars and boutiques.

"The floors are all original. They just need to be refinished," I say, tapping the toe of my black suede Gucci loafer against the scuffed parquet. These shoes are by far the most expensive thing I own and I still feel a little sick when I think about how much I paid for them. But the shoes are part of projecting an air of success, which is critical in this industry. Clients notice everything, including what I'm wearing (designer pieces I borrow from Rent the Runway) and the kind of car I'm driving (a grey Lexus, three-year lease, the monthly payment almost as much as my rent). It's those details that seem to reassure them that I know what I'm doing and that they're in good hands.

"I love the crown moulding," Ben says, glancing up at the decorative trim at the top of the walls. "It looks like it's in pretty good shape."

"The fireplace is nice," Jia says and I relax the tiniest bit—positive feedback, a good sign. But then she adds, "This room is a problem, though. It's way too small."

"That's an easy enough fix." I walk over to the wall that separates the living room from the dining area and rap on it. "You could knock this down," I say. "Make one big room."

Jia scrunches up her face, like she's trying to picture how that would look but can't quite see it.

We continue the tour. Ben and Jia are mostly silent, but silence is another good sign. Silence means they're thinking. If they hated the house they would have left already. I know that from experience.

"Some paint and modern light fixtures will really brighten this place up," I say as we walk down the hall towards the kitchen. "All it takes is some vision."

And money, of course—at least a few hundred thousand dollars of it—but I know they can afford it. I would never have brought them here otherwise.

My palms are sweating as I lead them into the kitchen. There isn't much worth saving in here, unless you're into ancient appliances, dull oak cupboards and worn yellow linoleum, and I'm expecting Jia to have a negative reaction but she surprises me by walking over to the huge picture window above the sink instead. The window overlooks the backyard, a large and private lot shielded from the eyes of prying neighbors by a tall boxwood hedge. A cherry blossom tree is planted in the corner and is just beginning to bloom with gorgeous pink-white flowers.

"Wow," Jia says. "It's like looking at a painting."

Ben is already opening the French door that leads to the patio. When we step outside, neither of them seem to notice the moss growing between the flagstones or the overgrown garden—they're too busy dreaming about all the summer mornings they'll spend sitting at a little wrought iron table, drinking coffee and listening to the birds. Or that's what I'd do, anyway, if I could afford to buy this house.

One day, I tell myself. *One day I'll be in a position to buy something just like this. And I will live there until I have to be carried out.*

I watch Ben and Jia as they explore the yard, knowing that the house has already won them over, so I'm not at all surprised when they walk back over to me a few minutes later and Ben asks me if there's any negotiating room on the price.

"One point eight is a bit high, don't you think?" he says. "Especially considering all the work we're going to need to do to get this place into shape."

I shake my head. Sadly, this is what almost two million dollars gets you in Vancouver. "Another home on this block sold for two-point six last year, but it was completely renovated," I say.

And because it's buyers' market, they don't have the luxury of time to mull this over—if they want the house, they're going to have to make an offer quickly because it will sell fast, probably within a day or two, possibly over the asking price.

Jia slides her arm around Ben's waist and looks up at him. "I think this house will make the commute worth it," she says. "I think that we should go for it."

Ben nods. "I think we should too."

This time when I smile at them they smile back at me.

We discuss the terms of their opening offer—thirty day close, contingent on inspection—and I leave them in the backyard to go inside and call the listing agent.

A bolt of excitement shoots through me. If I can make this deal happen—*please God let me make it happen*—I'm going to splurge and take my sister, Leighton, out for dinner to celebrate. Somewhere that doesn't have a drive thru.

I've just taken my phone out of my bag—a hot pink Chanel tote I rented from Bag, Borrow or Steal, all mine for the next month—when I hear the front door open. I frown. It's probably another realtor arriving early for their appointment. Sometimes an agent will show up when I'm still in the middle of a showing, which irritates me to no end. It's especially bad timing now that Ben and Jia have decided they want this house—the last thing I need is for another person to fall in love with it and force us into a bidding war.

I walk into the living room, preparing to tell the other agent to please wait outside until we're finished, but when I see who has come through the door I stop in my tracks and all the breath leaves my lungs.

Aiden Miller is standing in front of me, relaxed and tanned and as hot as ever in a peacock blue blazer worn over a white t-shirt, slightly rumpled khaki pants and grey leather sneakers. His dark blonde hair is a bit longer than I remember and when our eyes meet, a slow smile spreads across his face.

My chest tightens. I'd forgotten about Aiden's eyes. How could I forget about his eyes? They're two different colors, one blue and one hazel. Heterochromia. I looked it up after we first met, back when I thought something might happen between us.

And for one heart stopping moment I think that Aiden's come here for me, that maybe, *finally*, he's come to his senses and tracked me down so he could apologize for what happened two years ago. I feel my mouth automatically curving to return his smile but then my brain swoops in and saves me, reminding me that the simplest explanation is usually the right one…and in this case, the simplest explanation is that Aiden is the inconsiderate realtor showing up early to his appointment.

My stomach drops. I'm angry at myself for thinking, even for a second, that he might be here for me. That he might miss me, even a little. That he might be sorry for what he did.

"Piper," he says. His voice exudes warmth, like he's genuinely glad to see me. Which cannot be the case considering how we left things. But then again, Aiden's always been good at hiding his true feelings.

I quickly strengthen my resolve. I'm not going to be won over just because he has gorgeously hypnotic eyes. I can't forget that this is *Aiden Miller*, the guy who stole my very first client. Because of him and what he did I almost gave up on real estate. I almost gave up on myself. Something like eighty-five percent of real estate agents fail in the first five years and thanks to Aiden I could have easily become a statistic.

"I didn't realize you were back," I say flatly. Last I'd heard he'd quit his job and was travelling the world, living his best life and Instagramming every perfect moment. And that was fine with me. Better than fine, actually, because it meant that there was zero chance that I'd ever run into him anywhere. It meant that I could forget all about him.

Not that it worked very well. As embarrassing as this is to admit, I've kept track of him over the years, creeping on his social media, watching him adventure his way through China, Vietnam, Bali. I finally stopped checking up on him a few months ago after he posted a photo of himself lying on a hammock in Thailand, a straw fedora covering his eyes, no shirt to show off his chiseled chest and the raven tattoo on his right bicep. That photo did something to me, made me feel things for him that I didn't want to feel anymore, and I swore I'd never look at his account again. And I haven't. Although now I wonder if I should have—at least then I might have had a heads up that he was back in town. I could have prepared myself.

"I got tired of traveling, believe it or not," Aiden says. "Felt like it was time to come home."

Tired of traveling to amazing places, living on his own calendar, with no obligations to anyone? I want to roll my eyes at him but that wouldn't be professional—and I plan to keep things between us strictly professional this time around—so I look past him towards the door. "Are you here with a client?"

"Yeah, he's outside finishing up a phone call," he says. "The door was open so I figured we would just pop in and..."

He trails off when he notices the way I'm glaring at him. God, it's so typical. Aiden thinks he can just walk in anywhere he pleases with no regard for other people's time or plans. He's lived his entire life with the knowledge that no door is truly closed to him.

I wonder what that's like.

He clears his throat. "Sorry," he says. "I shouldn't have just barged in here. That was rude. It's just I have a really tight schedule today."

I don't care one bit about his tight schedule but his apology does knock me off guard. He gives me a hopeful smile, obviously trying to charm me. Well, I won't be charmed. I'm not as naive as I was two years ago. Aiden Miller may give off the air of a surfer with his too-long sun-bleached hair and laid-back demeanor, but he's actually a shark. I need to remember that.

I should kick him out, demand that he wait outside until I'm done with my showing, but I'm curious about who he's brought to see the house so I know what I'm up against. This house is pricey and out of reach for most buyers, but the kind of people Aiden usually represents are in another stratosphere altogether—they're interested in fifteen-million-dollar mansions in Point Grey or West Vancouver, spacious, impeccably decorated homes with stunning views of the North Shore mountains or the Pacific Ocean…not a simple three-bedroom Victorian that needs a lot of work.

I'm about to press him about his client when Aiden glances at the yellow silk scarf around my neck. I can tell from the way his expression softens that he knows about my surgery and my cheeks instantly go up in flames.

I guess I should have expected that someone would tell him—Vancouver is a relatively small city, we have a lot of mutual acquaintances and realtors are a gossipy bunch. And while it's not a big deal—plenty of people have had thyroid cancer, it's highly treatable and nothing to be embarrassed about, obviously—I'm still very self-conscious about the long, crescent shaped scar at the base of my throat, an inch too high to be hidden by a t-shirt. Leighton has been after me to ditch the scarves, but I'm just not there yet.

"How are you?" he asks.

My mouth tightens. I don't want to talk about this—not with anyone, but especially not with Aiden Miller.

"I'm fine," I say firmly.

And I am fine. Mostly. The cancer is gone and I'm so grateful for that, but if I'm totally honest, I'm not as over the whole experience as I wish I was. My scar is a constant reminder that life is unpredictable, that there are so many things that are out of my control, that my body could decide to betray me again and the cancer could come back. No matter how many times my doctor has reassured me that it's not likely to happen, that the odds are good that I'll live a long and healthy life, there's still a chance it will return. There's always a chance.

"Well, I'm very glad to hear that you're alright," Aiden says. "You know, I—"

"I need to make a call," I say, cutting him off to let him know the subject is closed.

"Oh. Sorry," Aiden says. He swallows. "I'll get out of your way."

Two apologies in less than five minutes from him, neither of them for the thing that he should actually be sorry for. I'm sure that's because he thinks that he didn't do anything wrong. To him, what happened wasn't personal, it was just business.

I was just business.

But just as he's about to leave to wait outside and give me some privacy, the front door opens and Tim Davidson walks in.

My heart drops. Tim Davidson is a big-deal developer. He's built several luxury condo buildings and mansions all over the city, although as far as I'm aware, he's never had a project this far east. The fact that he's looking at this house is not great news for Ben and Jia. If Tim decides that he wants to buy it then my clients don't stand a chance.

"Tim," Aiden says. "Have you met Piper Anderson?"

"Yes, we've crossed paths a few times," Tim says, extending his hand. "It's good to see you."

I shake his hand, surprised and flattered that he remembers me—in his line of work he meets a lot of people. It's nice to know that I made an impression on him.

"Piper's in the middle of a showing," Aiden says, clapping his hand on Tim's shoulder. "My fault, I should have double checked our appointment time. We'll have to wait outside for a few minutes while she finishes up."

"Oh, that's alright," I say, smiling at Tim. "Feel free to have a look around."

I'm not doing this for Aiden, I'm doing it because if I'm ever going to break into the big time I need people like Tim Davidson to like me. All it would take for me to get my foot in the door is for him to recommend me to a few of his powerful friends and I'd be set—the amount of commission I could make if I sold luxury properties would completely change my life.

Aiden raises an eyebrow and I know that he's onto me but I don't care. Once upon a time, his opinion may have mattered to me but it doesn't anymore. What matters is having enough money to take care of myself and my sister. And nothing—certainly not Aiden Miller—is going to stand in my way of that.

"Thanks for being so accommodating," Aiden says, the corner of his mouth lifting.

"Of course."

I wait until they've disappeared down the hall before I slip out of the house to call the listing agent, crossing my fingers that Tim won't want this house.

CHAPTER
TWO

LEIGHTON HANDS ME a blueberry smoothie before plunking down beside me on the couch, a well-worn dark green velvet sectional that she found at an estate sale last year. "There are no coincidences, Pips," she says. "The universe clearly wanted you to run into Aiden."

I roll my eyes. My sister thinks that everything is the result of divine intervention. "Why would the universe do that to me?" I reply. "Haven't I been punished enough already?" I mean, I had *cancer*, for goodness sake—you'd think that going through a life-threatening illness would entitle me to some good luck. And running into Aiden again was definitely not good luck.

"Maybe you need closure." Leighton rests her bare feet on the edge of the round Ikea coffee table she painted to look like a mushroom. The coffee table fits in perfectly with the rest of our apartment, which is all pale green walls, butterfly throw pillows and a zillion plants. "Fairycore" is not exactly my aesthetic but that doesn't matter—it makes my sister happy and that makes me happy. Leighton's given up so much for me the least I could do was let her decorate our place. Even if it means I now live in an enchanted forest.

I shake my head. "I don't need closure." I need for Aiden to stay far away from me. I need to never see him again.

I need to forget all about him.

Leighton sighs. "You know, holding onto anger is like drinking poison and expecting the other person to die."

I take a sip of the smoothie to give myself a moment before responding. My sister is full of platitudes and cross-stitch quotes and sometimes it makes me a little crazy. I love her to pieces and I know that she means well but we move through life very differently. We are pretty much polar opposites, not just in temperament but in appearance, too. Leighton inherited her dad's blonde hair and flawless skin, his tall, willowy frame and his cupid-bow lips, while I'm a carbon copy of my own father—pin-straight dark brown hair, vampire-pale complexion and blue eyes, too short to reach the top shelf of the kitchen cupboard without a footstool.

Also unlike me my sister can't stand silence, so when I don't immediately answer her she pokes me lightly in the arm and says, "You have to let it go. For your own sake."

"I have let it go," I say, wishing that I'd never brought Aiden up. Despite her unshakable, always look-for-the-silver-lining belief that 'everything happens for a reason' my sister worries about me a lot, to the point where she's put her own life on hold to take care of me. She's convinced that negative feelings will cause me to relapse and I usually just try to pretend that everything is fine—even when it's far from it—so I don't stress her out.

I hate that she worries about me so much. I'm the older sister—Leighton is eight years younger than me—so I'm used to looking out for her, but when I got my diagnosis last fall our roles suddenly switched. When we found out that I'd need surgery followed by a few courses of radiation, Leighton immediately dropped out of university and moved out of residence to live with me. I tried to talk her out of it—I didn't want her to give up her scholarship, never mind her life, for me—but she was adamant. And while I'm grateful that she didn't listen to me—I don't know how I would have gotten through those terrible months without her—I feel guilty, especially because without her scholarship we don't have enough money to send her back to school.

But we will. I'm going to see to it that my sister gets back on track without the burden of thousands of dollars in student loans that would take her the rest of her life to pay off. I won't let her give up on her dream of becoming a naturopathic doctor.

Leighton narrows her eyes. "Pips. You're forgetting who you're talking to," she says as I set my smoothie on the coffee table and grab my phone to make sure that I haven't somehow missed a call, even though I know the volume on my ringer is turned all the way up. I've been on edge all day waiting for the listing agent to respond to Ben and Jia's offer on the house. "I can tell when you're lying," she adds. "Your nose gets all scrunched up."

I sigh. "Okay, fine," I say. "Maybe I am still mad at Aiden, but I'll work on that, okay?" I will myself not to wrinkle my nose.

"You know, you haven't seen him in a few years," Leighton says. "Maybe he's changed. I'll bet he's really sorry for what he did."

"I doubt that," I murmur. My sister is someone who likes to believe that everyone is essentially good at heart and she forgives very easily, even when the person doesn't deserve it, and while I admire her ability to get over things quickly and always look for the best in someone, that's just not me. I know how to hold a grudge. In order for me to even entertain the idea of forgiving Aiden for stealing my client I'd need him to apologize for what he did…and he hasn't done that. And I'm not holding my breath that he ever will.

I'm sure there are some people who think I'm being too sensitive, that it was just business and I have no right to be this upset—technically, I hadn't yet signed the client so she was, for all intents and purposes, fair game. What I can't get over, though, is that Aiden knew how hard I'd worked to try and get that listing, he knew how many doors had already been slammed in my face as I tried to get a foothold in the market. He knew all about that but he didn't care. He swooped in and stole my client anyway.

He was my friend—or I thought he was—and that's why I feel so betrayed. I went to him for advice and he stabbed me in the back. How am I supposed to forgive him for that? And why would I even want to?

"Finish your smoothie." Leighton nudges my glass towards me before standing up and stretching. "I'd better get going or I'll be late for work," she adds unenthusiastically.

A pang of guilt zips through me. My sister hates her job—she works as a bartender at the Irish pub down the street—and she's only doing it because I can't afford to carry us both financially yet. But the commission from this sale should be enough to take care of her tuition and other expenses for at least a year. She'd be able to quit her job and concentrate on her studies full-time.

"Don't wait up," Leighton says, leaning over and booping me on the nose with the tip of her finger. "And don't forget to take your supplements!"

I nod. She has me taking ten different vitamins to boost my immune system and supposedly keep me from ever getting sick again, everything from vitamin D to garlic. She's also very bossy about what I eat, tossing out everything that isn't a fruit, vegetable or whole grain. While I appreciate her dedication to keeping me healthy, she has gone a bit overboard.

My sister picks up the Frank and Oak tote bag that she uses as a purse, slips into her black Toms and is out the door just as my phone starts to ring.

I look at the screen and my heart starts to pound. It's Viyaan Patel, the listing agent. This is it—the call I've been waiting for all day. The call that could change everything for me and my sister.

I take a deep breath and cross my fingers, then answer the phone.

"Hi Viyaan," I say. *Please, please, please let him be calling with good news.*

"Piper," he says. "How are you?"

Viyaan and I used to work together at Pinnacle Realty before he left to form his own brokerage. He's in his late forties, a nice guy with a deep, radio DJ voice. He is well known on the east side of town, a minor celebrity thanks to his bus shelter ads—Viyaan in a navy blazer and red tie, his arms crossed, a jovial smile on his face. *Trust me to bring you home* scrawled in big red letters under his photo.

"I'm good," I say.

"So listen," Viyaan says, dispensing with the small talk. "We have another offer on the property and it's a really strong one."

I sag against the couch. Viyaan can't share who the other client is or the terms of the other offer—it's confidential—but I'm certain that it's Tim Davidson. I knew there was a very real possibility that this could happen, of course, but I'd been holding out hope that Tim would decide that the house wasn't for him.

"If your clients want to submit a new offer, then we'd be happy to take a look at it," Viyaan adds. "But I'll be honest, they're going to need to come up quite a bit in order to compete."

I frown. Ben and Jia came in at the full asking price, which means that Tim must have offered well over that. He must really want this house. Trying to outbid him will be like going up against Goliath—he has all the money in the world to make this deal happen. And he doesn't like to lose.

"I'll call them right now and get back to you with their response as soon as possible," I say, forcing myself to keep my voice steady.

"Great," Viyaan says.

I hang up and stare into space for a minute, trying to gather my thoughts. This isn't the first time I've had to break news like this to a client—I've done it plenty of times before, it's the nature of this business—but while it's never easy, I'm not usually this upset about it. I know that my reaction is tied to how much I really need this commission, but I'm also really disappointed for Ben and Jia. This is the first place they've found that they've even wanted to put an offer on and now they just might lose it to a developer. To *Aiden Miller's* developer.

This really sucks.

I take a deep breath and call Jia. She picks up right away and puts me on speaker so I can talk to both of them at the same time.

"Hi," she says. "Have you heard anything?"

"Yes, the listing agent just got back to me," I say. "Unfortunately, there's another offer on the table."

I fill them in on my conversation with Viyaan and let them know that if they want to stay in the running they'll have to come up significantly in price.

"We don't want to get into a bidding war," Jia says, sounding peeved. "We're already almost at the top of our budget as it is. We can't go much higher, not with all the renovations we'd have to do to make the place livable."

"What if we offered them an extra twenty-five thousand dollars?" Ben asks.

"Ben. No," Jia says.

"What? That's not all that much in the long run, all things considered," he says. "I really don't want to lose this house. I know that it's the one."

I swallow. He's already so emotionally attached. I don't think twenty-five thousand dollars will make a difference, though—even if it's more than what Tim initially offered, Rob will just go back to him for a counter and Tim will outbid us again. I'm pretty sure that Ben and Jia aren't going to win this one, but I need to at least give them the opportunity to counter so they can feel like they went down swinging.

"What do you think we should do, Piper?" Ben asks me.

"Let's go back to them with your best and final number," I reply. There's no point in dragging out this negotiation in increments. And who knows, maybe a miracle will happen—maybe Tim will decide it's not worth it and he'll bow out. Maybe I'm calling this game too early.

Jia reluctantly agrees to go back with an extra twenty-five thousand dollars. "But if they don't take it then we're out," she says firmly.

It's almost eight o'clock when I text Viyaan with our updated offer—there's no such thing as nine to five in real estate, we all keep odd hours and are tied to our phones, especially when we're working on a deal. It's hell on the social life and part of the reason I've been single for the past year—although my sister says that I'm just using work as an excuse not to put myself out there again. She's not entirely wrong.

Feeling anxious, I get up and pace around my apartment, waiting for Viyaan to respond to the new offer, knowing that I might not hear anything until tomorrow—his clients might want time to consider both deals before they make a decision. I could be in for a long night.

I go into my bedroom and dig in my closet for the family-sized bag of BBQ chips that I keep hidden from Leighton and take them back to the living room, along with my laptop. I'm about to fire up Schitt's Creek and eat my feelings when my mind wanders back to Aiden and his role in all of this. I know it's a little unfair to rest all the blame on him—he's only doing what his client instructed him to do—but I can't help it. This situation feels infinitely worse because of his involvement.

What are you trying to do to me Universe? Why do I have to go up against Aiden Miller, of all people?

I'm halfway through David and Patrick's wedding—and the bag of chips—when Viyaan calls me back.

"Piper, I'm afraid I don't have good news," he says.

I squeeze my eyes shut as he informs me that his buyers have accepted the other offer and although I was expecting this, although I knew in my heart that this was probably the way this was going to go, my stomach still turns over.

It's a quick conversation—there's not much more to say after that—and I thank him and hang up, glad that Leighton isn't here to see me shot-putting her throw pillows around the room. I grab one of the pillows, hold it against my face and scream into it. Months and months of ferrying Ben and Jia around to showings and open houses all over the city, they *finally* decide on a place and it's cruelly snatched away from them. Now we have to start all over. Actually, this is worse than starting over because now that they've fallen in love with this house I'm not sure how I'll find something else in their price range that will ever compare.

Not to mention, that beautiful old house is going to be torn down, replaced with some ugly modern eye sore.

I lower the pillow from my face. I was so close. *So close* to sending my sister back to school and now she's going to be delayed for another year because I lost this deal. I think of Aiden, about the smug look on his face when he hears that he won, and I feel another scream building inside of me. It's so unfair. This commission won't make any kind of difference in his life. Not in the same way it would in mine.

Once I've collected myself—which takes several minutes—I call Ben and Jia. My mouth is dry as I tell them that they lost the house. I hate this part of my job.

Silence…followed by Ben, sighing heavily. "Well, that's very disappointing," he says. "I really thought we'd get it."

"I know it's a letdown," I say. "But I'm going to find you some-thing even better. I promise." I pull up MLS as I'm speaking to them to check if there's any new listings in the same area. Now that I know what they like I can narrow the search—who knows, maybe I'll strike gold and find another fixer-upper in the same neighborhood for around the same price.

"I don't know," Jia says. "Maybe this is a sign. I mean, I loved the house and I know I said I wouldn't mind the commute to work but I've been thinking it over and it would definitely suck."

"It would have been worth it," Ben says.

"You can say that because you're not the one who would've had to do it," she snaps.

I chew my lip. Buying a property is stressful—one of the most stressful events in life for most people—and it can cause couples to bicker. Most of them don't do it in front of me, but I have had to mediate occasionally.

"How about we check out some more condos," I suggest, hoping to distract them from their argument and get the conversation back on track. "There are a few pre-construction buildings downtown that we haven't looked at yet. We could visit their showrooms."

"I'm not sure I want to live in a condo, anymore," Ben says. "I think I want a backyard. And like you said earlier, Piper, if we buy a house then we won't have to deal with monthly fees."

I could kick myself. I never should have steered them away from condo-living—what was I thinking? I should have just kept my mouth shut. Now I've confused them and they're even further apart.

"I didn't expect this to be quite so stressful," Jia says. "Maybe we need to take a break. I think we should just continue renting for a while until we figure out what we want."

My heart sinks. This is my worst-case scenario. They're dis-appointed that they lost the house which has translated into disappointment in me, even though none of this is my fault. And despite their reassurances that they'll reach out when they're ready to start looking again, I know that this is probably the last time I'll hear from them. When they decide to try again they'll do it with another agent.

After the call ends I let out a long breath, trying to stave off panic. At the moment I have no other serious clients and no active listings. There's not much I can do about that right now, but tomorrow I'm going to have to work my contact list, see if I can drum up some new business. But tonight…tonight I'm going to get drunk. Very, very drunk.

I'm about to get up and retrieve the bottle of tequila I keep in my room, liven up this blueberry smoothie Leighton made me, when it occurs to me that maybe there is something I can do.

Aiden just cost me my clients. He might not have set out to do it, it might not have been deliberate (this time) but once again, my life is worse because of him. So it's only fair that I try and even the score.

And so I google Tim Davidson. Poaching another realtor's client is against the code of ethics and seriously frowned upon in this industry, but that didn't stop Aiden from doing it to me two years ago.

If I'm ever going to level up I need to associate with people who can help my career and get me to where I want to be. I could call Tim, I guess, and try and schedule a meeting, but even if he agreed to see me I'm certain that his schedule is packed for months and I don't want to wait that long.

Halfway down the results page I spot a link to Davidson Properties Instagram account. I click on it. There's a post from nine minutes ago—Tim at some fancy charity event at the Westin Bayshore, a gorgeous hotel on the Coal Harbour waterfront. And standing beside him is Aiden, dressed in a black tux, the ends of his blue bow tie hanging loosely around his neck. Those different colored eyes stare into the camera in a way that makes my pulse race, his wild blonde hair mussed from running his fingers through it. He's smiling in that annoyingly confident way, like the world belongs to him and nothing— and no one—will ever be able to change that.

I get up off the couch.

It's time to show Aiden Miller that he's not the only shark swimming around in this ocean.

CHAPTER THREE

SITA IS WAITING for me at the hotel entrance when I pull up in a Lyft. I wasn't quite brave enough to crash this event alone so I called her and begged her to come with me. Fortunately she was dying for an excuse to leave her husband and toddler at home for the night and agreed to meet me here. And I'm so grateful—unlike my sister, who would try her best to talk me out of what I'm about to do, Sita believes in revenge.

I thank the driver and get out of the car. Sita's eyes widen as I walk towards her in a sparkly midnight blue dress and strappy gold sandals.

"I'm having a flashback," she says, laughing a little. "That is your prom dress, right?"

I flush. Of course she'd remember that I wore this dress to prom. Sita has a photographic memory when it comes to clothes.

"I was desperate," I say. Almost everything I own (or rent) is business casual, not exactly suitable for a gala, so I had to go with what I had and what I had was my prom dress. It's a little too tight and a little too young for me, plus I had some trouble getting the zipper up, but it was the best I could do on such short notice.

"It's not terrible," Sita says, which is actually pretty high praise coming from her—she's a personal shopper at Holt Renfrew and has strong opinions about what clothing looks best on different body types. "Although it would look much better if you got rid of that necklace," she adds.

My fingers automatically fly to the chunky gold chain around my neck. I can't argue that it doesn't compliment the dress but it covers my scar so there's no way that I'm taking this necklace off.

"Piper." Sita's expression softens and she reaches for my hand, drawing it away from my neck. "I'm sure no one would even notice your scar."

I shake my head. That's just not true. My surgeon promised me that my scar will eventually fade, almost the point where it won't be noticeable, but it's still pink and raised and obvious. I'm just not ready for anyone to see it. Not my oldest and dearest friend, not my sister, and certainly not a roomful of strangers.

Sita sighs. "Alright. Keep the necklace. It's your fashion funeral," she says, but she smiles and loops her arm through mine.

Normally we're about the same height, but Sita's wearing sky-high black Louboutin's that put her a few inches taller than me. She's also wearing a gorgeous fuchsia jumpsuit that I'm sure is from some fabulous up-and-coming European designer and her long dark hair is twisted back from her face in a braided bun. Her makeup is perfect, her light brown skin has that perfect hot-girl summer glow. I'm more than a little jealous that she looks so stunning and perfectly put-together when I know for a fact that, like me, she was lounging around in sweatpants an hour ago.

We walk through the glass doors and into the marble lobby of the Westin Bayshore. Coal Harbour is one of my favorite areas of the city, on the edge of Stanley Park with a beautiful marina and a view of the North Shore mountains. Heaven to me is a summer morning sitting on a bench on the seawall, drinking a maple latte and watching the float planes land, although I've been working so much lately that I haven't made time to do that. I make a silent promise to myself that I'm going to come back here soon. Maybe I'll have sold a house by then and I can even come and stay at this hotel.

"What are we going to say if someone wants to see our tickets?" Sita whispers to me as we follow the event signage for "One Enchanted Evening", our footsteps echoing down the long hall.

"I'm hoping that won't happen," I reply. It's close to ten o'clock— the formal part of the night should be well over by now and with any luck all of the guests will be pleasantly tipsy, if not downright drunk. Since hundreds of people are attending this event I'm betting that we'll be able to slip in unnoticed.

Sure enough, the registration table outside the ballroom has been abandoned and Sita and I walk through a pink and white wisteria tunnel and into the party with no problem. Once inside we survey the crowd. As I expected, there are a million people here and thankfully all of them are too busy chatting, making their bids at the silent auction tables filled with high-end items or listening to the older gentleman playing the baby grand piano on a dais at the front of the room to pay any attention to us.

"So what's the plan?" Sita asks, raising her voice so I can hear her over the chatter and the music.

"Let's split up," I say. "I'll look for Tim." Hopefully he hasn't left yet or I gave up an evening of Schitt's Creek and BBQ chips for nothing. "You find Aiden and distract him for a while." I don't want him to see me talking to his client and get suspicious. If he figures out what I'm up to then he'll definitely try and come up with a way to stop me.

Sita nods. She's never met Aiden but she knows all about him, including what he looks like—I took a screenshot from his Instagram account and texted it to her earlier. She sent me back a fox emoji, which wasn't at all helpful. I don't need to be reminded how hot Aiden Miller is.

Sita and I head in opposite directions. I search for Tim as I snake my way through the crowd, weaving around partygoers and round tables draped in heavy white linens. The ballroom is lit with a rosy pink glow and smells like flowers, which makes sense because they are everywhere—in huge crystal vases on the tables, covering the top of the piano and twisted in the chandeliers. It's a rich people event, full of the city's most wealthy and glamorous.

I spot Tim a few feet ahead of me with his wife Annabelle—I recognize her from a spread in the copy of *Chatelaine* I thumbed through at the doctor's office last year. I suck in a breath. They're putting on their jackets, getting ready to leave. I'm steeling myself to walk over to them when I feel a hand on my arm. I spin around to find Aiden standing behind me, because of course he is. Of course I would run into him before I had a chance to talk to Tim.

"Piper," Aiden says, his stupidly handsome face warming with a smile. "I didn't expect to see you here." Just like this morning, he sounds happy to see me. Which makes no sense. Why would he be happy to see me when we're mortal enemies?

I smile coolly back at him. "Yes, well—" I start to say as someone squeezes behind Aiden, forcing him to move closer to me. No room to breathe close. Kissing distance close. He's as tall as lamppost and when he stares down at me with those magnetic blue-hazel eyes, the corner of his lip quirking, all rational thought leaves my head. Despite myself, my heart beats a little faster and I start to feel all mushy and warm inside. Yuck. It's pretty clear that my body hasn't got the message yet that Aiden Miller is off limits. And from the amused way that he's staring at me I can tell that he knows exactly what effect he's having on me, damn him.

I take a step back to put some distance between us. *Be professional,* I remind myself. *Don't give anything away. And don't let him charm you! Remember why you're here. You are on a mission!*

I clear my throat. "I like to do my part for charity," I continue, making a mental note to send a donation to the children's hospital foundation tomorrow.

I glance desperately around, looking for Sita. I really want out of this conversation—I need to talk to Tim before he leaves—but I can't just make a beeline for him in front of Aiden. He'll know something's up.

Seriously, where is Sita?

"Congratulations on the deal." I almost choke on the words.

Aiden's eyebrows rise slightly. "Thanks," he says. "Tim's been wanting to invest in that neighborhood for a while so I'm glad we were finally able to find him something."

I try not to grimace. I don't want to seem like a sore loser, even though that's exactly how I feel right now. Deep down, I know that it's not Aiden's fault that Tim outbid us—he was just doing his job. I would have done the same thing. I wish I were a bigger person and I could let go of this desperate need to get back at him for what he did to me two years ago, but I'm not.

"What's Tim planning to do with the house?" I ask, turning around to make sure he and Annabelle are still here. I'm not sure that I want to hear about how the house is going to be torn down to make room for a boring modern development, but maybe that information will help me somehow when I finally get to talk to Tim.

Aiden notices me glancing everywhere around the room but at him. "Are you looking for someone?" he asks, his brow furrowing.

I nod. "I've lost her somewhere in the crowd."

His shoulders relax. He obviously thought I brought a date, but I'm not sure why he cares who I came here with. He probably just likes the ego boost, knowing that I have feelings for him.

Had feelings for him.

"By the way, I saw your bus bench on Alma," Aiden says.

And I feel my spirit leave my body.

I have one bus bench—one measly bench!—in this entire city but of course Aiden saw it. I scowl. I know that *some* people might view this kind of advertising as cheesy but it's super common in real estate—just look at what it's done for Viyaan. Aiden wouldn't know about what it takes to try and build a business, though, because he works for his parents' brokerage. He's never had to hustle for anything. Life has just handed everything to him.

"Right," I say, which doesn't make any sense but my brain is short-circuiting. He's standing too close to me again and he smells good.

Aiden studies me for a moment. "Listen, I was hoping we could—" he starts to say just as Sita shows up with two glasses of champagne.

"There you are," she says, holding a glass out to me.

I shake my head. "I'm good." As much as I'd like to down the whole drink to calm my nerves, I need to be on my game and as sharp as possible when I talk to Tim.

Sita offers the champagne to Aiden, but he declines, too. "Thanks but I'm driving."

"Sita, this is Aiden," I say. "Aiden, Sita."

"So how do you two know each other?" Sita directs the question to him, batting her eyes as she double fists her drinks. Oh, she's good. A few more seconds of staring at him like that and Aiden will forget I'm even here. He'll probably even forget his name.

I try not to let that bother me. I did ask Sita to distract him, after all, and I know that she isn't the least bit interested in him—she's just really good at flirting. It's second nature to her.

"We met through work," Aiden says.

"Oh. You're a realtor, too?" she asks him, feigning surprise. As he gives her an abbreviated version of how we met—a story I've already told her—Sita finishes her first glass of champagne and sets it onto the tray of a passing waiter and then starts on the other glass. Her eyes flick to me, giving me permission to leave Aiden in her hands, so I casually glance over my shoulder again to check on Tim and Annabelle. My stomach tightens when I see their empty table. I look around frantically and finally spot them making their way towards the door.

"You know, I think I do want some champagne after all," I say. I leave Sita to handle Aiden and I hurry to catch up with Tim, hoping that Aiden won't figure out where I'm off to. I just need five minutes to try and convince Tim to let me represent him instead.

I catch up to him and his wife as they're walking down the hall.

"...for the last time." Annabelle says. "I mean it, Tim. I'm not going to do this again. Please don't ask me."

Tim mumbles something back to her that I can't quite make out, but I do hear the irritation in his tone.

My stomach drops. Oh shit, they're arguing. This is clearly a bad time to try and talk business to him. And it's too late to turn around—or pretend that I wasn't just eavesdropping on their conversation—because I'm practically beside them and unfortunately Tim has already noticed me.

"Piper," he says. His expression relaxes the tiniest bit and he gives me a warm smile. "What are the odds that we run into each other twice in one day?"

I smile back at him. The odds are pretty good, I'd say, considering I stalked him.

"I saw that you were leaving but I hadn't had the chance to say hi," I say. *And so I chased after you like a total lunatic.* My face burns. I'm not off to a great start. "So...hi."

Calm down. Deep breaths. You can do this.

"It was a lovely evening, wasn't it?" Tim asks me.

I nod enthusiastically. "Wonderful. Such a great cause."

"Annabelle is on the board of directors." He introduces me to his wife, resting his hand against her back. Annabelle Davidson is in her late-fifties and has the most beautiful silver hair that falls loose around her shoulders. She's wearing a beaded black dress that I'm almost sure I saw on the cover of last month's Vogue and a diamond on her ring finger that's so big you could probably see it from space.

"Piper is a realtor," Tim tells her.

"Oh?" Annabelle's smile widens. "Well, we're about to put our house on the market. I'd love for you to come and see it. Give us an idea on how much we should list it for."

"I'd love—"

"Anna," Tim interrupts. He grimaces. "I think we should probably—"

"Oh, I know what you think," Annabelle says, cutting him off this time. "But I'd like to know what Piper thinks."

My eyes dart back and forth between them. I'm not sure what's going on here, but there's a thick fog of tension that is making me super uneasy.

"Are you free tomorrow?" Annabelle asks me.

I swallow. I really don't want to make an enemy out of Tim Davidson—he could derail my career if he wanted to—but I'm also not about to let this opportunity pass me by. This is what I've been waiting for, after all. The chance to sell a luxury property.

"Of course," I say. "Just let me know what time works best for you and I'll be there."

Tim fidgets, hands shoved in his pockets, while Annabelle texts me her contact information.

"See you at ten o'clock tomorrow morning, Piper," she says.

I watch them walk away, my heart bursting with happiness. As soon as the Davidsons are out of sight, I google their address, almost dropping my phone when I see the photos of their house. I knew from the magazine article that they live in West Vancouver—one of the wealthiest neighborhoods in the entire country—but this house is *beyond*. It has to be worth at least six or seven million dollars.

I quickly do the math in my head. If I manage to sell their house for them I will earn well over a hundred thousand dollars in commission. Which means I'll be able to pay for Leighton to go back to school for the next few years. Not only that but selling a place at this level is the best advertisement I could ever ask for. It will definitely lead to more business. Clients will flock to me.

I will be set.

I let out a long, shaky breath. Okay, so I'm getting a little ahead of myself—I still have to get the listing—but I'm going to do everything in my power to make sure that I land it. This is my chance.

I grin and go back inside the gala to find Sita and tell her our plan worked.

CHAPTER
FOUR

"**P**LEASE TELL ME you haven't been up all night," Leighton says early the next morning when she finds me on the couch, staring blearily at my laptop screen.

"Okay, I won't tell you," I reply, stifling a yawn. Nailing this meeting with the Davidsons requires that I learn everything I can about them and their stunning 10,000 square foot European-inspired estate. The meeting is in a few hours and I still have to finish drafting a marketing plan that will knock them off their feet. There's no time for sleep.

My sister shakes her head. "Piper."

"One night of missed sleep isn't going to cause me to relapse," I say, because I know that's what she's thinking. I know because I'm always thinking about it, too. Not a single day has passed where I haven't worried that my cancer might come back. And that it might be worse the next time it does.

But I can't think about that now. I need to focus on landing this listing. I have one shot to get this pitch right. One chance to convince Tim and Annabelle Davidson to let me represent them.

Leighton sighs as I turn back to my computer. She doesn't understand how life-changing getting this listing would be because I haven't told her all the details—like how much I'd be making in commission. I don't want her to get her hopes up. Mine are already up enough for both of us.

"I'm going to make us wheatgrass shots," my sister says, bustling off to the kitchen.

I wrinkle my nose. I'm not sure there's anything more disgusting than a wheatgrass shot, but I'll do it if it will make her feel better. And who knows? Maybe it will give me the burst of energy I need to get through the rest of this day.

I'm making a list of recent sales in the British Properties—the ultra-exclusive area of West Van where the Davidsons live—when Leighton returns with the wheatgrass.

"Thanks," I say, taking one of the shots from her.

We cheers and clink glasses, then down the bitter green drink. I wince. "Yuck."

"It's not that bad," Leighton says, but I notice she's suppressing a shudder. "And it's worth it for the antioxidants."

I notice something on her face. "You have glitter on your cheek."

She rubs at her skin. "Must not have done a great job of washing off my makeup last night," she mumbles. As i 'natural' and 'organic' as my sister is, it's kind of weird how much she loves makeup. She's super into press on nails, too, and I'm constantly finding them discarded all over the apartment.

Leighton walks over to the window and yanks open the gauzy white curtains, letting in the rising sun, before disappearing into her bedroom to change for her yoga class.

"You sure you don't want to come with me?" she calls from her room. "I'm meeting Ryland afterwards for brunch."

I frown. Ryland is my sister's on-again/off-again boyfriend. He has a scraggly beard, smokes an obscene amount of pot and seems a little too invested in Game of Thrones, but he's nice enough. I would prefer if Leighton found someone who had a bit more motivation, though. Or at least didn't live with four roommates.

"Can't. I have to be in West Van in two hours," I yell back. In fact, I'm going to have to leave soon if I want to get there on time—it's normally only a twenty-minute drive, but traffic could easily add at least another half an hour. One of the drawbacks of living in the city.

"I'd wish you luck but I really don't think you're going to need it," Leighton says, appearing in front of me in her knock off Lululemon leggings and a blue sports bra. "You've got this. I can feel it."

I smile. My sister is my biggest cheerleader. My only cheerleader, really. My father was never in the picture and hers died in a car accident when I was eleven and Leighton was only three. Growing up, our mother was not the easiest person to live with, to put it lightly, and as a result neither of us is close to her now. I know Leighton has kept her up to date on my diagnosis, but our mother never offered to come out from Toronto to help, not even after my surgery. That was pretty much the final straw for me. We pretty much only talk through my sister now.

After my sister leaves for her yoga class, I finish my research, print out a copy of the marketing plan and head to our tiny green-tiled bathroom to take a shower. Almost every inch of the mirror is covered with sticky-note affirmations that Leighton insists we should be saying out loud several times a day, to make sure they really sink into our psyches. Words of wisdom from Brené Brown, Michelle Obama, Oprah.

Courage starts with showing up. I am a work in progress. Look inward—the loving begins with you.

I notice a new note, layered on top of the others, written in Leighton's bubbly cursive.

Ask, believe, receive! Once you make a decision, the universe conspires to make it happen!

She also drew lopsided happy face.

I'm not sure I believe in manifestation as strongly as my sister does, but it certainly can't hurt, so I close my eyes and tell myself that I'm going to get this listing. I'm going to be able to send Leighton back to school. Clients will flock to me and I will never have to knock on another door to try and get a lead again.

I open my eyes and let out a deep breath.

For once, I'm going to be an optimist. I'm going to believe that everything will work out.

AN HOUR LATER, I pull my car into the circular brick-paved driveway of the Davidsons house. Although *house* feels like an understatement—this place looks more like a hotel with its white stone exterior and floor-to-ceiling windows, thick columns and wrought-iron balconies. The house is set on an acre of lush, well-tended land with an incredible view of Burrard Inlet and Lions Gate Bridge, the skyline of the city rising in the background.

My palms are clammy as I climb out of the car. I figured that Annabelle would probably best respond to understated elegance, so I chose a cream silk blouse with a pair of black tailored pants, along with low black heels and the pink silk scarf that Leighton bought me for my birthday a few months ago.

Annabelle waves to me from the arched doorway. I smile, but my stomach is in knots as I walk towards her.

"Piper," she says warmly. She's wearing a blue linen shirt and white capri pants, her silver hair loose around her shoulders. "So glad you could make it. Come on in."

"Thank you for inviting me," I say, following her into the foyer. I take in the glossy Brazilian walnut floors, the high ceilings, the massive bronze chandelier. Over-the-top luxury that still somehow manages to be welcoming. Kind of like Annabelle herself.

"Why don't I give you the grand tour and then we can sit down and discuss the details," she says, starting up the curved staircase.

"Perfect," I reply.

Annabelle was involved with every bit of the design of the house and that, along with the sheer size of the place, means it takes us almost an hour and a half to get through it. But I don't mind. I love architecture and interior design—it's one of the reasons I got into real estate in the first place.

"How long have you lived here?" I ask, as she punches in a code that will let us into the temperature-controlled wine cellar.

"Fifteen years," Annabelle replies. "Brynn, our daughter, isn't too happy that we're selling. She'd like us to stay here forever, but that's just not possible. Not now, anyway." She chews her lower lip as she studies me. "I assume I can count on you to be discrete?"

I nod. "Of course."

"We're selling because Tim and I are getting a divorce," she says.

I blink. Unfortunately, divorce is one of the main reasons that people decide to put their homes on the market, but somehow it didn't occur to me that might be the case for the Davidsons. I guess because I just saw them together at the gala last night. I figured, given their age, that they were thinking about downsizing.

"I'm so sorry," I say.

Annabelle waves her hand. "It's a long time coming. And it really is for the best," she says. "It's important that we keep it between us, though, because we haven't broken the news to anyone besides our family and a few close friends. I don't want word getting around."

I'm touched that she trusts me enough to confide in me. "I understand," I say, squeezing her arm. "I won't tell a soul."

Annabelle shows me the wine cellar, the butler's pantry—where she hands me a crystal glass of spring water—and the pool house, before finishing the tour in an all-white living room with a massive marble fireplace.

"So," Annabelle says as we sit down on the plush white couch. "How much do you think we should we ask for the house?"

I swallow. Price can be a touchy subject with clients—they often overvalue the amount of their home, so it can be tricky to get them to agree to a realistic price without insulting them. Price too high and the property could just sit on the market for months. Price too low and they can feel cheated when it sells. That's where a list of recent sales in their neighborhood comes in handy.

"Well, I've done a bit of research," I say, pulling a sheaf of papers out my black crocodile bag. "And a few other places in this area have recently sold for around six million."

Annabelle nods. A good sign—I haven't offended her.

"Now, those places don't have all the amenities that your house does, so in my professional opinion, I think six-five is a realistic price."

Annabelle nods again. "That seems reasonable." She glances at me. "Have you sold anything at this level before?"

My heart sinks. I knew she'd probably get around to asking me this question eventually. This is my make-or-break moment, my last chance to convince her that I'm the one she should hire for the job.

"Honestly? Not at this level," I say. "But I've been working towards this for the past few years and I'm ready. More than ready." I smile at her. "I know I can do this. I just need a chance."

Annabelle's expression falters for a moment, but then she smiles back at me. "I have a good feeling about you, Piper," she says. "You remind me a little of myself when I was young. Someone gave me a chance once and I'd like to pay that forward. So if you want this listing, it's yours."

I'm so happy I could hug her. "I definitely want the listing," I say. "Thank you, Annabelle. I promise you won't regret this."

"Don't thank me just yet—there is a condition," she says. "This is a co-list. Tim has his own realtor, so you're going to have to work with him." She shifts on the couch. "Do you know Aiden Miller from Miller Realty?"

My throat closes. I feel like I'm breathing through a straw, but I somehow manage to squeak out a "yes, we've met."

"Tim wanted to just give the listing to him, but I'm more comfortable having my own representation," she said. "It's not that I don't trust Tim, but divorce can change people, especially when it comes to money. I don't want to end up getting screwed."

Somehow I'm still smiling. "Co-listing is no problem," I say, my mind racing ahead to all of the contact I'm going to have to have with Aiden over the next few months.

This is terrible. Amazing, because I got the listing, but also really terrible because it means that not only am I going to have to work with him, but we're also going to have to split the commission. And, okay, it's a very large commission and even half of it is still a lot of money—more than I've ever made before—but to get it I have to be around Aiden Miller. The guy who almost ruined my real estate career before it even started.

The guy who broke my heart.

"Great." Annabelle beams at me.

"Great," I repeat.

CHAPTER
FIVE

LATER THAT AFTERNOON, Tyler bursts into Madeline's office with a bottle of champagne, his Shih Tzu, Freddie Mercury, trotting behind at his heels.

"It might be a little early for champagne," I say, smiling tightly at him. He clearly eavesdropped on our conversation about my meeting with Annabelle Davidson. My fault, I should have known better than to leave Madeline's door open.

"It's never too early for champagne." Tyler uncorks the bottle and pours each of us a glass. He's in a light blue seersucker suit and a straw hat as if he's planning to go on a picnic in 1925. And this isn't even the strangest outfit he's ever worn. "Besides, it's five o'clock somewhere," he says.

"I meant that it's a little too early to celebrate this listing," I say as Freddie jumps into my lap and makes himself comfortable. "I haven't sold the house yet." I also haven't told Madeline that I have to co-list with Aiden Miller, something I probably should have done before I agreed to do it. She is my boss, after all, and I know she's not exactly keen on co-listing with other agencies.

"You'll sell it." Madeline says, smiling at me as she rests her elbows on her glass-topped desk. "And when you do we'll break out the really good stuff."

I smile back at her. Madeline is who I want to be one day. She's a great boss, someone who knows the balance between propping me up and lighting a fire under my ass. She started Pinnacle Realty on her own ten years ago and she now has seven agents working under her—a phenomenal accomplishment for someone who's not even forty years old.

Freddie licks my hand as Madeline and Tyler pepper me with questions about the Davidsons house. I tell them everything except for why they're selling. I don't want to lie to them, but I made a promise to Annabelle that I wouldn't tell anyone about the divorce, and that includes my team, so I just say that they're downsizing.

"You should definitely offer to help them find a new place," Madeline says.

I nod. "I mentioned that to Annabelle," I reply. In fact, I've already drawn up a list of amazing waterfront properties to send her. "She'd like to stay in West Van but she said she'll go as far as Horseshoe Bay if she loves the house enough."

Madeline's brow furrows. "They downsizing into another house?"

My chest tightens. The woman doesn't miss anything.

"They are," I say quickly, hoping she won't be angry with me when she finds out I kept the Davidsons situation a secret. "They'd just like to be in something a little smaller, a little easier to maintain."

Another lie. Annabelle doesn't care about maintenance because Annabelle doesn't have to maintain anything—she has people to do that for her. She was clear with me that she doesn't want to her lifestyle to change, she just wants something that belongs to her alone. A house that isn't tainted by memories of her soon-to-be ex-husband.

"Ooh, there's an incredible listing in Altamont that just hit the market yesterday," Tyler says. "It's right near the beach. Four bed, five bath, all the trimmings. I'll send it your way."

"Thanks." Technically Tyler is Madeline's assistant but he helps all of the agents in the office when he can. Which is probably more than he should.

"There is one other thing," I say, ready to confess that I'm going to be working with Aiden Miller. But the universe clearly likes to screw with me, because the words are just on the tip of my tongue when the front door of the office opens and the man himself walks in.

My stomach drops. I think about trying to hide, but that's impossible in a building made almost entirely out of glass. I knew that I was going to have to talk to Aiden once Tim informed him that we'd be working together, but I was hoping that when the time came I'd be a little more prepared. He's caught me totally off-guard, showing up at my office. Which I assume is the point.

"What is Aiden Miller doing here?" Madeline asks, her champagne glass lifted halfway to her mouth.

"Annabelle had one condition," I say quickly as Aiden spots us staring at him. He starts walking towards us and he is not smiling, so yep, he's definitely not happy about this arrangement either. "I have to co-list with him. We have to sell the Davidsons house together."

Tyler laughs. "Well, this just got interesting."

There's no time to ask exactly Tyler what he means by that because Aiden is now standing in Madeline's office. Towering over me. Scowling.

I scowl back at him. He must have come here straight from the gym because he's wearing track pants and a white t-shirt that shows off his perfect arms—arms that could easily lift a girl into the air, carry her to his bed. The bottom of his raven tattoo, the one I've drooled over in his Instagram photos, peeks out from his sleeve.

It's really unfair how hot he is.

"Aiden," Madeline says coolly. "Nice to see you."

"Hi, Maddy," he replies.

Maddy?

I glance at Madeline, but her face is unreadable. I was aware that they know each other—his name has come up between us before—but I didn't realize they were close enough for nicknames. I'm not sure what to make of that.

"Hi Aiden," Tyler says, offering his hand. "I'm Tyler."

"Nice to meet you." Aiden's big paw closes over Tyler's hand. He pumps up and down once before letting go.

"Would you like some champagne?" Tyler asks him, flexing his fingers. "We're just celebrating Piper's new listing."

"Nah, I'm good," Aiden says affably. "I would like a minute with Piper though, if that's alright."

Of course he would.

"Is there somewhere a bit more private we can talk?" Aiden glances around, but aside from Madeline's office, our space is open concept, nary a bit of privacy to be found.

He must not want any witnesses, which probably means he intends to tear me a new one for weaseling my way onto his listing. The *nerve*. It's not like I'm shutting him out of this deal (although, to be totally honest, I definitely would if I could). And it's not like he wouldn't do the very same thing if our roles were reversed.

Well, I dare him to get angry with me. If he does, he'll soon realize that I'm not the same girl he screwed over two years ago. I sit up a little straighter. I can handle myself. I'm not going to let him intimidate me.

"You can talk in here," Madeline says, standing up. Tyler plucks Freddie from my lap and the two of them walk out of the office, pulling the door shut behind them. Leaving me alone with Aiden for the first time in years.

I frown as he walks around Madeline's desk and settles into her white leather chair instead of the perfectly good chair next to me—it's a power move, a way to not-so-subtly convey that he's in charge. Thinks he's in charge, anyway.

We look at each other and I can feel the tension rising between us, degree by painful degree. It's like we're playing that kids game, the one where you stare at each other until one of you blinks. Unfortunately for Aiden, I have this game down. I am not going to look away first. I am not going to let him win.

And so we continue to silently stare at each other, seconds turning into minutes. I study Aiden and his two different colored eyes, his full lips and shaggy blonde surfer hair, his slightly crooked nose and his beautifully full lips, until my heart starts to beat faster. I'm irritated that my body is responding to him, like it doesn't care that he's the last person on earth I should be attracted to.

I realize I'm glowering at him and I force my face to relax. I don't want Aiden to know that he gets under my skin. I don't want him to think that he has any power over me. He doesn't need to know how warm I'm feeling or that I'm wondering what he would do if I got up and sat in his lap, ran my fingers through his thick hair.

What is *wrong* with me? I shouldn't be thinking about Aiden that way. Or any way. I let him charm me once before but I'm not going to fall for it—I'm not going to fall for him—again. Not ever.

Aiden's lips quirk, like he's just read my dirty thoughts. My cheeks flush, but I won't let myself look away from him, even though inside I'm curling up with humiliation. The worst part of all this is that he knows how I felt about him. He knows but he didn't see me as more than a friend. Actually, he didn't even see me *as* a friend. If he had, then he wouldn't have done what he did to me.

"So," Aiden says finally, breaking the silence but not our eye contact. He laces his hands behind his head, the picture of cool and unbothered. "The Davidsons have thrown us quite the curve ball."

"Yes. They have."

"You know, I'm kind of a lone wolf. I normally don't co-list," he says. "I'm only doing this as a favor to Tim."

A flare of anger shoots through me, but I manage to tamp it down. I can't afford to blow this opportunity just because Aiden's an ass. For better or worse, we're going to have to work together and that means I have to play nice. I can bawl him out after we've sold the house. And I will.

"This is new for me, too," I say, fiddling with my scarf. Bad move because Aiden's eyes are immediately drawn to my neck and now he's wondering about the scar underneath.

His expression softens. His obvious concern is what gets me to finally look away from him. I drop my hands back into my lap and tell him I took a crack at the listing pitch, just to change the subject.

"That was quick," he says.

I shrug and reach for my phone, then forward him the file. "I assumed we'd want to get it on MLS as soon as possible. Annabelle is anxious to sell."

Aiden nods. His phone buzzes. He takes it out of the pocket of his track pants and opens up my email. "She's told you about the divorce, I take it?"

"Yes," I say. "She also asked me to keep it on the down low."

Aiden sighs. "I haven't said anything to anyone about it either," he says. "I feel terrible for Tim. He's pretty broken up about it."

I blink. "Tim doesn't want the divorce?" I'm not sure why, but I assumed that it was amicable. Maybe because Annabelle told me that it was a long time coming.

"No. He doesn't," Aiden says. "They've been married almost forty years. How many couples make it that long?"

Not many, it seems. I haven't even made it past the six-month mark in a relationship yet.

Aiden scans my listing pitch, nodding to himself. "This isn't bad."

Why does he sound surprised? And it's better than not bad. It's really good. I tell him that I've drafted a marketing plan, too.

"Oh, cool," he says. "Send it to me. I'm sure I'll have a few things to add to it."

"Please," I say, frowning at him. "Send it to me *please*."

Aiden laughs. Laughs! "Please send me your marketing plan, Piper," he says, grinning at me, like this is all some big joke. Like I'm a big joke.

He must realize that I'm annoyed with him because he straightens his face. "We can focus on the marketing plan later," he says. "What we really need to discuss is what we're going to do about the commission."

"What do you mean?" We're working on this together, so I assumed it would be a fifty-fifty split. But of course it isn't going to be that easy. Nothing with Aiden ever is.

"I'm thinking an eighty-twenty split is fair," he says. And there's the shark, the guy who is always looking out for number one.

Now it's my turn to laugh. "I don't think so," I say. There's no way that I'm going to do all the work required to sell this place just to hand him eighty percent of the commission. No. Way.

Aiden smiles. "I have a lot more experience than you do, P," he says. "Not to mention my brokerage has more resources. That's worth eighty percent right there."

I scowl at him. He's not wrong about the experience or the resources—I don't have access to a social media team or a list of high-end buyers the way he does. And the Miller name goes a long way in this town. But that's still not enough to make me settle for less than I deserve.

"That may be true, but I'm going to work my ass off on this listing," I say, folding my hands on the desk. "That's worth a lot more than twenty percent. And don't call me P."

Aiden's smile widens. "You drive a hard bargain," he says. "Let's say seventy-thirty, then."

"Nice try, but no," I say. "Fifty-fifty." I'm not going to agree to anything less. And I'm prepared to sit here all day until he gives in.

Aiden rubs his chin and I hear the scratch of his stubble. I flush, wondering what that stubble would feel like against my thighs. *This is just my hormones*, I tell myself. *That's all this is.*

"If you're so confident, then how about we make a bet?" he asks me.

I narrow my eyes. "A bet?"

He nods.

I'm not sure I like where this is going.

Aiden leans towards me. "Winner takes all," he says. "If I find our buyer, then the commission is all mine. If you find our buyer, then it all goes to you. Every last cent. No hard feelings."

No hard feelings on his end, maybe—he can afford to lose this commission. I can't. But even if I could, it's not just my money that I'd be gambling with. I pay Madeline a percentage of every commission—I'd still need to pay her if I lose and that would put me in even worse financial shape than I'm in right now.

Still…it's tempting. So very tempting. I could do a lot with all of that money. And beating Aiden, taking his commission from him, well that would definitely be sweet.

I swallow. Am I really thinking about taking him up on this?

Yup. I am. Because here's the thing: I've spent most of my life being risk adverse, of taking the safe route, and it hasn't really gotten me anywhere. I'm suddenly tired of being that girl. I'm ready to try something different.

Maybe it's time to bet on myself.

"All or nothing, P," Aiden says again, holding out his hand.

"All or nothing." I take his hand and his fingers are warm and soft. I feel that touch zip right through me and I pull away as if I've been burned. Like I've just made a deal with the devil.

"Then may the best person win," Aiden says as he pushes the chair back and stands up.

"Oh don't worry," I say, smiling up at him. "I will."

CHAPTER
SIX

TO: Piper Anderson <piperanderson@pinnaclerealty.ca>
FROM: Aiden Miller <aiden.miller@avenuerealty.ca>
RE: Marketing plan

I think we should up the budget to fifty thousand. We really need to do a listing video as well as a broker's open.

A.

STARE AT MY computer screen, my stomach churning. Aiden wants to spend fifty thousand dollars on a video and a party? That's more than three times the budget I originally sent him.

I feel sick. The expectation is that each of us will front half of the money required for marketing the property—money that will eventually come off our commission, provided that we sell the house in the allotted ninety days. If we don't manage to sell it, however, then we will lose every cent of our investment.

Which would put me even deeper in the hole than I already am. So deep that it could take me years to climb out of it.

I wipe my sweaty palms on my skirt. I don't have twenty-five thousand dollars just lying around, so I'm not sure how I'm going to pull this off. But if I want to play in the big leagues then I'm going to need to find a way. Maybe I can ask Madeline if the brokerage can front the costs. She won't be happy about that, but I don't really have any other options. I'm certainly not going to admit to Aiden that I can't afford it.

All of my earlier confidence leaks out of me. I should have just agreed to a seventy-thirty commission split and let Aiden take the lead instead of making this stupid bet. I'm going to end up losing everything because I'm an impulsive idiot, too prideful to back down. Not only have I put my own future on the line, but Leighton's as well. If I fail, if I don't sell this house, then I'm not even going to be able to pay for my half of our rent—my sister will be taking care of me. Again.

My breathing starts to quicken. I rest my hand against my chest—a trick my therapist taught me to help regulate my nervous system—and close my eyes. *Whatever happens, it's going to be fine,* I tell myself. Well, maybe not *fine,* but it will be okay. I will live through this. I hear Leighton's voice in my head, chanting her feel-good sticky-note mantras: *I am capable. Everything I need is within me. I am grateful.*

Feeling slightly calmer, I open my eyes. My phone buzzes. Aiden's now texting me, wanting to know if I'm free for dinner tomorrow night. He quickly follows up with another message to clarify that he wants to "talk about the broker's open" just in case I got it in my head that he's asking me out, I'm sure.

Once upon a time, I might have misread his intentions but I know better now. My cheeks flush. I don't need him to point out that it's only a business meeting. I know there's nothing between us and that there never will be.

I frown at my phone, wondering how best to respond. Technically, yes, I am free tomorrow night but I'm not sure why we have to meet in person—I'd been hoping that we could do almost everything over email so I could severely limit how often I have to see him. It's much better for me that way.

> **ME:** Why don't you just send me your ideas.

> **AIDEN:** I'd really rather talk about it over dinner. 7:30?

Ugh, I should have known that he's going to be difficult to work with. He never takes no for an answer. Which is probably part of why he's so successful—he doesn't let anything stop him.

> **ME:** Fine, whatever.

Freddie paws at my leg and I lean down to lift him into my lap. I'm praying that Aiden doesn't pick anywhere too fancy, but my hopes are dashed when he sends me the reservation details to a pricey steakhouse on Granville Island, the kind of place you'd take a date if you wanted to impress them.

Except this is not a date, it's a business meeting. Between two people that don't even like each other that much.

My mouth tightens. Aiden's just doing this to screw with me. I know it. And here I am, letting him get away with it, the way I always have. I'm debating whether I should text him back and insist that he just send me his thoughts on the broker's open so I don't have to waste an evening on him when Freddie distracts me by standing up in my lap and trying to French kiss me.

"You really should get a dog," Tyler says from his desk a few feet away. "You're so good with him."

"I'm not home enough," I reply, gently nudging Freddie away from my face. Sadly, this is the only kiss I've had in the past year. Working in real estate means keeping odd hours—most clients are only free to look at properties in the evenings or on weekends, so it's hard to have a social life. I mean, not for me—I don't have any clients at the moment, other than Annabelle—but Aiden is at the top of his game so I'm surprised that he has the time to go for dinner with me.

"You should come with me to the shelter," Tyler says, spinning his chair towards me. "I volunteer there a few times a week."

"Stop tempting me," I say. "It wouldn't be fair to adopt a dog right now."

Someday I'll have one, along with a cute little house and season tickets to the Canucks. I'll have anything—everything—I want. Someday I'm going to have it all. And the first step towards having it all starts with selling the Davidsons house and winning that bet.

"You could fill your puppy love tank by volunteering at the shelter," Tyler says. "We always need more walkers."

"Okay," I agree. "But I'm telling you right now if your master plan is to get me to fall in love with one of them and take it home with me it's not going to work."

Tyler just gives me one of his enigmatic smiles and turns back to his computer.

AIDEN IS ALREADY at the restaurant when I arrive for our dinner meeting the next evening. The hostess leads me through the dimly lit, cozily romantic room to a table tucked in the back corner by a floor-to-ceiling window with an amazing view of False Creek.

Aiden stands as I approach. He's wearing khaki pants that, for once, aren't wrinkled, and a blue dress shirt that matches his left eye. The first two buttons of the shirt are undone, revealing a tuft of golden chest hair. I like a guy with a little chest hair, which sucks because I don't need another reason to be attracted to him.

This is not a date, this is a business meeting, I remind myself again as I sit down across from him. It's why I'm still in the suit I wore to the office today. It's navy and sensible, nothing sexy or suggestive about it. Even my jewellery—a seed-pearl necklace that rests in the hollow of my neck—is ladies-who-lunch boring.

"Hi P," Aiden says.

"Don't call me P," I snap. How many times do I have to tell him that?

Aiden's lips tighten like he's holding back a smile. He seems to enjoy riling me up. Maybe irritating me is his kink. I'm going to have to learn how to not give him the satisfaction if I'm going to survive working with him.

"So, tell me your big idea for the broker's open," I say, getting right down to the reason he asked me here. I pick up the thick, leather-bound menu so I don't have to look at him—less because I'm annoyed and more because he makes me nervous. I scan the menu for the cheapest item, which turns out to be a side salad. Eleven dollars for a handful of micro greens, topped with thinly sliced radishes and grated carrots that won't even come close to filling me up.

"I think we should have a yacht party," Aiden says.

I peer at him over the top of the menu. "You want to have a party on a boat instead of showing the house?" That makes no sense.

"No, we'd be at the house," he says. "It's just a theme. I'd be the spirit of a yacht party."

"What does that even mean?" Big surprise, I've never been on a yacht. No surprise, I'm sure Aiden has, many times.

He grins. "It means we would have a champagne bar and a seafood tower," he says. "We could even hire Rock the Boat, this amazing yacht rock cover band. Wait until you hear them—they're incredible."

"That all sounds very expensive." I frown at him. "And I don't understand how any of this is going to help us to sell the Davidsons house." Really, I think Aiden just wants to have a party. And wear a captain's hat.

"It's going to help us get agents to the house, which will help us sell the house," Aiden explains, leaning back in his chair. "We need to do something exciting to draw them in, P."

I bristle at "P" but decide it's not worth correcting him again. This is me, not reacting. Look how good I'm getting at it already.

"The chance to check out a seven-million-dollar property should be enough to draw agents in," I point out. I've been to plenty of broker opens and the most I've ever been offered are branded bottles of water and store-bought sandwiches. "Surely the commission for bringing us a buyer is enough to get them in the door."

Aiden shrugs. "A seven-million-dollar property isn't that big of a deal in West Van," he says. "It's kind of average, actually, for the luxury market."

As crazy as that sounds, he's right.

"Agent expectations are much higher in this bracket," he adds. "We can't just do branded water bottles and store-bought sandwiches."

I sigh. "Okay, but are their expectations yacht party high?"

He nods. "Yes," he says. "The last broker's open I went to had synchronized swimmers and a Botox station."

As much as I hate to admit it, Aiden's right about this, too. He has years more experience under his belt, so I'm going to have to trust that he knows what he's doing. Even if I don't trust him on anything else.

"Come on, it'll be fun," he says.

Maybe I would be more excited if we weren't the ones stuck paying for a soft rock cover band and a mountain of crab legs.

"Fine," I say as the waiter stops by to take our order. Aiden orders wine, along with wagyu beef, two of the most expensive things on the menu. I stick with the salad and tap water just in case he's expecting me to split the bill.

When the waiter leaves, I assume we're going to chat about logistics or maybe some of our other marketing strategies, but Aiden steers the conversation in another direction instead.

"So, Piper," he says. "It's been a while since we last hung out."

Two years, actually, and I'm not sure I'd classify this dinner as 'hanging out'.

The story of Aiden and me goes like this: I was brand new to the business, had just gotten my real estate license a few weeks before, when I met him at an industry event. We had an our-eyes-met-across-a-crowded-room moment, the kind that seems to really only exists in movies, and, sadly, that was all it took to hook me.

My face burns. It's embarrassing to think about how I chased after him. Humiliating, really. And my unrequited feelings weren't even the worst part—that came when he betrayed me by stealing my client.

"Catch me up," Aiden presses. "How has life been treating you?"

"Good," I say.

"Good? That's it?" he asks.

I shrug. That's all he's going to get.

He plays with the stem of his water glass. "Are you seeing anyone?"

I narrow my eyes. Why is he asking me that?

"Not that it's any of your business," I say. "But no. I'm not." Dating in this city is difficult even when you have the time, which

I don't. And I'm not sure I'm up for it, at least not right now. I haven't felt like putting myself out there again since Rob and I broke up, right before my cancer diagnosis.

"I'm not dating anyone either," Aiden says.

"Okay," I say, because I don't know what else *to* say. Why does he think I care if he's seeing someone? Because I don't. Not even a little bit.

"I know we didn't end on the best terms, but I have missed you." He stares at me in that intense way that makes me flutter inside. *Used* to make me flutter inside. I'm sure what I'm feeling right now are just hunger pains. "I've been hoping that we can move on and be friends again."

"We were never friends," I say, tensing. "A friend never would have done what you did."

Aiden's smile droops. "I really am sorry about poaching your client," he says. And to his credit, he does look sorry. But an apology, even a sincere one, can't turn back the clock. It can't make me trust him again. "It really was nothing personal, Piper," he adds. "Just business."

It may have been just business to him, but it was entirely personal to me. I'm not sure why he doesn't understand that.

"I did have my reasons, however unforgivable they might seem—"

"It's fine," I say, cutting him off. It's totally not fine, but I don't want to talk about this anymore. Thinking about it is just going to make me angry and I don't want to be angry. I want to sell the Davidsons house, collect the commission and go on with my life. Without Aiden in it.

An awkward silence descends in which we avoid looking at each other. The waiter arrives with the wine, breaking some of the tension. He pours a splash of malbec into a glass, which Aiden swirls around before taking a sip. After he gives his nod of approval, the waiter looks at me, his eyebrows raised.

"Yes, please," I say, nudging my glass forward. I'm going to need something to take the edge off and help me get through the rest of this dinner. Plus, I might as well enjoy the wine if I'm going to be paying for some of it.

The waiter fills my glass halfway and then leaves us alone again.

"I've been travelling a lot over this past year," Aiden says, attempting to re-start conversation.

I already know about his globe-trotting adventures from snooping on his socials, but I obviously don't want him to know that I've kept an eye on him, so I say, "Oh yeah? Where did you go?"

"Southeast Asia, mostly," he says. "Thailand, Vietnam, Laos." He sighs. "It wasn't a vacation, although it probably looked like it was."

It sure did to me.

"What was it then?" I ask, taking a sip of wine. It's delicious, dry and smooth, kind of smoky tasting. A lot better than the cheap bottles I usually buy.

Aiden shrugs. "Me running from my life," he says somberly. "My dad had just died and my mom had all these expectations of me that I never seemed able to live up to." He shakes his head. "One day I woke up and realized that I just couldn't do it anymore, so I bought a one-way plane ticket and I took off for six months." He lifts his glass to his mouth and I notice that his hand is trembling slightly.

"I'm sorry about your dad." Ray Miller was a real estate magnate, known not only for his brilliant business sense but also for his warm, charismatic nature. Everybody loved him. I thought about sending Aiden a message when I'd heard that Ray had passed away, but it felt awkward. I was also dealing with my own health issues by that point, which I was sure he must have heard about and since he hadn't reached out to check on me, I figured we could call it even.

"Yeah. Cancer sucks," Aiden says. His eyes flick to the pearls around my throat. "But I guess you know that first-hand."

"I do, yes."

I catch myself starting to soften a little towards him. My chest tightens. Is he telling me about his father so that I'll be nicer to him? Easier to manipulate, maybe?

I chew the inside of my cheek. History has taught me to believe the worst of Aiden, so maybe I'm a fool for believing him now. But I do believe him. Whatever his motive may be for telling me about his dad, he's still opening up. Of course, that doesn't mean I have to return the favor—I'm not about to share my own experience with life-threatening illness—but it does convince me to let my wall down the tiniest bit.

"I thought about never coming back," Aiden continues. He gazes at me but he's not really looking at me, he's lost in his memories. "Buying a bar on a beach somewhere, spending the rest of my life slinging drinks and swimming in the ocean."

"Why did you change your mind?" I ask him.

He grimaces. "I realized that where I lived wasn't the problem," he says. "I was the problem. I could run to the ends of the earth but I'd still never be able to escape myself." He gives me a small smile. "So I came back to face my fears."

My stomach flips. Aiden is not someone who comes across as being afraid of anything. I have to give him credit, I suppose, for working on himself. Maybe, like me, he's not the same person he was two years ago. Maybe he's grown up. Maybe he's realized he was a jerk.

I glance away from him, my heart pounding. Hope kept me afloat during my fight with cancer, but when it comes to love it can be a dangerous thing. I need to quash these feelings before they start to sprout again. Because even if I could somehow get over Aiden's betrayal—and I'm really not sure that I can—that doesn't change the fact that I told him how I felt and he didn't feel the same way. How do you go back to being friends with someone after that?

The answer: you can't.

Dinner arrives. Aiden stares at my meager salad, his brow furrowing. "That doesn't look very filling. You need to eat more than just a salad."

I would if I had the money. "You sound like my sister," I say.

"How is Leighton?" Aiden asks, cutting his steak into two and depositing half onto my plate without even asking.

"She's good." I don't tell him that she dropped out of university to take care of me, that I need to win our bet so I can send her back. I don't need him pitying me even more than he already does.

Aiden smiles. "Good? Is that your standard answer for everything?"

"Yes." It's not the honest answer, but it is the easiest one. It's the only one that most people want to hear. I save my real feelings for my therapist.

The conversation turns back to business. Aiden tells me how important this listing is to him.

"I haven't sold anything since I've been back," he says. "Taking time off was great for my mental health, but it wasn't exactly the best move for my career."

I understand that completely. I lost a lot of momentum when I took time off to recover. When I returned to the office a few months ago it was like starting back at square one.

"What do you think about keeping the house as a pocket listing rather than putting it up on MLS?" Aiden asks me, referring to the platform realtors use to post properties. "I have a few heavy hitters in mind that the house might be perfect for."

I shake my head. I don't have access to the same calibre of clients that Aiden has, so not spreading the word wide would only give him a huge advantage. We already aren't on a level playing field. It's going to be twice as hard for me to sell this house, so I'm not about to make it any easier for him.

God. I never should have made that stupid bet.

"Nice try, but I don't think so," I say, cutting into the steak.

Aiden shrugs. He doesn't push and I'm surprised that he's giving in so easily. Surprised and suspicious. Why is he being so agreeable? I know he wants to win this bet as badly as I do.

"I've hired Greg Li for the listing video," Aiden says. "He's only available on Friday. Does that work for you?"

I nod. "I'll clear my schedule."

Aiden doesn't need to know that my schedule is already pretty clear. I was planning to do some door knocking, try to drum up some new clients, but I can do that another day.

We probably don't both need to be at the shoot, but there's no way either of us are going to let the other take charge. Aiden because he's not used to giving up control, me because I still don't entirely trust him. One dinner isn't going to change that. A lifetime probably won't change that.

After we finish eating, I excuse myself to go to the washroom. When I come back, Aiden is no longer sitting at our table. I spot him at the bar, talking to a stunning redhead in a blue dress. I watch him for a moment, smiling, relaxed, and the surge of jealousy that goes through me is so strong I know that I've just been kidding myself about my feelings for him.

Being around Aiden is a bad idea. Probably the worst idea. Without even really trying he's already pulling me back in and I don't know if I'm strong enough to fight him off. It was hard enough to get through losing him the last time, and I didn't even really *have* him. The spark I felt was all in my head and it still messed me up.

I straighten my spine and grab my purse. I'm going to need to put my wall all the way back up again. There's just no other choice. Not if I don't want to repeat history, anyway.

CHAPTER
SEVEN

"**D**ON'T FORGET YOU have a blood test this afternoon," Leighton says the next morning as she hands me a glass of homemade peach kombucha. "I can come with you, if you want."

Since I lost almost all of my thyroid during surgery I have to go for semi-regular blood tests so the doctor can monitor my hormone levels. I also have to take a hormone pill every day for the rest of my life if I don't want to end up with a whole host of terrible symptoms, like fatigue, panic attacks and heart palpitations.

"I don't have time. I'm going to reschedule," I say, taking a sip of the kombucha. I'm working from home so I can catch up on some administrative work. Other than a short walk with Tyler, who coerced me into taking a couple of rescue dogs from the shelter out with him later this evening, I'm not planning to leave this couch until I get through every last email.

My sister crosses her arms and stares down at me.

"You are not skipping this appointment, Piper," she says sternly. "Your health is important. More important than anything else you've got planned today."

I sigh. I know it's important and I also know that Leighton's only trying to help, but a blood test is just not at the top of my very long list right now. Shifting my appointment by a week or two isn't going to make a difference.

"I'm feeling fine," I say. And I am. Mostly. I'm anxious, but that's not a side effect of the medication, that's just me. Anxious is how I roll.

Leighton shakes her head. "You're going for the blood test this afternoon. No argument."

"Okay, okay." She's right, I guess. I shouldn't push off the appointment. And it won't take that long—half an hour, tops. I'll eat lunch on the way there. Two birds, one stone.

Now that I've given in, Leighton's shoulders relax. She grabs the off-white chunky knit blanket she made for me from the back of the couch and spreads it over my lap. It drives me crazy when she fusses over me like this but it's hard to be mad at her when I know that it's coming from a good place. A place of love and care. I don't have nearly enough people that fill that role for me in my life.

"Do you want some blueberry pancakes?" she asks, knowing that I haven't eaten anything this morning.

"You know I do," I reply. I feel a rush of gratitude for my sister as she heads into our tiny galley kitchen to make our breakfast.

When I got diagnosed, the dynamic between Leighton and me shifted, our big sister/little sister roles switching the instant my doctor gave us the news. I'm healthy now but we still haven't switched back. I'm not sure either of us knows how to.

As the smell of vanilla and cinnamon wafts into the room my phone dings with a notification. I glance at the screen, surprised to find that Aiden has just followed me on Instagram.

There isn't much to see on my profile—I'm more of a lurker than a poster. Certainly there's nothing to be embarrassed about, but I'm still a little uneasy. Aiden is clearly trying to kick down the door and get back into my life but I'm just not convinced that it's a good idea. Even more so after what happened last night.

When I came back from the washroom and saw him talking to another woman at the bar I decided to flag down the waiter, pay my half of the bill and hightail it out of there. But as it turned out Aiden had already paid for dinner—not because we were on a date, obviously, but because he can write our meals off as a business expense. I was relieved but I also wished that I'd ordered something more fortifying than a stupid side salad. While it was nice of him to share his steak, I was still hungry.

I was preparing to take off without saying goodbye—let Aiden flirt with the redhead all night, whatever, they could leave together, wouldn't make a difference to me—when he came back to the table. He made a point to tell me that the woman was a former client, even though I didn't ask about her. Even though he didn't owe me any explanation. For whatever reason, I guess he didn't want me to get the wrong impression.

And I'm not sure what to make of that. The Aiden I knew before wouldn't have bothered to explain himself. He probably wouldn't have even come back to the table—I would have left the restaurant mad and he would have let me go.

I take another sip of kombucha as scroll through his photos. I've seen them all before—many, many times, because I am a stalker—but I've never picked up on the sadness beneath his smile. Aiden was grieving and I somehow missed it.

My heart aches for him. I know what it's like to lose people. And while I knew he and his dad were close, I guess I didn't realize just how hard his father's death had hit him. His mother, Grady, is also a realtor and the most intimidating person I have ever met, so it's no wonder that Aiden felt the need to get away for a while. I get it. Leighton and I moved clear across the country to get away from our mother.

My finger hovers over the follow back button. Aiden might have changed, but that doesn't mean that we should be friends again. It's not just about him stealing my client—although that betrayal still stings every time I think about it—it's about how I felt about him back then. How he made me want him, whether he meant to or not. It would be so easy to be sucked right back in, but I have to guard my heart. And to do that I need to maintain some boundaries.

So I'm not going to follow him back. We're not going back to the way things were. We can't.

I can't.

But even as I set my phone aside, I wonder if it's really going to be that easy.

A FEW HOURS later Leighton and I eat almond butter and honey sandwiches on the way to the clinic. After I have my blood drawn we stop at Whole Foods to grab a few things for dinner and then I get a few more hours of work done before Tyler shows up.

He texts me that he's in front of my building and I slip on my sneakers and my green hoodie, call goodbye to Leighton and head outside to find him and Freddie and a mid-sized brown and white dog waiting on the sidewalk.

"And who is this?" I ask, bending down to pet the new dog.

"Piper, meet Maisie." Tyler passes me her leash. "She's a Siberian retriever. She just arrived at the shelter a few days ago."

"Hi beautiful girl," I say. Maisie blinks at me with the softest brown eyes and my heart instantly fills up with love for her. I sternly remind myself that I can't adopt a dog right now. Not even one as adorable and sweet as Maisie is. My apartment is too small and cramped and besides, Leighton would kill me. She's more of a cat person.

I live just a few blocks from Kits beach, so that's where Tyler and I decide to head.

"How's it going with your new listing?" he says, glancing at me. He's wearing a navy-blue porkpie hat. He's very committed to hats. "I didn't realize you and Aiden knew each other."

Right. He started working for Madeline while I was off on medical leave, which means he wasn't around to witness Aiden double crossing me. Tyler and I are work friends and while I know almost everything about his life (he lives to overshare), I haven't opened up to him in quite the same way yet. This is actually the first time we've even done something together outside of the office.

I let out a long breath. Maybe it's time to let him in a little more. I've gotten too comfortable with keeping people at arm's length and I really do want to change that, so I fill him in on my history with Aiden.

"Wait," Tyler says, holding up his hand. "He stole your client?"

I nod.

His face scrunches up in such an expression of disgust that I can't help but laugh. Whether he realizes it or not he's just been promoted from work friend to real friend.

"Well," I say, because this is where things get a bit murky regarding what Aiden did to me. "*Technically* she wasn't my client yet. But she was ready to sign the representation agreement." Aiden just beat me to it. Was it shitty of him to do that? Yes. But unethical? To be honest, that's kind of a grey area. What he didn't wasn't illegal but it was still wrong, at least in my eyes.

"But you guys were friends," Tyler says, shaking his head. At the stop light he digs into the pocket of his coat for a treat for each of the dogs.

"Yes." At least I thought we were.

"Aiden seems too nice to be a villain," he says.

"It's all an act." My mouth tightens as I remember how sorry/not sorry he was when I found out what he'd done. He couldn't seem to grasp why I was so mad, which just made everything worse. I know he didn't expect that poaching my client would mean the end of our friendship—he figured I'd eventually get over it, that we could just go back to the way things were. Clearly he didn't know me as well as he thought he did (and vice versa).

Even now, two years later, I don't think Aiden realizes how badly that experience shook me. The only reason I didn't quit real estate altogether was because Madeline talked me out of it.

Thinking about this brings all those awful emotions to the surface again. It's a good thing that Aiden isn't here right now or I'd probably flip out on him again.

"I really can't picture him with Madeline," Tyler says as the light changes and we cross the street. "I know she likes her men a little younger, but he really doesn't seem like her type."

I stop walking in the middle of the street. I feel like he just punched me in the chest. "What?"

Tyler turns around, eyebrows raised, and waits for me to catch up to him. "You didn't know they used to be a thing?"

"No." But I guess that explains Madeline's strange reaction when Aiden showed up at our office the other day. Apparently I'm not the only one at Pinnacle Realty who has a past with him.

"When were they together?" I ask, relieved that my voice sounds normal and not like I'm reeling from this news. The idea of Aiden and Madeline shouldn't bother me but it does. Quite a bit.

"It was a few years ago," Tyler says. "But they weren't really *together* together. They only went out a handful of times. Madeline really liked him, though. She was pretty bummed when he ended it."

I frown. Unlike Tyler I don't have in-depth personal discussions with my boss, so it's not exactly a surprise that Madeline didn't tell me about her relationship with Aiden—or whatever it is you want to call it. Especially because it's not really any of my business.

But just because it's not my business doesn't mean I'm not going to dig for a little information. When it comes to Aiden I can't seem to help myself.

"Why did he break up with her?"

Tyler shrugs. "I guess he just wasn't feeling it."

This just confirms my theory that Aiden is never going to settle down with one woman. Madeline is gorgeous and kind, a total catch. She's basically perfect. If he didn't want her, then what exactly *is* he looking for?

Maybe that's the problem—he doesn't know.

"Were they dating while I was working at the brokerage?" What I really want to know is whether they were seeing each other before or after Aiden swooped in and stole my client. If it was after, then I'm probably going to meltdown right here on the sidewalk—I might not confide in Madeline about much, but she was aware of how that particular situation affected me. I'm definitely going to feel betrayed if she kept her involvement with Aiden a secret while I was sobbing about what he did to me in her office.

"I don't know," Tyler says. "I didn't grill her on the timeline."

I shake my head. No. I can't imagine Madeline would have done that. She has too much integrity. She and Aiden must have been together before he stole my client, because when I told Madeline about it she was angrier than I'd ever seen her before. She called him and cussed him out right in front of me, which now that I think about it was really out of character. I gave her a reason to yell at him and she probably needed that.

"I'll bet the sex was really amazing," Tyler says. "How could it not be? They're two of the hottest people alive."

I grunt. I don't want to think about Aiden and Madeline having sex. I don't want to think about Aiden having sex with anyone, but especially not with my gorgeous, kind, perfect catch of a boss. And it's not because I want to have sex with him—I may have wanted to once, very badly, but I'm over that now—it's because…well, I don't know why. I just don't want to think about it.

Tyler and I walk the rest of the way to the beach in silence. The sun is about to set and the lights of the downtown core are spread out before us, twinkling to life.

"You're into him," Tyler says, bending down to take Freddie off his leash. "I can tell."

"What?" I laugh hollowly. Unconvincingly. "I am not into Aiden."

He nudges me gently with his elbow. "Come on. It's written all over your face."

Awesome.

"It's okay. I don't blame you. He's ridiculously sexy," Tyler says.

I flush. I can't argue with him about that. I wish I could, but I can't.

"Don't worry. I'm not going to tell anyone." He mimes zipping his lips.

"There's nothing to tell," I say, but I'm relieved that he's planning to keep this conversation to himself. I don't want him blabbing my business all over the office. Especially knowing what I know now about Aiden's relationship with my boss.

Tyler gives me a look.

"Fine," I say. "I *was* into him but that was years ago. I'm over it now."

Tyler smiles. "I can see that."

"I am," I insist.

I'm over Aiden. I am *so* over him. And, okay, I still find him attractive—I can't exactly control that—but that doesn't mean I want to be with him. It doesn't mean that at all.

I steer the conversation to work-talk. Tyler and I are real estate nerds, which means we can discuss the housing market for hours on end and never get bored. And so that's what we do as we take the dogs to the off-leash area.

Tyler pulls out two small red rubber balls and Freddie and Maisie start to dance around in excitement. I throw Maisie's ball down the beach. She races after it and then brings it back to me in a matter of seconds. I lean down to pet her and she is pure joy, her tail wagging so hard her whole butt sways.

"Are you sure you don't want to adopt her?" Tyler asks me once we've tired the dogs out and have arrived back at my apartment building.

"Of course I want to adopt her," I say. "I love her. But my circumstances haven't changed in the past hour. I can't have a dog right now." It's not just up to me, anyway—Leighton would have to be on board and I know she isn't going to want all the responsibility that comes with having a dog. I'm enough responsibility for her.

I give Maisie a final hug and reluctantly pass her leash to Tyler.

"Make sure she goes to a great family," I say, just as my phone rings. I slide it out of my pocket. "It's Madeline. I'd better take this."

Tyler waves. I answer the call as he walks away with the dogs.

"Hi, Madeline," I say.

"Piper," she replies, sounding harried. "Are you free tomorrow night? I need you to do me a big favor."

CHAPTER EIGHT

THE NEXT EVENING I park in front of the Yaletown condo building where I'm hosting Madeline's open house and switch on my hazard lights. Rain drums against my windshield as I grab a yard sign from the passenger seat and dash outside to plant it in a small patch of grass near the front door. A minute or two later I'm back in my car, shivering but mostly dry, at least underneath my raincoat.

I spend the next fifteen minutes circling the block before I manage to find an open parking spot. I plug the meter for three hours and then walk back to the building, trying to shield the supplies for the event from getting completely soaked. I've stepped in to do open houses for Madeline before and I usually don't mind, but this one is coming at a bad time—I have to be at the Davidsons house early tomorrow morning to meet Aiden for the video shoot and I feel totally unprepared.

It's going to be another late night of playing catch up.

Madeline left the keys to the building on my desk this after-noon. I enter the fancy, all glass lobby and take the elevator up to the fourth floor. There's lots of competition in this area of the city, a lot of similar condos for sale in the same price range, but this unit faces the marina so hopefully the million-dollar view will be enough to draw people in on this cold and miserable rainy night.

I slide the key into the lock of 4A. When I step inside, my heart sinks. The owners haven't cleaned up and the place is a mess. Well, a mess by realtor standards anyway. The tiniest thing can turn a buyer off, so everything needs to be spotless—the baseboards wiped of dust, the counters free of clutter, the bed properly made. No hair in the shower or fingerprints on the windows. Family photos and tchotchkes taken down and hidden away. The place needs to look as fresh and faceless as a hotel room, otherwise it will never sell. Or it will sell, but for lower than the asking price.

I pull off my purple Hunter boots and hang up my raincoat before frantically running around straightening towels and shoving all the owner's loose crap into closets. I spritz clouds of cinnamon-scented air fresher in every room and set a plate of oatmeal cookies and bottles of Pinnacle Realty branded water on the kitchen counter, along with a stack of Madeline's business cards. She's paying me a flat rate to take over for her tonight, but the commission—if/when it comes—will strictly be hers. But I still want to help her sell this place.

I'm just touching up my makeup when the first arrival knocks on the door. I put on my brightest smile, take a deep, cleansing breath and walk over to let them in.

Two hours later, my voice is hoarse and my cheeks hurt from smiling. Almost thirty people showed up, which isn't great but it isn't too bad either considering how nasty the weather is. I'm about to call it a night and start packing up when Bowen Clarke walks in with a young couple.

"Piper," Bowen says, smiling at me. He has an amazing smile. He's sexy in an understated way, the kind of guy you might not notice at first but when you do you can't believe you've never noticed him before. We've run into each other at open houses and industry events a bunch of times over the years and I always enjoy talking to him.

"Nice to see you," he adds, running a hand through his rain-damp curly brown hair. "Sorry we're dropping in on you so late."

I smile. "That's alright. Come on in."

Bowen introduces me to his clients, Aaron and Savannah, and they all kick off their shoes and shed their wet outerwear. I show them around the condo, pointing out all the features that make this unit special. "In-unit laundry," I say, opening a closet near the bathroom to reveal a stacked washer/dryer. A huge selling point, in my opinion. I would kill to not have to trek down to the basement in our building to do my laundry.

I lead them through the kitchen with its stainless-steel appliances and into the bedroom with its floor-to-ceiling window that overlooks the wharf. It's grey outside, sure, and rain is pattering steadily against the glass, but that doesn't diminish the incredible view. Rows of sleek white boats and yachts bobbing in the water below, the Cambie Street bridge curving gently to the left, the huge round glittering ball of Science World in the distance.

I study Aaron and Savannah's reactions closely but they're not giving me much so I have no clue what they really think of this apartment. Bowen, like any good realtor, keeps his face unreadable, and I'm guessing he must have coached them to keep their own faces blank. Which is exactly what I would have done if I was representing them. The worst thing a client can do is show how excited they are about a property in front of the seller's agent—it tips the balance during negotiations. Ask me how I know.

After we've completed the tour, Bowen tells his clients he'll meet them downstairs in the lobby. "I just need to have a word with Piper," he says to them.

Interesting. Maybe they are going to make an offer. This may not be my listing but I'll still come out looking good if I sell it for Madeline. And I like looking good to Madeline. I know she values me as part of her team, but I'm also painfully aware that I haven't brought in much business for a while and there's only so long that can continue without some kind of consequence. That's another reason why selling the Davidsons house is so critical for me.

Bowen waits until we hear the ding of the elevator in the hall before he lets out a long, tired sigh. "God help me," he says, shaking his head. "I've shown those two just about every condo in this city and they've managed to find something wrong with every single place. I hate to do it, but I think I'm going to have to break up with them."

I laugh. "I get it," I say, thinking of Ben and Jiya and all the hours I've invested over the past six months ferrying them around to different properties with nothing to show for it. "Time wasters are the worst."

Bowen nods. We stare at each other for a few seconds, and just when I'm beginning to wonder if he actually wanted to talk to me about something or if he just needed a break from his clients, he says, "So, I thought maybe we could hang out sometime. Go for coffee or a hike or something?"

I blink. I get asked out pretty regularly on the dating apps, but it hasn't happened in person in a long time. So long, in fact, that it catches me completely off guard.

I briefly worry about crossing professional lines—if we date and it goes badly, then we'll have a lifetime of awkward run ins at work-related events to look forward to. Then again, what if it doesn't go badly? Maybe it's worth taking the chance to find out. Bowen is sexy and funny and interesting. I genuinely like him. And, okay, he might not make my heart race in the same way that Aiden does but maybe that kind of attraction isn't what I need. Maybe what I need is someone who is the total opposite of Aiden Miller.

And so I find myself saying yes, I will go out with him.

"Great," Bowen says, grinning at me. "I'll text you and we'll make some plans."

"Looking forward to it," I say. And I am. Bowen is cute and he's charming and he's not Aiden and that's a very, very good thing.

I WAS SO busy getting ready for the open house that I skipped dinner and so by the time I get home I'm starving. Leighton catches me taking a box of macaroni and cheese out of the cupboard and insists on making me something healthier.

"You don't have to do that," I say.

"If I don't then you're just going to eat that crap."

True. But it's such tasty crap.

Leighton gently pushes me aside and whips up a chickpea curry, which is delicious, and we eat it on the couch in our pajamas from the misshapen bowls she made last year in a pottery class.

"Mom called me earlier," Leighton says as she scrolls through all of the Hallmark movies she has saved on our DVR, trying to find one we haven't watched ten times already. "She says she hasn't talked to you in weeks."

I shrug. "I've been kind of busy."

"You really should reach out," she says. "I think her feelings are hurt."

I snort. "Her feelings are always hurt." Our mother is an emotional vampire and talking to her depresses me so I try to do it as little as possible. "And what about my feelings?" I add, jabbing at a chickpea. "What kind of parent isn't there for their child when they have cancer?"

Leighton sighs. "Yeah, that was pretty inexcusable," she says. "And I fully support you setting boundaries with Mom. I don't want you to think that I'm not on your side, because I am Team Pips forever." She leans over and hugs me. "But I still feel bad for her. I can't help it."

That's because my sister has a soft heart. Leighton so badly wants to believe our mother can change, but I made peace with the fact that she's never going to be who I need her to be a long time ago. It sucks but that's just the way it is.

Leighton gives up trying to convince me to call her and we settle on *Hometown Hero*, a movie about a woman forced to take care of her client's dog. I keep sneaking glances at my sister as we watch it, wondering if I should use this as an opening to talk her into adopting Maisie…

"Aw, that dog is so adorable," I say.

"The vet is pretty cute, too," she says.

She's right, he is very tall dark and handsome, but she's missing the point completely. I'm going to need to be direct.

"We should rescue a dog," I say, smiling at her as if the thought had just occurred to me. "Imagine all the good karma that would come our way."

"Nice try, but no way," Leighton says. "Dogs are a lot of work and we both know who would be stuck taking care of it." She sets her empty bowl on the coffee table. "Why don't we get a cat? They don't require as much attention."

"We can get one if you want." I don't mind cats. I'd rather have Maisie, but I get where my sister is coming from. It's not fair to saddle her with all the responsibility that comes with owning a dog.

"Really?" Leighton says, surprised.

"Sure. Why not."

She smiles. "Let's go to the shelter tomorrow."

"I can't tomorrow," I say. I have the listing shoot at the Davidsons and it's going to be an all-day thing. "You pick one. I trust your judgement."

After the movie ends, Leighton gets up to take a shower and I check my phone. Aiden has just emailed me the latest version of the script for tomorrow. This video needs to be perfect—it's going to be blasted to every luxury realtor in town next week, along with some of Aiden's big-fish clients.

I sigh. I've been compiling a client list of my own with Madeline's help, but so far I don't have a lot of prospects—finding people who not only have enough bank to buy a mansion but are also willing to talk to me, a relative newbie to the game, it isn't easy. It's hard not to feel discouraged.

I make some changes to the script and then send it back to Aiden. He texts me almost instantly.

> **AIDEN:** Hi.

> **ME:** Hi.

> **AIDEN:** ...

I stare at those three little dots as they disappear, reappear. Disappear again.

> **AIDEN:** You want to grab a drink? We could go over the script in person.

I frown. Two years ago, I would have agreed to meet him anytime, anywhere. But Aiden and I aren't friends anymore. We're colleagues. And colleagues don't meet up for a drink at ten o'clock at night.

ME: No.

AIDEN: Aw, come on. It would be faster than sending it back and forth.

ME: No, it wouldn't.

I don't know if he's bored or lonely or what, but giving in would require that I change out of my pajamas and no thanks. Nothing good can come from meeting up with Aiden tonight. For me, anyway.

AIDEN: 😞

I can't help smiling. It's getting harder to keep a fence around my feelings when he's always looking for a way to climb it.

ME: I'll see you tomorrow.

AIDEN: 😃

CHAPTER NINE

"MORNING, P," AIDEN says, handing me a red mug. "Made you a maple latte."

"Thanks," I reply, surprised and touched that he remembered my usual coffee order. I glance around the Davidsons kitchen. Aiden also brought bagels and muffins and—my favorite—banana bread. It's such a small thing, remembering the things I like, but it makes my heart pound a little faster. That and the fact that he looks so good. He's dressed in jeans and a black t-shirt, his blonde hair artfully mussed. But what really gets me is his thick-framed black glasses. Hot guys in glasses are kind of my thing.

I briefly wonder if Aiden knows that, if he's wearing them on purpose just to make me weak-kneed, but then I remember that he's not interested in me so why would he bother? He made it clear a long time ago that he's only wants to be friends.

"Hi, Greg," I say as I help myself to a slice of banana bread.

Greg Li, our videographer, looks up from the storyboard spread out on the Davidsons enormous marble island. We've hired him to take the listing photos and video—Aiden's used him before but this is my first meeting him in person.

"Piper," Greg says warmly, extending his hand. He's older than Aiden and me, maybe late-forties or early-fifties, and he has the most gorgeously thick silver hair. "I thought we'd start here and then make our way upstairs," he adds as his assistant Brittany comes into the kitchen carrying a light meter. There's a bunch of photography equipment—lights, a tripod—already set up in the corner of the room.

I nod. "Okay."

The plan, Greg tells me, is to take the photos first, followed by the video shoot this afternoon, which Aiden and I are both going to be featured in.

As Greg and Brittany continue setting up, Aiden gestures for me to follow him. Greg knows what he's doing—he's shot thousands of high-end houses before—so really, our job this morning is to stay out of his way and just let him do his thing. He won't actually need us until he's ready to shoot the video.

Aiden leads me into the same all-white room where I met with Annabelle last week. We have the house to ourselves today— Annabelle and Tim are staying at the Fairmont Pacific Rim for two nights on our dime (in separate rooms, at her request). Another expense added to an already very expensive day—one that's costing us almost ten thousand dollars. Five of which I'm going to be responsible for coughing up. Of course, it will be worth it if we sell this property. If we don't…well, then I can kiss that money goodbye.

My stomach hurts thinking about it.

Aiden sinks down onto the couch. I sit across from him and take a small bite of banana bread, careful not to spill any crumbs anywhere.

"I'm exhausted," he says.

"Me too."

We were up ridiculously late last night, emailing the script back and forth, nitpicking over every little thing until we were both finally happy with it.

"You don't look tired," Aiden says. "You look great."

"That's the magic of makeup." I slathered on quite a bit of concealer this morning to cover my undereye bags.

He shakes his head. "It's not just makeup. You always look beautiful, P."

I frown. I know Aiden thinks he's being nice, that paying me a compliment will make me feel good, but I really wish he wouldn't say things like that. The first time around, when we were friends, I believed every word out of his mouth. I couldn't tell the difference between harmless flirting and real feelings, and because of that I ended up with a broken heart.

Well, that's not going to happen again. I'm wiser now. And I'm not going to take his flattery so seriously.

As Greg and Brittany move through the house taking photos, I steer us towards business chat and industry gossip. Half an hour later, they come into the living room and Aiden and I move back to the kitchen where he quickly polishes off two everything bagels and a blueberry muffin.

"So I've decided to delete all my dating profiles. I'm kind of over trying to meet someone online," Aiden says as he washes his dish in the big farmhouse sink. "What about you? Are you having any luck on them?"

I narrow my eyes. Is this his way of telling me that he's seen my dating profile? I think it is. And why is he even asking me about this, anyway? Is he simply trying to make conversation or is there another reason he wants to know if I'm active on the apps?

It's tiring, analyzing every word that comes out of his mouth. Too bad I can't trust anything he says. Or does.

"I'm probably going to take mine down, too," I say, even though up I hadn't thought about it until right this minute. "Now that I'm seeing someone."

It's not exactly a lie but it isn't exactly the truth, either. I have a date with Bowen on Monday to do the Grouse Grind, a notoriously punishing hike straight up a mountainside. While I'm excited to spend some time with Bowen, I can't say I'm all that jazzed about the hike itself. Even if he has promised to buy me breakfast afterwards.

"You are?" Aiden says, his eyebrows rising. "You told me you were single when we went to dinner a few nights ago."

I shrug. "Circumstances have changed."

I mean, they haven't. Not really. But Aiden doesn't need to know that.

He scowls and starts to scrub the plate a little harder than necessary. So hard, in fact, that I worry he'll break it.

Wait. Is he jealous?

No. There's no way. And it's dangerous for me to think that he might be. This is how I got so confused before.

Still, if Aiden's going to pry into my personal life, then I'm going to pry into his. Let's see how he likes it.

"I heard about you and Madeline," I say, grabbing a dishcloth and taking the plate from him.

Aiden glances at me. "Yeah? What exactly did you hear?"

"That you dumped her."

He snorts. "Is it really considered dumping someone if it wasn't serious? It was just a casual thing. It's not like we were in a relationship. She wasn't my girlfriend."

I flinch. Opening up this conversation might have been a misstep on my part—I don't want him to think that Madeline has been bad-mouthing him. She would be horrified if she found out we were talking about her. Not to mention it's totally inappropriate and completely unprofessional to gossip about your boss's sex life. I need to correct this quickly.

"For the record, Madeline hasn't said a word about you," I say. "I heard this from someone else."

Aiden shakes his head as I put the plate back in the cabinet and hang up the towel. "So you're just repeating gossip," he says.

"Basically."

He's quiet for a moment. "I wouldn't use the word dumped, but I did decide that we should stop seeing each other."

"Why?" I probe, despite my better judgement. What can I say? I'm nosy. "Madeline's amazing. She's beautiful and intelligent and she has such a good heart. Any guy would be lucky to have her."

"You're right," Aiden says, nodding. "Maddy's all of those things. But that doesn't mean we were a good match."

He's being honest, I'll give him that, but I'm still annoyed on Madeline's behalf.

"I don't understand what men want," I say.

Aiden laughs. "I could say the same about women."

"I'll tell you exactly what we want: someone who is respectful and thoughtful, supportive and emotionally available," I say. "And if he can make us laugh, even better." It really doesn't feel like that much to ask for, so why is it so damn hard to find?

"In my experience, a guy can tick every box on that list and still fall short," he says. "As for Maddy, the truth is that I liked her…just not quite enough. And I didn't want to waste any more of her time."

I grunt. I guess I can't fault him for that. Even if I still don't get it. I mean if Madeline isn't his type then who is?

I'm still wondering about that when Greg comes in to show us what he's captured so far. Aiden and I huddle around the camera, his arm brushing against mine as we flick through the pictures. I do my best to focus on what's in front of me instead of the way he smells, like a mixture of citrus and wood chips, but it's almost impossible. Standing this close to him is completely scrambling my senses. Making me feel things that I don't want to feel for him.

After Greg leaves again to finish taking the rest of the photos, I grab my laptop out of my tote bag and sit down at the kitchen table to do some work. Aiden sets up his own computer directly across from me. His legs are ridiculously long and he keeps accidently-but-maybe-on-purpose bumping my foot with his own.

A few minutes later, I'm concentrating deeply on an email when Aiden jump-scares me by shouting, "Yes!"

I glance up to see him pumping his fist in the air, more excited than I've ever seen him before.

He beams at me. "We got Rock the Boat! They're free for the night of the broker's open."

I roll my eyes, but I can't help smiling back. When did he become so horny for yacht rock?

Once he settles down, we work in relative silence for the next two hours, getting up only to refill our coffee mugs at the built-in expresso station. My only other interruption is a text from Tyler, who insists that 'inquiring minds want to know whether Aiden and I have made out yet', which I ignore.

More work and then we pause for lunch, diving into the fancy sandwiches and salads Aiden's assistant had delivered. Greg and Brittany join us while we eat and then Aiden and I are sent to get ready for the video shoot.

I go out to my car to retrieve the dark green Tori Burch belted shirtdress I borrowed from Rent the Runway. After I've changed in one of the guest bedrooms, I stand in front of the gilded full-length mirror to touch up my makeup before re-tying the cream silk scarf around my neck.

Aiden is in the foyer. He's traded in his jeans and t-shirt for a navy suit and a red tie. He must be wearing contacts because he's gotten rid of the glasses (boo). He watches me descend the stairs with a strange expression on his face.

"What?" I ask, feeling my cheeks start to burn. I thought this dress would be perfect but maybe I was wrong. I start to panic. I didn't bring any other options, which seems very short-sighted now.

He clears his throat. "Nothing. You look great."

Am I…am I making him nervous?

I think I am.

Weird.

"Ready?" Aiden asks.

I nod.

Greg has set the camera up on the other side of the door. The plan is for us to throw it open and welcome the viewer inside the house. Almost like we're a couple, inviting people into our home.

We run through the scene a few times and I think we've got it, but then Brittany says, "Piper, can you lose the scarf? It's a bit distracting."

"The scarf stays," Aiden says firmly, before I can even form an answer.

Brittany blinks, clearly confused to meet resistance on what must seem like a very simple request. I'm grateful that Aiden has spoken up so that I don't have to explain why I don't want to take the scarf off. Now I don't have to tell her the story and watch pity creep into her expression.

Fortunately, my scarf is only a minor speed bump and the rest of the afternoon goes well. Aiden occasionally flubs his lines, but we laugh it off and still manage to wrap up on time, just before sunset.

"We're all dressed up with nowhere to go," he says as he arms the security system. Greg and Brittany took off half an hour ago, but we had to do another walk through the house to make sure all the lights were off and everything was left as perfect as we found it when we arrived this morning. "You want to grab some dinner?"

I shake my head as we step outside. "Too full." I snuck a blueberry bagel during our last break.

"How about a drink, then?" Aiden asks as he locks the front door and pockets the keys.

Going out with him tonight is tempting, but that's exactly why I need to go home instead. A drink may just be a drink to him, but it would just lead me to getting my hopes up. I don't want to make that mistake again.

"I don't think that's such a good idea," I say.

Before he can try and convince me otherwise, I wish him good-night and get into my car. But as I'm driving away, I can't help looking in my rear-view mirror. Aiden's leaning against his car, his hands tucked into his pockets. Just watching me leave. Like a sad puppy.

It's almost enough to make me turn the car around, agree to grab a drink with him after all. Almost, but not quite. My fingers tighten on the steering wheel and I keep driving.

CHAPTER
TEN

I SPEND MOST OF the next morning knocking on doors in the richest neighborhoods in West Vancouver on the off chance I might find someone interested in buying the Davidsons property. Door knocking sucks. I hate it. But I make myself do it because it sometimes reaps results and right now I desperately need results.

I've been standing in front of a beautiful Tudor for a few minutes—I know someone's home, I saw the curtains twitch—but when it becomes evident that they're not going to answer, I sigh and leave a small pot of lavender honey on the welcome mat. The honey is my calling card, the label contains all of my contact details. I've also included a fact sheet about the house and a handwritten note to let whoever's hiding behind the curtains know that I'd be delighted to help them with their real estate needs.

Dejected, I walk back to my car just as the rain starts up again. This morning has been a total bust. I haven't gotten any leads, although I still have a kernel of hope that the honey will convince someone to reach out to me. All I need is one buyer. Just one.

To cheer myself up, I decide to get a coffee before I head into the office. The Starbucks drive-thru line is way too long, so I place a mobile order and wait in my car until the designated pick-up time. While I'm waiting, I check my emails.

Tyler has sent me a message, the subject line a long string of exclamation marks, his way of preparing me for something he thinks I'm not going to like. I get at least one of these emails from him a day, so I'm not too worried—until I open the message and find that he's sent me a link to the MLS listing for the Davidsons house.

My jaw tightens. I wasn't expecting the listing to go up today. Aiden just went ahead and uploaded it without discussing it with me first, which is super annoying. He should have given me a heads up, at the very least.

But that's not even the worst part. That comes when I click the link and see Greg's beautiful photos—a handful of which he sent us late last night—and the listing description, along with Aiden's email and phone number beneath a headshot of him looking stupidly handsome.

What I don't see? Anything about me. There is no mention that I'm co-listing this property anywhere on this page.

My vision narrows. All the goodwill from yesterday drains away. My heart is pounding so hard I can hear it. Aiden did this on purpose! He knows that every realtor in town checks for new listings daily, sometimes multiple times. Those that have already seen it will assume that Aiden is the only realtor the Davidsons are working with and they're going to call him for information and to book showings. He's cheated by starting the race before the pistol has even been fired.

From the outside, it might seem like this is a small, easily fix-able thing, nothing worth getting angry over, but it doesn't feel that way to me in this moment. It feels like Aiden's trying to gain an advantage. The stupid part is, he already has one—he's more established than me, he has more contacts than me. The odds are stacked heavily in his favor. He doesn't need to play dirty to win. So, what is this about then? He gets a kick out of making sure I don't even have a chance?

My hands are shaking as I call him. Aiden might have screwed me over once before, but I'm certainly not going to just sit back and let him do it again.

He picks up on the first ring. "I know, I know," he says, his voice harried. "I'm sorry, P. I swear it was just an oversight."

"How do you just 'forget' to include your co-realtor?" I ask.

"My assistant is new and he's a little eager," Aiden explains. "We're fixing it right now, I promise. It should be updated shortly. I really am sorry. I know how this looks."

Okay, but blaming the assistant is what everyone does when something goes wrong. Is it right? No. But that doesn't mean it doesn't happen all the time.

Still, my shoulders relax the tiniest bit. Aiden sounds genuinely remorseful and I want to believe that he's telling me the truth, but it's not that easy to take his word on anything. It's not that easy to trust someone who betrayed you. At the back of my mind I'm always going to be wondering if he's playing me for a fool.

"Let me know when the listing's been changed," I say, hanging up on him.

I'm sure Aiden thinks I'm freaking out over nothing, but I don't care. He doesn't understand the position I'm in. And he never will. He was set up to succeed from the beginning when he walked into a job at his parents' brokerage. I've had to fight to get where I am and I'm not even anywhere close to where I want to be yet. And there's no guarantee that I'll ever get there.

This just strengthens my resolve to find a buyer and win this bet. Not only will it mean that I'll get all the commission, but it will teach Aiden Miller to never mess with me again.

THAT AFTERNOON, A huge bouquet of pink peonies arrives at the office. I assume they're for Madeline—she gets flowers delivered to her fairly often—so I'm surprised when Tyler carries the vase over to my desk.

"Looks like someone's really sorry," Tyler says, setting the vase down beside my laptop.

My eyebrows rise. "You think these are from Aiden?"

He shrugs. "Guess you won't know for sure until you open the card."

So I do. And sure enough I recognize Aiden's handwriting. The fact that he went to the extra effort of going to the florist himself instead of just dictating a message over the phone makes my stomach flip.

I know I have a lot to apologize for, but I hope that you can somehow find it in your heart to forgive me. I really am sorry, P.

My cheeks flush. Is he asking me to forgive him for what happened this morning or for everything else, too? I'm not sure, but I feel myself waffling. Holding a grudge against him has been hard, but I'm still afraid that if I let my guard down, even just a little bit, he'll end up breaking my heart again. Even if he doesn't intend to.

"You two are cute together," Tyler says. "But maybe don't tell Madeline I said that. And maybe don't tell her who the flowers are from. She might get weird about it."

I shake my head. "There's nothing to get weird about. He sent the flowers to smooth things over. That's all."

"Okay," Tyler says.

"Okay," I reply, but I take his advice and stow the flowers beneath my desk just in case. "Did I tell you I have a date this week?" I fill him in about Bowen, hoping it will get him off my back about Aiden.

"Bowen Clarke?"

I nod. I'm not surprised that Tyler knows him—he knows everybody in the real estate world.

He taps the end of his fountain pen against his lips, digesting this bit of information. "I approve," he says finally. "Bowen's sexy, in a wholesome, boy-next-door kind of way. And he's nice. A little strange, maybe, but nice."

I laugh. "He's not strange."

"He is, but that's okay. Strange isn't always a bad thing." Tyler says. He opens his desk drawer and digs out an energy bar. "Where is he taking you on your date?"

"We're doing the Grouse Grind."

Tyler wrinkles his nose. "I beg your pardon?" he says. "There are a million amazing restaurants and bars in this city but he wants to scale a mountain with you instead?"

"I don't know. Maybe it'll be fun."

"No," Tyler says. "It won't. The grind is the furthest thing from fun. I did it once and it almost killed me." He rips open his energy bar. "Seriously, Piper, you're going to hate it. And you'll hate him for making you do it." He shakes his head. "Take my advice and tell Bowen you want to do something—anything—else."

"It'll be fine," I say. Tyler exaggerates everything. I mean, I've heard the grind is hard, that's not exactly news, but I'm in pretty good shape. I'm sure I can do it.

Tyler laughs. "Well, don't say I didn't warn you," he says.

WHEN I GET home that evening, I'm kicking off my shoes in the hall when a paw darts out from the closet and swipes at my ankle. I screech, causing Leighton to come running in from the kitchen.

"Oh, I see you've met Mr. Tumnus," she says, smiling at me.

Of course my sister would name a cat after her favorite character from *The Lion, the Witch and the Wardrobe*.

"Yep. We've met."

"Isn't he adorable?" she asks as the cat peers out at us from the closet with narrowed, evil eyes.

"So adorable," I reply, bending down to dab at the three thin lines of blood on my ankle.

"Mr. Tumnus is a little spicy," Leighton admits. "The shelter said that he has some trust issues. But I'm sure he'll come around. We just have to smother him with love."

"I think I'm okay with loving him from a distance," I say as the cat decides to make a break for it. He darts out of the closet, a comet of orange fur, and squeezes himself under the couch.

"Poor guy," Leighton says with a sigh. "He's been hiding all day. He's terrified."

I'm sure he is. I'm also sure that my sister chose the hardest case from the shelter, the cat that no one else wanted, the one with the attitude problem. I should have known better than to send her there alone.

"Look," Leighton says, showing me all of the stuff she's bought to make Mr. Tumnus comfortable—toys and a water fountain and a three-story cat tree. She stocked up on tins of food and placed a litter box in the bathroom, which I notice when I go in to get a Band-Aid for my ankle.

"I had to get rid of Azriel," she says sadly when I come back out. "I gave him to Mrs. Chomsky downstairs."

I stare at her blankly.

"Our sago palm," Leighton says. "It's poisonous to cats. All the other plants are fine, though, thank goodness."

Yes, thank goodness we don't have to get rid of any more plants—otherwise our apartment would lose that forest-feel.

Mr. Tumnus avoids us for the rest of the night, remaining hidden under the couch despite Leighton's repeated attempts to coax him out with treats. Instead, he waits until we're both on the edge of sleep to explore the apartment, knocking over who-knows-what and pawing at my door because he's suddenly in the mood for company.

I put my pillow over my head but it doesn't do much to block out the yowling. Eventually I hear Leighton get up to shush him but when he doesn't shut up I wonder if she still thinks that cats are less work than dogs.

CHAPTER
ELEVEN

OKAY, I DEFINITELY should have listened to Tyler—the Grouse Grind is even worse than he claimed it was. It's twenty-eight hundred steps of pure, punishing hell.

"You're doing great," Bowen says, holding his hand out to me. I take it and let him help me up the next step and the next one after that. Before this morning I thought I was in good shape, but this hike has proved that I'm far from it—my legs are burning, I can't catch my breath and I've completely sweated through my t-shirt.

I groan. I hate this. I hate everything about it. We've been climbing for over and hour and we're not even halfway to the top yet. I can't even turn around and go back down because this is a one-way trail. I keep having to move aside to let other people pass by us, which would be embarrassing if I had the energy to feel anything other than total exhaustion.

"You got this, Piper," Bowen says, but I *don't* got this, at least not at the pace he wants us to keep. He's barely out of breath, but that's because for some reason he puts himself through this torture three times a week. He's used to it.

"Why don't you go on ahead," I pant at him when I stop to rest for the fifth time. I wipe my forehead with the red bandana tied around my neck. "I'll meet you up there."

"Are you sure?" Bowen asks, but he looks relieved. I know he's dying to make it up the mountain in his usual time, which is never going to happen if he sticks with me.

I nod. At least now I can plod along without feeling guilty that I'm holding him back. Let every single person on the trail pass me, I really don't care.

"I'll get us a table at the restaurant," Bowen says.

I nod again, too tired to form words. Even the promise of pancakes and bacon waiting at the top of the mountain isn't enough to inspire me to move any faster. All I really want is to go home, take a long shower and then rot in bed for the rest of the day. Except I can't do that because I have to work. Aiden and I are meeting to go over the last-minute details for the brokers' open this coming weekend.

Bowen smiles and then turns and starts to jog up the stairs. I quickly lose sight of him as he disappears around a curve. A few minutes later, I force myself to start climbing again. Leighton's voice is in my head, cheering me on, insisting I take in the all the beauty surrounding me—the enormous, ancient Douglas Fir trees, the clean mountain air, the twitter of birds. I can't argue that it's beautiful, but I would enjoy it more if I wasn't sweating so much.

I stop a bunch more times to drink water and rest my aching legs, but finally, after an hour and a half, I crest the mountain. The relief I feel is so intense I almost burst into tears. Thank god that's over and I'll never have to do it again.

I walk stiffly over to the restaurant. Bowen's snagged a table at the back, near the huge picture window that offers an impressive view of the city.

"You made it," he says, beaming at me as I plop down in the chair across from him. He slides a champagne glass filled with orange juice towards me. "I ordered you a mimosa."

"Thanks." I chug it down. I can't help it. I drank a litre of water on the way up but I'm still thirsty.

"Have you eaten?" I ask him. He's been waiting for me for quite a while, so I wouldn't really blame him if he did.

Bowen shakes his head. "No," he says. "I feel kind of bad about leaving you behind. We're on a date. I should have done the gentlemanly thing and stayed with you. My mom would kill me if she knew."

"Don't worry about it," I say. After all, I told him to go. And it really was for the best —I was free to wheeze and huff without worrying about what he thought of me.

The waitress arrives with two glasses of ice water. Bowen orders yogurt and berries, which is hardly anything at all, while I get the works—pancakes, bacon, sausage, scrambled eggs and sourdough toast. Along with another mimosa. Because I've earned it.

"So, I noticed you got Tim Davidsons listing," Bowen says, leaning back in his chair. "How did you pull that off?"

"What do you mean?" I ask, polishing off my water.

Bowen shrugs. "I'm surprised, that's all. Aiden Miller doesn't like to share."

"He didn't have a choice." I tell him about Annabelle hiring me, leaving out the part about the Davidsons getting divorced.

Bowen laughs. "I can't imagine Aiden took that well," he says. "I worked at Avenue with him a few years ago and let's just say he's a big part of why I left."

I blink, surprised. I didn't realize Bowen had worked at Avenue Realty. He's never mentioned that before.

"It was ridiculous what Aiden got away with there," Bowen continues. "But I guess you can do whatever you like when your parents own the firm."

I've had the same thoughts myself but for some reason it bothers me to hear Bowen dragging Aiden. Okay, yes, nepotism got him the job—no one can dispute that—but he's worked hard and proved himself over and over again. He deserves some credit for that.

I'm not sure how much Bowen knows about my own history with Aiden, but I decide not to bring it up. From the sounds of it, I don't need to give him another reason not to like him.

"I did love his dad, though," Bowen says. "Ray was the greatest. Too bad Aiden doesn't take after him."

"Oh, come on. He's not that bad." I actually think he got the best parts of his dad—he's charming and confident, he has an innate ability to put people at ease, which are perfect qualities for someone in sales. Of course, he's also a shark, but Ray was a shark too. He just hid it a little better.

Bowen snorts. "Just be careful, Piper. I don't want to see you get screwed over."

That warning is coming about two years too late, but it's sweet that Bowen is looking out for me. I'm tired of bad-mouthing Aiden, though, so I change the subject and ask Bowen how work is going for him. We talk a lot about business before we turn to our personal lives. I learn about his family—his parents have been married for thirty years, he has a younger brother who's trying to make it as an actor, they're all very close. When it's my turn, I tell him about Leighton and my own fractured family, but I leave out my cancer diagnosis. I know Bowen knows about it, but he doesn't push me for details, which I appreciate.

After breakfast we take the gondola back down to the parking lot. Since Bowen and I live on opposite sides of the city we decided to meet here, so this is where we say goodbye.

"We should do this again sometime," he says.

I nod, hoping he means that we should go on another date, not that he wants to do the grind again. Because no.

I can tell he's waiting for a signal from me, a sign that I'd welcome him making a move, so I smile. He steps closer and kisses me. And it's nice. Very nice, actually. So nice that I'm almost able to completely push thoughts of Aiden out of my mind.

CHAPTER
TWELVE

LATER THAT MORNING, I've just settled onto my couch and turned on my laptop when I get an email from a woman thanking me for the honey I left on her doorstep the other day. She's wondering when she can take a look at the Davidsons house. My calling card worked!

I grin and quickly reply to set up a time to chat. It turns out that she's free right now, so I call and it goes very well. Her name is Lynn and she and her husband have been renting in the area while they wait for the perfect home to come on the market. Even better, they aren't working with a realtor, which means if I help them buy this house I could double end the deal. Two commissions in one!

Of course, we're still a long way from an offer, but it's a promising start.

Mr. Tumnus leaps up beside me as I text Aiden to let him know I'm going to bring someone through

tomorrow, feeling smug that I'm the one who found our first potential buyer.

> **AIDEN:** How do you know these people can afford to buy the house?

I frown. I mean, I don't know how much is in their bank ac-
counts, obviously, but they're renting a huge place in West Vancouver
and that's not cheap.

> **ME:** What, I'm supposed to ask them for bank statements?

> **AIDEN:** Yes. The Davidsons are going to want proof of funds before you bring someone through their house. It weeds out anyone who doesn't actually have the cash. Pretty common ask when you're working with clients at this level.

I sigh. I know he's right (damn it), but I have no idea how to ask
Lynn if she can prove she can buy the house without insulting her.

> **AIDEN:** And I would question how serious these people are if they don't already have a realtor. But we can talk about it more tonight.

Right. We're getting together later to go over the final details of
the brokers' open. I'm supposed to meet Aiden at his office at six
o'clock, but I'm still sore from doing the grind this morning and I
really don't feel like putting on work clothes, getting in my car and
driving across town in rush-hour traffic.

ME: Can we just FaceTime instead?

AIDEN: Nah. I'd rather crack through this in person.

I grimace. What's the difference? I don't get why he's so hellbent on us being in the same room together all the time. It's annoying.

AIDEN: Why don't I come to you?

ME: I'm not at the office, I'm working from home. But I guess you can come here if you want.

Leighton is out with friends for the evening, so Aiden and I will be able to work undisturbed. If she was home we'd never get anything done—our apartment is tiny and I'd be all too aware that my sister was in the next room, eavesdropping on every word we said. Not that she'd hear anything all that exciting.

AIDEN: Great! You're still in Kits? Same place?

ME: Yes.

He's been to my apartment before, back when we were friends. Of course, the decor has changed quite a bit since he was last there, thanks to my sister.

Just before six, I get up off the couch with a groan to move the apology peonies Aiden sent me yesterday from the kitchen table to my bedroom—I don't want him to read into why I brought them home instead of leaving them at the office. It's not because I'm still hung up on him, it's because I didn't want to have to explain to Madeline that the guy who dumped her sent me flowers. Even if

Aiden didn't send them as a romantic gesture, it's still not a conversation I want to have with my boss.

I trade my old yoga pants and cropped sweatshirt with a grease stain on the sleeve for a more presentable version of the same outfit, tying a silk scarf around my neck to cover up my scar.

Aiden buzzes and I let him up, my stomach flipping. When he knocks, I take a deep, cleansing breath before I open the door.

"Hi," he says, smiling at me. My heart skips. He's in a suit, fresh from the office, and he's holding a white bakery box. "Brought some pistachio cannoli. I know how much you like them."

"Thanks. That was nice of you," I reply as he hands me the box. He's sure going all out to try and win my friendship back, I'll give him that.

Aiden kicks off his black oxfords, revealing socks with tiny yellow polka dots all over them. He briefly sets his leather messenger bag on the floor before shrugging off his suit jacket and hanging it off the coat rack that's built to look like a tree.

"You've redecorated," he says, taking in the dried floral arrangements, the macrame plant hangers, the gauzy white curtains entwined with fairy lights.

"This is all Leighton." I'm slightly embarrassed, but he doesn't make fun of it, so who knows, maybe he has matured a little. The old Aiden definitely would have cracked a joke or two.

"That makes sense," he says. "You guys live together now?"

I nod and set the bakery box on the mushroom-painted coffee table before slowly lowering myself onto the couch.

"Why are you moving like an old man?" Aiden asks.

"Because I feel like an old man," I say. "I did the Grouse Grind this morning and now I'm paying for it."

"You surprise me, P," he says, plunking down beside me and rolling up the sleeves of blue button-up shirt as I try very hard not to stare at his arms. "I didn't think you'd be into hiking up a mountain."

"Well, you're right, I'm very much not into it," I say. "It wasn't my idea."

Aiden busies himself with taking his laptop out of his leather messenger bag. "Did you go with your boyfriend?"

"Bowen isn't my boyfriend. We just started dating." And yes, I dropped his name on purpose, just to see if Aiden reacts to it. And sure enough, he whips his head around to stare at me.

"Not Bowen Clarke?" he asks.

I nod.

His jaw tightens. "Oh god, really? He's such a slimeball. I *hate* that guy."

"Yeah, well, turns out he isn't too fond of you either," I say. "And he's not a slimeball."

If it was any other guy I'd wonder if he was jealous but this is Aiden. He made it pretty clear two years ago that he wasn't interested in me and I can't imagine anything's changed since then. So he can shove his opinions.

"Believe it or not, it doesn't matter to me if you like him or not," I add. "What matters is that I like him."

And, okay, maybe Bowen doesn't give me butterflies in the same way that Aiden does, but I would much rather be with someone who is genuinely into me than waste time pining after someone who isn't.

Aiden scowls. "I don't want to talk about this anymore."

"You're the one who brought it up," I say. I know I should just leave it alone, but something in me always needs to get the last word with him.

"My mistake," he replies.

"Don't ask if you don't want to know."

He nods. "Got it."

"Good."

"Yup. All good."

"It is good."

"It really is."

I glare at him. He can't even let me have the last word! In an argument that he started! And this isn't something we should even be arguing about. Who I date is none of his concern.

I silently fume as he opens up our event spreadsheet. We stiffly update each other on the status of our individual tasks, until finally the tension starts to dissipate.

"I think we should hire another bartender," Aiden says, looking at me for the first time in ten minutes. "I know it's another added expense, but it'll be —" His face stills as his eye catches on something across the room.

"What?" I ask, following his gaze. He's staring at the bookshelf, which is crammed with thrift-store romance novels and a zillion little porcelain fairies that Leighton has collected over the years.

Instead of answering me, Aiden stands up and walks over to the bookshelf. He picks up the cute little brown and white wooden bird carving that my sister gave me when I first got sick.

"I didn't think you'd still have this," he says, weighing the bird in his palm.

I stare at him, wondering what on earth he's talking about, when it hits me: Leighton never specifically said that the carving was from her—I just assumed that it was because she handed it to me.

My breath catches. "Wait. Did you...did you buy that for me?"

Aiden nods. "I dropped it off after I heard about your surgery," he says, glancing at me. "Leighton didn't tell you?"

I shake my head. I can't believe she never mentioned that. I also can't believe that Aiden did something so thoughtful, but then I remember the apology flowers and the pistachio cannoli and realize that maybe I've been so angry with him that I haven't been able to see him clearly. Maybe he's not quite the villain I thought he was.

"I got it from this little shop on Granville Island," he adds. "It reminded me of you."

I narrow my eyes, confused. I remind him of a bird?

"It's a sand*piper*," he clarifies, his cheeks flushing a deep red. "It sounds kind of stupid now that I say it out loud."

"It's not stupid," I say. It's actually very sweet. Aiden reached out to me at the worst time in my life, even if I didn't know it, and now I feel really bad that I didn't contact him when his father died. I absolutely should have put my pettiness aside and sent my condolences.

"I was really into birds when I was a kid," Aiden says, and that is definitely not how I pictured him as a child. Sports and rough-housing, yes. Snapping girls bras, definitely. Birds? A total surprise.

Our eyes meet. We stare at each other for a long moment and something electric shoots through me. From the expression on his face, I'm sure Aiden feels it, too. Or maybe he doesn't and I'm just deluding myself into thinking that he does because I want to believe it so badly.

My stomach twists. This all feels very familiar. I'm being sucked back in, despite my determination not to be.

I break our gaze, turning back to my laptop, my heart galloping wildly in my chest. Aiden sets the sandpiper back on the shelf and comes back over to the couch. My senses are on high alert as he sits back down beside me, but I force myself to keep staring at the screen.

Mr. Tumnus strolls out of Leighton's room. He doesn't hide as much as he did when we first arrived, but he's still not overly friendly. We've made a silent pact to avoid each other.

"I didn't know you had a cat," Aiden says.

"He's Leighton's," I say. I make no claim on this demon cat.

To my surprise, Mr. Tumnus walks over and jumps on the couch beside Aiden. Aiden extends his hand to pet him.

"Watch it or he'll scratch you," I say. Or bite, as I unfortunately discovered yesterday.

But for some reason Mr. Tumnus has taken an instant shine to Aiden because he crawls into his lap and starts to purr. It's super irritating, considering that I've repeatedly tried to win him over.

"What are you going to wear to the broker's open?" Aiden asks me as he scratches Mr. Tumnus under the chin.

"I don't know. I haven't really thought about it yet." I probably should have, but I've been so busy with everything else. "A black dress, I guess." That's pretty much the only formal wear I have in my closet right now, besides my prom dress.

Aiden shakes his head. "You can't just wear any old thing, P," he says. "This is a theme party. We're the hosts! We have to dress like we belong on a super yacht."

I frown. "What does that even look like?"

Aiden pulls up photos of models in silk maxi dresses and bright, drapey caftans. I definitely don't have anything even close to what they're wearing. I chew my lower lip. Maybe there's still time to order something from Rent the Runway…or I could call Sita, she'd probably have something I could borrow.

I guess Aiden can tell I'm starting to panic, because he says, "Why don't I ask my assistant to get you a dress? He's arranging something for me to wear anyway."

Must be nice to have an assistant to do your bidding. #goals

"That would be great. Thanks," I say. One less thing for me to worry about.

"Hey, are you hungry?" he asks. "Because I'm starving."

I assume that means he's going to crack into the cannoli, but he surprises me by asking if I want to order in some dinner.

"I could really go for some coconut chicken," he adds. "Spring rolls, mango salad, pad thai."

I should probably boot him out, tell him to pick up dinner on his way home, but now that he's mentioned it I really want Thai food. And so, when he offers to buy I give in.

"Your boyfriend isn't going to care that we're having dinner alone together in your apartment?" Aiden asks as Mr. Tumnus jumps off his lap.

"This is a working dinner not a date, so no, he won't care," I say. "And I already told you Bowen's not my boyfriend." Although who knows, maybe he will be soon. Maybe we'll get married and buy a house together and have two point five kids and a dog and open our own brokerage. Maybe we'll live happily ever after.

Aiden is studying me intently—so intently that I almost wonder if he's thinking about kissing me. Waiting for a signal that it's okay to lean in.

But that's crazy. He can't be.

I blush and look away from him. I'm doing it again, reading too much into a situation. On the cusp of making a fool of myself over him for the second time in my life.

I get up and go into the kitchen to grab us some water, just to give my racing a heart the chance to slow down. When I return, Aiden is on the phone ordering our dinner and the moment has passed. We're back on solid ground, the place where we need to stay if I'm going to get through working with him.

I set the water glasses on the coffee table and sit as far away from him on the couch as possible. If this evening has shown me anything, it's that Aiden and I can't be friends. Not because I'm still angry at him for stealing my client—although I am—but because it would just be too hard. I already feel myself slipping back into old feelings. The sad truth is that I'm always going to want more than Aiden can give me, so for my own sake I need to sell this property, win the bet, and move on with my life as quickly as possible. I need him to become part of my past again.

And that can't come soon enough.

CHAPTER
THIRTEEN

"WHAT'S WRONG?" TYLER asks the minute I sit down at my desk. Freddie is curled in his lap, wearing a red tartan tam to match the one on Tyler's head. It's adorable and ridiculous and if I was in a better mood it would make me laugh, but I'm not, so I don't.

"Nothing. I'm fine," I say. I don't want to dump all my problems on him. I've done that too much lately.

Tyler narrows his eyes. "Your face isn't giving fine," he says. "Your face is giving black cloud. So spill."

I sigh. I can't tell him about the argument Leighton and I had this morning over the bird carving because it will just reinforce his belief that something is going on between me and Aiden and I won't be able to convince him otherwise. Just like my sister, Tyler will swoon and insist that the sandpiper was a romantic gesture when really it was just Aiden feeling bad for me. It was a 'sorry-you-got-cancer' present. Nothing more. (also,

Leighton claims she didn't tell me who gave me the carving because she was worried I'd throw it out. And she's right—I probably would have. In fact, I still might).

And then there's the Madeline of it all. Tyler's my friend but he's her friend too and it's not right for me to expect him to keep anything from her. But I don't want my boss knowing that her ex-boyfriend got me a gift, even if it was just a pity-gift, so I need to keep the bird carving to myself.

"My client didn't take it very well when I called to tell her she needs to provide proof of funds before she can see the house," I say, logging into my computer. That's the other reason why I'm cranky this morning—I've lost my potential buyer. I've had no other requests about the property yet and while it's still early—we've only been on the market for a few days—I'm already panicking. Barely out of the starting gate and the pressure is beginning to get to me.

"I guess I'm just overwhelmed." To put it mildly.

Tyler nods. "I would be, too. This is a career-making listing," he says, which doesn't make me feel any better. "But you're going to sell it. I can feel it," he adds, which does.

I smile.

"And just imagine how good it's going to feel when you're spending all that sweet, sweet commission."

My smile slips. I haven't told Tyler about the bet, the one that means I won't see a dime if I don't find a buyer before Aiden does. When the truth comes out—and it will eventually—I'm going to have to explain myself to Madeline. And I'm really not looking forward to that because I don't think she'll react well to someone on her team gambling their commission. It's not only unprofessional, it's also incredibly stupid. She could fire me for this.

I swallow. I should probably tell Aiden that I want to call off the bet, save myself all this extra stress and probably my job in the process, but I just know that he'll gloat about winning by default and I won't be able to stand it. Aiden Miller can't win at everything in life. His ego needs to be knocked down a few pegs and I'm all too happy to be the one to do that.

I decide to put the bet and all of its possible horrible repercussions out of my mind for now—plenty of time to worry about it when I wake up again in the middle of the night.

Tyler's just asked me about my date with Bowen when he's interrupted by our colleague, Sherry, who accidently deleted something from the database. By the time he's corrected her mistake and she's walked away he's forgotten what we were talking about. Which is great because if I don't come across super excited about Bowen then Tyler will assume it's because I'm actually in love with Aiden, when in reality I'm just too tired to muster up enthusiasm for anything right now.

"I walked Maisie last night," Tyler says. "She wanted me to tell you that she misses you."

"I miss her too," I say. "She's such a sweetheart. I'm surprised she's still at the shelter. I would have thought someone would have adopted her by now."

He shrugs. "I don't get it either." He adjusts Freddie's tam so it doesn't fall into his eyes. "I'm taking her out again tomorrow night," he adds. "Want to come with?"

I probably shouldn't. For one thing, I should be spending every spare second trying to find a buyer for the Davidsons house. And for another, I don't want to fall more in love with Maisie than I already have. Much like Aiden, the less I'm around her, the less chance I have of getting hurt when she's inevitably taken by someone else.

I know this, but I still say yes, I'll go for a walk with them. I'm a glutton for punishment, I guess.

"But no more pressuring me to adopt her," I tell him.

"No promises," Tyler says with a grin.

THE REST OF the morning flies by in a blur of cold-calls and emails. I follow up with Ben and Jiya in the hope that they're over their disappointment about losing the house in East Van and are ready to start the search again, but unfortunately they haven't changed their minds. I look over a few contracts for Madeline, then comb through our client database for the tenth time, hoping to find someone with a fat enough wallet to buy the Davidsons place, but once again I come up empty-handed.

I've just gotten up to reheat the leftover coconut curry in the microwave when Sherry wanders back to my cubicle and drops a big fancy white box on top of my desk.

"For you," she says, somewhat obviously. "Fed-ex just brought it."

"Ooh, what is it?" Tyler asks, getting up from his chair and standing beside Sherry. They both look down at me, waiting for me to open it.

"I don't know." I'm not expecting any packages.

Wait. I blink. The return address is from Aiden's office. This must be the outfit for the broker's open he promised to send me. My yacht-wear.

Sure enough, when I lift the lid off the box I find a deep blue maxi dress with kimono sleeves.

"Oh my god, it's stunning," Tyler exclaims as I hold the dress up. It's conservative while somehow still being very sexy—exactly what I would have picked out for myself if I had any idea what to wear on a yacht.

"Gift giving is clearly Aiden Miller's love language," Tyler adds. Because of course he didn't miss Aiden's name on the return label.

Like me, he reads too much into things. It's good that I listened to my instincts and didn't tell him about the bird carving.

"It's not a gift," I insist. And it isn't love, it's business. "And it's not from Aiden. His assistant, Gil, sent it over."

Of course, Gil wouldn't have done that if Aiden hadn't asked him to. Aiden has done something nice for me—again—and even though I agreed to let him send me a dress last night, the scales are suddenly beginning to feel very unbalanced. It makes me uneasy. I mean, I love getting gifts as much as the next girl, but I can't help wondering if these ones come with strings. Like Aiden is trying to buy my friendship back or something.

"Well, Gil has fantastic taste," Tyler says.

Sherry raises her over plucked eyebrows. "Is this for your yacht party?" she asks.

I nod. I know she thinks the theme is dumb but I also know that she'll be there—she wouldn't miss the opportunity to rub shoulders with high-end clientele. No realtor in their right mind would.

"What's that in the bottom of the box?" Tyler asks. He reaches inside and pulls out a long wispy scrap of fabric, pale blue silk patterned with tiny, intricately detailed sailboats.

"It's a vintage Hermés scarf," he whispers reverently as he passes it to me.

But the brand name isn't what puts a lump in my throat—it's the fact that Aiden must have told Gil to send a scarf along with the dress, knowing that I'd want something to cover my scar.

My heart starts to race. Because now I'm the one reading more into this gesture more than I should. I know better and I still can't help myself. Maybe giving gifts really is Aiden's love language.

Love.

No. I give myself a mental shake. This is what I used to do when Aiden and I were friends. He would do something nice for me, or look at me a certain way, and I'd convince myself it was proof that he was into me. When in reality he wasn't. And I know he wasn't because I actually mustered up the nerve to bring it up once.

It's humiliating to think about how I misread all the signs. To remember the pained look on Aiden's face when he told me that he was seeing someone. He'd never mentioned that he was dating anyone before, so I assumed it was just an excuse. A way to let me down easy. That he didn't want to ruin our friendship and I meant too much to him to take the risk. He told me he didn't want to lose me.

And I bought it. I actually thought he was being sincere. Right up until a week later when he stole my client and destroyed our friendship all on his own.

So no. Aiden doesn't love me. He doesn't want to be with me. And the only thing that's changed is that I'm wiser now. I'm not going to let myself romanticize everything he does or the way he sometimes looks at me, because it isn't real. This dress, this scarf, he sent them so I will match the theme of the party. That's all.

Sherry frowns. "Am I supposed to dress on theme? Because I was just going to wear a pantsuit."

"A pantsuit is fine," I reply. We're not expecting the other realtors to show up in cruise wear.

"Well, I'm going all out," Tyler says. "Wait until you see what I've got cooked up."

I smile. I can only imagine.

As Sherry walks away muttering to herself, I carefully fold the dress and scarf back into the box and tuck it under my desk before Madeline comes back from lunch. I don't know how she'd feel about Aiden sending me this package—maybe she wouldn't care, but maybe she would and I don't want to risk hurting her if she does still have feelings for him. I may know that what Aiden sent me means nothing but I also know that it doesn't look like nothing, and it's all just too awkward and embarrassing to have to explain to my boss.

When Madeline breezes in a short time later, I stop her as she walks past my cubicle to ask if she has time for a quick meeting. Thankfully, she offered to pay my half of the party and I want to reassure her that her money is being well spent and that everything is under control.

"Sure," she says.

I stand up and follow her into her office, closing the door behind me. Madeline and I have worked together for a few years and I was never nervous around her before Aiden came back into the picture. But now I'm anxious every time I see her, mostly because I'm trying so hard not to let on that I know about the two of them. It shouldn't be a big deal and yet it feels like one.

"How's the listing going?" Madeline asks as she settles into the white leather chair behind her desk. "Any bites on the property yet?"

"Not yet." I don't tell her about the potential buyer I lost because she didn't want to show proof of funds, because honestly I should have already known to ask for that upfront. I don't want Madeline to starting questioning if I know what I'm doing. Me questioning myself is bad enough.

"Well, it's still early," she says. "And as you know the buyer pool is a lot smaller for properties in this price range. It could take a while."

Ugh, I hope not. Aiden and I only have ninety days to sell the house. After that, there's no guarantee that the Davidsons will extend our contract. In fact, it's more than likely that they'll decide to work with another realtor. And then who knows how long it will be before another opportunity like this comes my way. Maybe never.

"The broker's open should help, though," Madeline says. "Those connections are what's going to sell this property."

Well, if that's true than that sucks for me because Aiden already knows most of the realtors on the guest list. I'm really going to have to work the room if I'm going to convince anyone to bring their buyers to me instead of him.

I fill Madeline in on the rest of the details for the party. Overall, she seems pleased with how her money is being spent, although she isn't too happy that Aiden's hired a yacht rock band.

"Of course he did," she says, sighing as she tucks a strand of platinum blonde hair behind her ear. "This theme has his sticky fingerprints all over it."

I frown. I don't want Madeline to think that Aiden is in control, that I'm just sitting back and letting him do whatever he wants. Okay, so I didn't push back on the theme or the video, but I would have if I thought that we weren't going in the right direction. I'm smart enough to accept that we need to lean on his experience to sell this property. Of course, letting him convince me to bet my entire commission was pretty stupid—but only if I lose.

"Although quite a few people have reached out to me about getting on the guest list, so maybe Aiden is onto something," Madeline says, drumming her nails against the desk. "Everyone seems to want to be there."

I've been getting a lot requests, too. We've been pretty strict about keeping the guest list exclusive, a strategy that has made everyone in town want to be there.

"You sure you can't make it?" I ask her.

Madeline hesitates before shaking her head. "I can't reschedule this meeting. It's with a very important client."

I don't think she's lying, but do I think she deliberately scheduled a meeting for the night of the broker's open so she would have a built-in excuse not to come? Yes, I do. Because if I were in Madeline's shoes, I wouldn't want to go to a party hosted by the guy who dumped me, either. Even if it was a great business opportunity.

"What's it been like, working with Aiden?" she asks. I can't read her expression— Madeline has perfected the blank face—so I'm not sure if she's genuinely curious or if she's actually fishing for information about him. Or about him and me. Because of course she knows all about what happened between us. Professionally, at least.

"We've had a few little bumps, but overall it's been okay," I say.

Madeline nods. "Hopefully it stays that way, but you never can tell with Aiden. He can turn on you pretty quickly."

I'm all too aware. But at the same time, there's a part of me that really wants to believe he's changed, that he wouldn't do anything to hurt me again. I want to be able to trust him, but I'm not sure I should.

The door opens and Tyler pokes his head in to let me know I've monopolized enough of Madeline's time today. Which is fine because I have some more work of my own to get done.

"Thanks, Madeline," I say, standing up.

"Of course."

When I get back to my cubicle I find Freddie curled up in my chair, fast asleep. I don't have the heart to kick him off—he looks so peaceful—so I take my laptop over to an empty desk in the corner and settle in to do some more cold calling.

CHAPTER FOURTEEN

AFEW HOURS LATER I'm getting ready to leave the office when I get a text from Aiden informing me he's planning to show the house to one of his clients tonight.

I frown at my phone. He hasn't asked if I want to come along—not that I really expected him to. We may be co-listing the house, but we're still competitors. He made that crystal clear with this stupid bet.

If I'm being honest, I wouldn't invite Aiden to my showing if our roles were reversed, so that's not really why I'm mad. I'm upset because he's now officially one step ahead of me. I didn't think it was possible to feel even more pressure to land our buyer before he does, but here I am. Anxious and desperate.

I have to win this bet. I *have* to.

And so I pull my laptop out of my tote bag and sit back down at my desk. I could go home and work from the comfort of my couch, but I know I won't get anything done with Leighton bullying me into taking a break every ten minutes.

Two hours later I'm the last one left in the office. I've researched and strategized until my brain hurts and my eyes are blurry. There's nothing more I can do tonight. I'll just have to pick up the search for potential clients again tomorrow.

I'm walking out to my car, the last one left in the lot, when Bowen texts to ask if I want to meet up for a drink. I should probably say no—I'm exhausted, I really do need to go home and get some rest—but I would like to see him. And I could use the distraction.

One drink and then I'll go home, burrow under the covers and try to get some sleep.

I drive across town to the trendy, dimly lit restaurant Bowen suggested. I find him sitting at the bar, scrolling through house listings on his phone.

I tap him on his shoulder and he looks up, startled.

"Hey," he says, sliding off the stool to give me a hug. He's a great hugger and I melt into him, my head resting on his chest. He also smells really good. Like freshly laundered linen.

"Glad you could make it," he adds as I shrug off my jacket and sit down on the black leather bar stool beside him. "I know it was kind of short notice."

Some of my friends would be horrified to know that I agreed to go out with him at the last minute, but honestly I'm done playing games with men. If Bowen is going to be turned off simply because I happened to be free when he called then he's definitely not the one for me.

I hope he is the one for me, though, because boy am I tired of dating. I don't even put myself out there much and I'm still so, so tired. Finding someone good and kind and decent, not to mention compatible, feels next to impossible sometimes.

Bowen hands me the drink menu. "I'm kind of an amateur mixologist," he says with a trace of smugness. He excitedly talks me through his recommendations, each of which seems to have an out-there ingredient like pickle brine or bone broth.

"I think I'll have a strawberry margarita," I say, coming across the one thing on the menu that actually appeals to me.

Bowen's face falls. "Really? A margarita is so basic. Why don't you try the mushroom martini instead?"

"I don't like mushrooms," I say. But even if I did, I'm pretty sure I wouldn't want them in my martini.

"I bet this drink would change your mind," he says.

I'm not willing to chance that, so I stick with the margarita, much to his obvious disappointment.

I study Bowen while he orders for us. He's a carbon copy of almost every guy I've ever lusted after—slightly geeky, dark hair and five o'clock shadow, a lean, wiry frame. Physically, he couldn't be more different from Aiden, with his blonde hair and blue/hazel eyes, his broad shoulders and muscular, sweep-a-girl-off-her-feet arms. And yet two years ago I fell harder for Aiden than I ever have for anyone else.

Make it make sense, I think as the bartender sets down our drinks.

Bowen and I lock eyes as we clink our glasses together—clearly neither one of us wants to be saddled with seven years of bad sex. Although it's been a minute since I had any kind of sex, good or bad. Well before my surgery, anyway. It's not that I don't want to do it—I do, very badly—but I've let my scar hold me back. It's been a hard thing to get past and it makes me squirm, thinking about showing it to him or anyone else.

"So, I hear you're having a brokers' open tomorrow night," Bowen says.

I stop, my drink raised halfway to my mouth.

Okay, so I guess Madeline was right—word is definitely getting around. I haven't mentioned the event to Bowen because we already have someone more senior from his brokerage attending, someone who could potentially bring us a VIP buyer, which is the whole reason we're throwing this party. Bowen is a good realtor, but as far as I'm aware he doesn't have any really rich clients, so he didn't make the cut.

"I'd love to come and support you," he adds.

I hesitate. I'm not going to have a lot of time to hang out with him—I'll be in full party-hosting and working-the-room mode—but it's nice that he wants to support me. Of course, I'm not naïve—I know that's not the only reason he's asking if he can come. Bowen is no dummy, he's aware that this event is the perfect opportunity to make high-level contacts. And I can't blame him for wanting to be there. I mean, I crashed a charity gala just for the chance to talk to Tim and Annabelle.

I chew my lip, thinking. Aiden won't be happy if I invite Bowen—the guest list is already getting out of control and also, he hates him—but who cares what Aiden thinks? He's not the only one hosting this party. If I want Bowen to come, then Bowen can come.

"Okay. I'll put you on the list," I say.

Bowen beams at me. He offers me a sip of his tamarind bourbon (gross, do not recommend). He's in the middle of telling me about running into an ex-girlfriend at his ten-year high-school reunion last month, when my phone buzzes. I flip it over to check the text. If I were on a date with someone who didn't work in real estate I would ignore all messages, but I know that Bowen gets that it's part of the job—he's checked his phone at least five times since I arrived.

> **AIDEN:** Do you have a minute? I want to fill you in on the showing.

I frown. He probably just wants to brag that his buyer is planning to make an offer.

ME: I'm kind of busy right now.

AIDEN: Busy doing what?

ME: That would be none your business.

Two seconds later, my phone rings.

I sigh. "Sorry. I've got to take this," I say to Bowen as I slide off the stool. If I don't answer then Aiden will probably just keep calling. And I have to admit, I am a little curious to hear how the showing went. Might as well know if he's about to win the bet.

I walk outside so Bowen won't overhear our conversation. The night air is cool and I left my jacket in the bar, so I hope this is quick because I'm wearing short sleeves.

"You're with him right now, aren't you?" Aiden asks as soon as I pick up.

I roll my eyes. He sounds like a jealous lover. Which is ridiculous.

"I'm out with Bowen, yes," I say, and he grunts. "Now tell me about the showing."

"It went okay," Aiden says. "I don't think this guy is our buyer, though. He's planning to submit an offer, but he's going to lowball us. I told him that would be a big waste of everyone's time because Tim isn't going to take one dollar less than the asking price."

I frown. "Tim doesn't even want to negotiate?" I view every offer as a starting point, even if it's way under the asking price. I'm surprised to hear that Tim won't even want to consider it.

"No," Aiden says. "He's already annoyed that Annabelle agreed to sell the house for six five. He thinks it's worth a lot more."

I narrow my eyes. Is that a dig at me, for setting the asking price?

"I would have recommended six five, too," Aiden adds quickly. "I think you were bang on with your assessment. This guy is just trying to get a deal. I think he must have heard that Tim and Annabelle are splitting up."

"Well, I haven't told anyone,," I say, my chest tightening. I don't want Aiden thinking I'm the leak. One of the reasons why Annabelle wanted to keep their divorce quiet was to prevent vultures like this guy from swooping in and lowballing them, assuming they'll want to dump the place quickly.

"Yeah, I haven't either," Aiden says. "Honestly, it's Tim. He hasn't been himself lately and it's obvious to anyone who comes in contact with him that something's wrong. He can't hide it."

I feel a stab of sympathy for Tim. It must be awful, having your wife leave you after forty years.

"Look, where are you?" Aiden asks. "I'll come by and we can talk more about this in person."

I laugh. He wants to crash my date? Why? So he can chase Bowen off? Because I can't imagine he'd want to stick around if Aiden showed up. Or maybe he would and that would be worse.

"I don't think so," I say.

"Then come to my place after you're done," Aiden says, lowering his voice in a really sexy way.

I stop laughing. Is he hitting on me?

No. No, he can't be.

Stop it, I scold myself. I'm doing it again. Reading too much into what he says. If he's feeling possessive over me it's only because he hates Bowen. No other reason.

"It's getting late," I say. "None of this is urgent, anyway. If you really want to talk in person then we can meet tomorrow. I have some time after lunch."

"Can't tomorrow," Aiden replies. He doesn't tell me why he can't, so now I'm wondering if the reason is business or pleasure. I hope it's business. I don't like to think about what—or who—he does for pleasure.

"Then I guess I'll see you at the party on Saturday," I say. "And thank you again for the dress and the scarf. They're beautiful." I texted him earlier, but that gesture deserves another thank you.

"You're welcome," Aiden says. "I'm glad you like them."

We're both silent for a moment, almost like neither one of us wants to hang up. But I need to because Bowen is waiting in the bar for me. Also, I'm freezing.

"I've got to go," I say, hugging myself to try and warm up.

"You sure you don't want to come over?" he asks.

"I'm sure." But I know I don't sound as sure as I should.

"I moved recently," Aiden says. "I'm going to send you my new address, just in case you change your mind and feel like..." he trails off.

My breath catches. Feel like what?

"...watching a movie," he says.

Is he bored? Or lonely? I'm not sure why else he'd want me to come over after my date. If this were any other guy I'd assume he was after a late-night booty call, but this is Aiden. He's made pretty clear in the past that he's not interested in seeing me naked.

"I'm not going to change my mind," I say firmly, but my phone buzzes with a location pin anyway.

"You'd have a lot more fun with me," he says.

And for a moment—one moment—I consider giving in. Because maybe I have been reading him right. Maybe he's jealous because he actually does have feelings for me.

I shake my head, coming to my senses. This isn't Aiden wanting me, it's just his competitive side coming out—he doesn't like Bowen so he wants to ruin this date for me. But I'm not about to let him to do that. I'm not going to drop everything and come running just because he snaps his fingers. I would have once, but I'm not that girl anymore. I haven't been her in a long time.

Aiden Miller is not going to mess with my emotions again. This isn't a game, this is my life. I need to let my head rule over all my other body parts.

"Don't wait up," I say.

Aiden laughs softly. I know he still thinks I'm going to give in and show up on his doorstep, because that's the me that he's used to.

"Goodnight, Aiden," I say, hanging up before my body talks my head into doing something I will definitely regret.

When I get back into the bar I discover that Bowen has ordered us each another drink.

"I know you said you don't like mushrooms, but I really think you should try this," he says, passing me a martini glass.

I purse my lips. It's annoying that he's being so pushy about this stupid drink, but I take a sip just to show him what a good sport I am. And I'm instantly sorry because it tastes even worse than the tamarind bourbon. Worse than anything I've ever tasted, actually.

"Yuck," I say, wrinkling my nose. God, that's disgusting. I hand the glass back to him.

"Really?" Bowen shakes his head in disappointment. "I was so sure you'd love it." He offers to order me another strawberry margarita to make up for it, but I decline—I won't be able to drive if I have another drink. I do take him up on BBQ pork steamed buns, just to get the gross earthy mushroom-y taste out of my mouth.

An hour later, Bowen has downed both martinis, plus another bourbon. By the time we're ready to leave, he's good and drunk. But he's a cheerful drunk, at least. A life of the party drunk. He's chatting with everyone around us, laughing and bright-eyed.

I yawn, ready to go home, but Bowen doesn't want to let the night end just yet.

"Oh come on, it's still early," he says, putting his hand on my knee. "How about we head back to my place. I just live a couple of blocks away."

For the second time tonight I'm tempted to go to a man's house. The idea of having sex with Bowen is very appealing. Maybe getting under him is the best way to get Aiden out of my mind. And when he leans over and kisses me, I'm so dizzy that I almost agree to go home with him.

But when I open my eyes, I know I'm not going to go through with it. I like Bowen a lot, but I'm not ready sleep with him just yet. I won't be ready until I've managed to push Aiden completely out of my thoughts.

I just hope that I'm going to be able to.

CHAPTER
FIFTEEN

ANNABELLE HASN'T YET left for the hotel when I arrive on Saturday afternoon to set up for the broker's open. Aiden and I sprung for another night at the Fairmont Pacific Rim for her and Tim (once again in separate rooms) to get them out of our hair, so I'm surprised she's still here instead of enjoying the extremely pricey facial I booked for her at the hotel spa.

"I can get a facial any old time," Annabelle says after she directs the caterer to the kitchen. "I thought I'd stay for the party. It just sounds like so much fun. And to be honest I prefer to be here when there's a bunch of strangers wandering around my house."

I smile but inwardly I'm sighing heavily. The strangers she's worried about are all top of their game real estate professionals who are hopefully going to bring us a buyer, not randoms wandering in off the street.

"Of course," I say. "We're happy to have you join us."

I hope I sound sincere, because I'm not at all happy that Annabelle is sticking around. And Aiden won't be either. Her presence is going to make this event awkward, but it's not like I can tell her to get out. It is her house, after all.

Aiden arrives a few minutes later. Just as I predicted, he's wearing a captain's hat, along with a starched white dress shirt with black and gold epaulets on the shoulders and tight black pants.

My stomach flips. I do love a man in uniform.

We make eye contact and I smile. Although we've texted back and forth a million times I haven't talked to Aiden since the other night, when he tried to convince me to ditch my date and come over to his place. I can just imagine how smug and unbearable he'd be if he knew I actually drove past his house.

My cheeks heat up as I remember slowing down in front of his cute little bungalow. Aiden lives in a quiet neighborhood just off Main Street, a far cry from his old apartment in a sleek high rise downtown.

I told myself I was just curious to see where he lived, that there was no way I'd go inside, but the sad truth is I almost did. I almost backslid to being that girl again, the one who believed that if she just stuck it out, Aiden would one day come to his senses and realize that we were made for each other.

Fortunately, I managed to talk myself out of knocking on his door.

Now, I stand back as Annabelle greets Aiden with a hug before she heads upstairs to change into something she probably wore on an actual yacht in the Mediterranean. He waits until she's disappeared from view before turning to me, his eyebrows raised.

"Why is she still here?" he asks.

"She's staying for the party," I reply.

He shakes his head. "Great."

"What can we do," I say, shrugging. "We can't exactly kick her out of her own house."

"Kick *them* out of their own house," Aiden replies. "Tim's coming, too."

I sigh. I wish Tim and Annabelle would just trust us to handle this party ourselves. Having them here is going to change the whole vibe. I want the other realtors to be focused on which of their clients might want to buy this property, not on trying to talk their way into doing business with Tim. Which is one hundred percent what's going to happen now.

Not to mention I have no idea how Tim and Annabelle will behave around each other. I know Annabelle claims their divorce is amicable, but who knows if that's really true. They certainly didn't seem too friendly when I saw them at the gala.

"You look amazing, P," Aiden says, his cool blue/hazel eyes running over me in a way that almost feels like he's touching me. And my traitorous body is responding—I'm getting warm just from him *looking* at me. I can't imagine what would happen if he actually put his hands on me.

I shouldn't be thinking about that.

"Thanks," I say, fiddling with the vintage scarf he sent me. I'm happy with the dress—it fits me perfectly—and Leighton helped me with my hair, twisting it a high bun. She also lent me her clear quartz bracelet, which is apparently supposed to bring good luck. I'm not sure if I believe in the power of crystals, but I'll take all the luck I can get tonight.

My eyes meet Aiden's again and something passes between us that I'm too afraid to name. I want to believe that his heart is racing as fast as mine is, but I've been fooled before. And I'd be an even bigger fool if I let myself believe that he's feeling what I'm feeling now.

I clear my throat. "The band is setting up in the white room. You want to meet them?"

The mention of Rock the Boat makes Aiden's whole face light up. "I definitely want to meet them," he says.

He follows me through the hall and into the other room. Like Aiden, all five members of the band are dressed in sea captain costumes. He fangirls over them for a few minutes before the caterer pulls my attention away with a question about dry ice for the seafood tower.

I'm fanning out a stack of my business cards on the kitchen island when Aiden appears, bobbing his head to *Margaritaville*. He grabs a shrimp from the seafood tower, then convinces me to get a drink. We head over to the bar where we each order a sea breeze, the signature cocktail for the night. I've just taken my first sip when the front door opens and Aiden's mother swans in.

He almost spits out his sea breeze.

"Mom. What are you doing here?" Aiden asks. "I thought you weren't coming back from Toronto until next week."

"I decided to come back early," she says, giving him an air kiss. "I didn't want to miss your event. Although quite frankly I'm still not sold on the theme." Grady's pointed gaze lands on me and my stomach does a nosedive. "Was this your idea, Piper?"

"No, Mom. This is all me," Aiden says, before I can answer her.

It might sound like he's taking credit for everything, but I know that isn't what he means—he's just trying to spare me his mother's scorn. And I'm grateful. Because Grady Miller intimidates me. Underneath that tan Ferragamo suit beats the heart of a great white shark. Given the chance, she could rip me—and my career—to pieces in seconds.

"Hm," Grady says, studying me carefully. "Well, I've certainly heard a lot about you lately."

"Oh?" I say, glancing nervously at Aiden. He's blushing to the roots of his hair.

Which is weird, because of course my name would have come up at some point—Aiden and his mother work together, so obviously she knows we're co-listing. My brow furrows. I'm not sure why he's acting like he wishes the floor would open up and swallow him whole, though.

"I must say, I wasn't too happy when I heard that Aiden was being forced to co-list with you," Grady says, and I stiffen. Okay, so that's why he's embarrassed—he complained to his mother about having to share this listing with me, not expecting that she'd bring it up.

"Tim and Annabelle are old friends," Grady continues. "So naturally I assumed that the listing would go to our brokerage alone—"

"Mom," Aiden interrupts. He inches closer to me until our arms are touching. "Stop. I'm happy to be working with Piper," he says. "She's been working her ass off to get this house sold."

I'm surprised that Aiden's defending me so fiercely, but I definitely appreciate it. And it seems to work because Grady backs down.

She gestures at our drinks. "Where can I get one of those?"

"Over here." Aiden leads his mother away, shooting an apologetic look at me over his shoulder.

I relax a little. I no longer think he complained about me to her, but he must have said *something* that he doesn't want me to know about. Otherwise why would he react like that?

The door opens again and a crew of realtors arrives, several of whom I've met before. I smile and walk forward to greet them. I spend the next hour taking different groups on tours of the house, catching the occasional glimpse of Aiden as he does his own tours. It's a strange position to be in, working together but competing for a buyer at the same time.

Currently, I'm in the wine cellar with Olivia Ng, an agent I've met a few times.

"I think my clients would really love this place," Olivia says, snapping a photo to send to them. "They're coming into town next weekend. I have to bring them through."

"Perfect," I say, buzzing with happiness. Three other realtors have told me they have clients who are the perfect match for this house. So far this night has been a great success, worth every penny that's been sunk into this party.

A few minutes later, I take Olivia up to the kitchen to finish the tour and I find Tyler and Sherry filling their plates with crab legs.

"Best broker's open ever," Tyler says, raising his voice so I'll hear him over the band's slightly off-key rendition of *Sailing*. He's taken the theme to heart, as I knew he would, and is dressed up as a yachtie in a blue polo shirt, khaki shorts, deck shoes and aviator sunglasses.

"You've done a really good job, Piper," Sherry says. She's wearing a pink pantsuit, but I notice she's added a little silver anchor pin to her blazer.

"Thanks." It means a lot to me that they showed up tonight, especially because most of the people here are Aiden's colleagues and contacts.

Speaking of Aiden, here he comes, walking over to us. My stomach twists. He does not look happy.

"Great party," Tyler says to him through a mouthful of crab.

Aiden's face changes, his professional mask sliding into place. "Thanks, man." He shakes Tyler's hand and then Sherry's. I watch silently as they all chat for a moment, mostly about interest rates and market predictions.

Something's obviously bothering Aiden. He's smiling, but there's a stony look in his eyes when he turns to me and asks, "Piper, can I have a word?"

Uh-oh. Calling me by my name instead of P isn't a good sign—I must be the reason he's annoyed. He puts his hand on my elbow and leads me into a quiet corner of the foyer.

"Care to explain why Bowen Clarke is here?" Aiden asks.

Oh. Right. I *may* have accidently-on-purpose left Bowen's name off the guest list—that way Aiden couldn't ban him from attending tonight. I figured he wouldn't be thrilled about it, but I didn't expect him to be quite this mad.

"I invited him," I say, wondering when Bowen arrived and why he hasn't searched me out yet.

"Yes. I guessed that," Aiden says. "But why did you invite him to *our* party, when you know I can't stand him?"

I stare at the vein popping out on his forehead. "I thought he might be able to bring us a buyer," I say.

Aiden snorts. He knows I'm lying—we both know that Bowen doesn't have those kinds of contacts. But if I tell him that Bowen flat-out asked if he could come then Aiden might decide that's a good enough reason to toss him out on his ear.

"He's been talking to Tim for the past twenty minutes," Aiden says. "He's trying to poach him. He's not going to be successful, but he's trying. The dirt bag."

I narrow my eyes. Aiden Miller of all people should not be complaining to me about someone trying to steal his client. And I can track the exact moment when he realizes this because his face reddens.

"He's networking," I say. "The same as every other realtor here. That doesn't make him a dirt bag."

I mean, I can understand why Aiden is annoyed—I would be, too—but I don't think he has to worry about Tim changing agents. So why get so angry about it?

Aiden shakes his head. "Why are you defending him? What do you see in that guy?"

"Why do you care what I see in him?" I hold my breath, hoping he's finally going to admit that there's something between us. Because I can't be the only one who feels this way. This thing between us, whatever it is, can't all be in my head.

Aiden's silent for a long moment. He glances away from me. "You're my friend," he says. "And I don't want to see you get hurt."

Friend, I think bitterly. *Right.* Once again I've deluded myself into thinking we could be something more. There's nothing going on between us. There never has been and there never will be.

Aiden doesn't want me. He just doesn't want anyone else to have me. It's laughable that he's so concerned about me getting hurt when he's the one who's hurt me more than anyone else, ever.

"Just trust me on this, P," he continues. "You don't want to get involved with Bowen. You don't know him the way I do."

That may be true—we've only just started dating, I'm still learning about who he is—but Aiden hasn't given me a single concrete reason why I shouldn't trust Bowen. Aiden's the one who has given me reasons not to trust him.

"Who I spend time with is none of your business," I say.

Aiden's jaw tightens. "Fine. Whatever," he says before storming off.

I take a breath and set out to find Bowen. I circle the main floor twice. He's not in the kitchen picking at the seafood tower. He's not with Tim in the white room, listening to the band play Fleetwood Mac. He's not in the wine cellar or the movie room or out by the pool.

I frown. Bowen wouldn't have left without talking to me, would he? My stomach sinks. Did Aiden find him first and kick him out? He better not have. But now that I think of it, I don't see Aiden, either.

Oh, wait. There he is, standing by the bar with his mom and Annabelle. He catches me staring and quickly looks away.

I pull out my phone and send Bowen a quick text to ask him where he is before heading upstairs. I check the guest rooms, but they're all empty. When I come to the end of the hall and find the door of Annabelle and Tim's room closed a strange, prickly feeling settles over me. I hear a peal of laugher coming from the room, so

I knock but I don't wait for permission to enter before I throw the door open.

"Piper," Bowen says, startled. He's lying in the centre of the California King with Olivia. He quickly pulls his hand out of her blouse.

I scowl. Bowen doesn't owe me anything—he's not my boyfriend, we're not exclusive—but still. Making out with another woman at a party I'm throwing? Super rude. And completely unprofessional. And stupid! What if Annabelle or Tim had walked in? They would lose their minds if they found him rolling around in their bed.

"Wait," Bowen says, struggling to his feet. His pants are unbuckled and he grasps at them to keep them from falling down around his ankles. "This isn't what it looks like."

I laugh. Because *what*?

Olivia shoots him a dirty look. "Are you kidding?" she hisses as she buttons up her blouse. "You told me you were single, Bowen."

"Don't worry, he's very single," I say to her.

"And it looks like he's going to stay that way." She stands up and smooths down her skirt. She grabs her purse and walks past me out of the room.

"Piper, let me explain," Bowen says. "Please?"

But there isn't anything to explain because there isn't anything he can say that would make this better. Deep down, I'm not even that mad about catching him with someone else—I liked Bowen, sure, but I'm not heartbroken that it isn't going to work out between us. No, I'm mad that I defended him to Aiden. I'm mad because he was right all along.

Ugh.

"Goodbye, Bowen," I say, following Olivia out of the room and pulling the door shut behind me.

CHAPTER
SIXTEEN

BOWEN MUST HAVE slunk out of the house at some point because I don't see him again for the rest of the night. I'm not sure if he tried to text me because I blocked him as soon as I got back downstairs. Olivia is everywhere, though, telling everyone what a dick he is. She ends up getting very drunk on sea breezes, so I take her keys and bundle her into an uber.

Aside from that, the rest of the night passes without any drama, thank goodness. The broker's open appears to have been a resounding success—I've made some great contacts, just the calibre of people I need to level-up my career. Hopefully one of them will bring me a solid offer on this house.

After everyone has left, I walk into the kitchen to see if the catering team needs any help. Aiden and I agreed earlier that we'd both stick around after the party while they pack up, but I have no idea where he's disappeared to and I'm not about to go looking for him. Thanks to Olivia's big mouth I'm sure he's already caught wind of what happened with Bowen and I'm not in the mood to hear I-told-you-so.

The catering team is bustling around, loading crates with dishes and wrapping up leftovers. I end up just being in their way, so I decide to go outside and get some air. As soon as I slide open the door I smell cherry blossom trees and fresh cut grass. I kick off my heels and walk barefoot across the lawn to the infinity pool. The underwater lights change color every few seconds, purple to blue to green and back again. I hike my dress up to my thighs, lower myself to the edge of the pool and dangle my feet in the water with a sigh of relief. This is the first time I've sat down in hours.

The glittering lights of downtown are directly across the Burrard Inlet but the city somehow feels a world away. It's peaceful here, silent except for the chirp of crickets and the footsteps coming up behind me.

"Apparently Annabelle took the car service we hired back to the hotel," Aiden says. "She didn't wait for Tim. I had to call another car for him."

I frown. That's kind of petty of Annabelle, but then again they are going through a divorce. Amicable or not. "I guess we should have seen that coming," I say as Aiden rolls up his pants. He sits down beside me, so close that his thigh rests against mine, and sticks his feet in the water. Somewhere along the way he's lost his captain's hat and his blonde hair is rumpled.

"I guess we should be grateful they didn't decide to go nine rounds at the party," he says, smiling ruefully at me.

"You mean like we did?" I ask. I've been mulling over whether or not I need to apologize to Aiden about our argument and I've settled on not. He's the one who overstepped with his unsolicited advice about my love life, after all. My only mistake was coming to the defense of someone who obviously didn't deserve it.

"Yeah, about that," Aiden says, rubbing his hand over his jaw. His face creases with worry and I can tell he's afraid that he's permanently wrecked the fragile peace we've managed to create over the past few weeks. "I'm sorry. I don't have any right to weigh in on who you're dating. Even if I do hate his guts."

I guess he hasn't heard about Bowen yet—if he had he definitely wouldn't be apologizing to me.

I sigh inwardly. Aiden's being the bigger person by admitting he was wrong to interfere, so I guess it's only fair to give him the satisfaction of knowing that Bowen and I are no longer a thing.

"Well, get ready to say I told you so," I say. I recount the story of discovering Bowen with Olivia. "You were right. He's definitely a dirt ball." Obviously I need to do some serious inner work to figure out why I keep picking the wrong men. Why can't I fall for someone who is emotionally available? *Why?*

Aiden's face hardens. "That motherfu—"

"It's okay," I say, laying my hand on his arm. I'm surprised at his reaction. What Bowen did was screwed up, sure, but I expected Aiden to be delighted that I'm no longer interested in his arch nemesis, not to want to punch him for it. "We only went out a few times," I add. "It's not like I was planning to marry the guy."

"That doesn't matter." He shakes his head, disgusted. "He should have had more respect for you than to try and bang someone at a party you're hosting."

He's right. But he didn't. And that's why Bowen is now in my rear-view mirror.

"I'm just glad I didn't waste any more time on him," I say. "And I'm sorry that I didn't listen to you when you tried to tell me about him. I know you were only trying to help."

Aiden gently bumps my shoulder with his. "That's because I want the best for you, P."

Unexpectedly, my eyes fill with tears. I glance away, hoping it's dark enough that he doesn't notice. The tears aren't for Bowen—he doesn't deserve them—but because I know deep down that Aiden does want me to be happy. He's proved that in a number of ways over the past few weeks. He's trying to be my friend. Despite the fact that I haven't exactly made it easy for him, he still keeps trying. And that means a lot.

If anyone had asked me even a week ago if Aiden Miller and I would ever be friends again, I would have laughed in their face. But things change. People change. And the more I'm around him, the harder it is to stay angry at him.

Aiden clears his throat. "So, P, I'm glad we have a second alone because I wanted to talk to you about something—"

I hear my name being called from the house. The caterer must be ready to leave. I start to stand but Aiden beats me to it, getting to his feet first and extending a hand to help me up. Touching him sets off fireworks inside of me, but I try my best to ignore the feeling. Which is pretty much impossible.

"Thanks," I say, my heart pounding as I drop his hand.

Our feet are wet from the pool, so Aiden darts into the cabana to grab us each a towel so we can dry off before we head into the house.

Five minutes later, the catering team is gone. I ask Aiden which floor he wants to take—we need to do a final walk-through to turn off lights and make sure all the doors and windows are locked before we leave for the night.

"Are you in a hurry? I thought we could have some coffee," he says. "Maybe do a quick recap of the event. Compare notes."

I shake my head. If I have coffee now then I'll be up all night. "Can we do that tomorrow? I should go before I'm too tired to drive home." As it is I'm not going to get a lot of sleep tonight—I drew the short straw so I have to be back here early in the morning to let the cleaning service in. Another expense that Aiden and I are on the hook for.

"You know, we don't have to go home," Aiden says. "We could just stay here. Tim and Annabelle have a million guest rooms. I don't think they'd mind if we borrowed two of them."

My stomach flips. It is tempting to just stay over—I mean, when will I ever get the chance to sleep in a mansion again? And it would save me from having to drive all the way back here tomorrow morning…

"Annabelle keeps extra toothbrushes and robes in all of the bathrooms," Aiden adds. "So we have everything we need."

That settles it, then. "Okay. I'm in."

Aiden grins at me. He looks so happy that I'm staying here with him that I can't help but smile. Since neither of us has to drive now he makes us each a White Russian, loads a bunch of mini sugar cookies shaped like lobsters onto a plate, and gestures for me to follow him.

We end up in the white room. While Aiden flicks on the massive stone fireplace, I send Leighton a quick text to let her know I won't be coming home tonight. I leave out the part where Aiden is staying with me. Well, not *with me* with me. Unfortunately.

No, not unfortunately. I give myself a mental shake. Aiden and I are friends. Or becoming friends again, anyway. Yes, I'm attracted to him, but I'm determined to get over that. His friendship is more valuable to me than his insanely hot body.

Of course, it would be a lot easier for me to forget about that body if Aiden wasn't still in his captain's uniform.

Costume, I correct myself. It's just a costume. And it's embarrassing that I'm so turned on by it. And even more embarrassing that I can't stop thinking about what's underneath those tight black pants.

These are not thoughts a friend should be having for another friend.

"So," Aiden says, plunking down beside me on the couch. "Great turnout tonight. I got some really good leads." He puts his feet up on the coffee table.

My heart sinks. I made some good contacts tonight, too, and some of them even mentioned having the perfect buyer but I'm not confident that any of them will come through.

Panic starts to set in again. Why did I ever agree to this bet? I never should have gambled my commission. If I'd kept pushing Aiden for a more even split then we both could have won. Instead one of us is going to end up with nothing. And there's a very real possibility that it will be me.

I should get out of my own way, put aside my pride and suggest that we call the whole thing off, but then Aiden will assume I'm backing out because I'm worried I'm going to lose. Which is true. And while I'd like to believe that I won't hold a grudge if he does win, I know myself better than that. This stupid bet could easily torpedo our friendship again. And there'd be no coming back from it this time.

"You okay?" he asks.

I smile because I don't want him to know that I'm spiraling. "I'm fine," I say, taking a sip of my drink. "Your mom wasn't too happy that we're co-listing."

Aiden shrugs. "She'll get over it."

I wonder what she'd think if she knew he'd bet his commission.

"I don't think she likes me very much," I say.

"She doesn't *not* like you," Aiden says. "She's just super competitive. She always wants to win at everything. To her it's the most important thing."

So that's where he gets it from.

He plucks absentmindedly at a loose string on the button of his uniform. "I love my mother, don't get me wrong, but 10/10 don't recommend working with her," he says. "Grady Miller is all business, all the time."

I can only imagine.

"You could always work for a different brokerage," I suggest. "Or start your own." He has the money, the contacts and the experience to pull it off.

Aiden snorts. "No. I couldn't." He glances at me. "My parents built this business. The plan has always been for me to take over one day. I can't just walk away from that."

"I mean, you could," I say. "If it's not what you want."

"Maybe I could have done something else if my dad was still around," he says. "He would have understood. But my mom would never get over it if I quit. She still hasn't forgiven me for taking off to travel for six months."

I guess I never thought about the pressure Aiden's under as the crowned prince of his parents agency. Trapped under the weight of his mother's expectations.

"She's always on my back about bringing in more listings," he says.

"Is that why you stole my client?" I ask. The White Russian has loosened my tongue and the question is out of my mouth before I can think about whether it's a good idea to have this conversation or not. I don't want to dredge up all the bad feelings. Not when we're finally getting to a good place.

Aiden grimaces. "I definitely owe you an explanation for why I did that, but I'm not sure I can explain it without it sounding like I'm just making an excuse," he says. He lets out a long breath. "Yes, I was under a lot of pressure, but I knew taking your client was wrong. I knew it and I did it anyway. I figured you'd be mad but that you'd get over it." He shakes his head. "Ridiculous, right? I was so impulsive and arrogant. But that's who I was back then."

He twists on the couch so that he's facing me. "I am really, truly sorry, P," he says.

"And I promise you that I'm not that guy anymore. I hope you can see that."

I nod. I do. Aiden has grown up a lot. And I'd like to believe that he'd never do anything like that to me again, but then I remember our bet, how I'll get nothing if I lose, and I wonder if I'm giving him too much grace—he knows I'm the underdog and the odds of selling the house first are not in my favor. He knows that and he still suggested that I bet my entire commission.

And, like an idiot, I agreed to it.

So I guess I still don't fully trust him. I want to, but I don't. And I'm not sure there's anything he can do to change that, which makes me sad. Because how can we truly be friends if I can't get let go of the past?

Aiden rubs his palms against his pant legs and clears his throat. "So there's actually something else I've been wanting to talk to you about," he says. "And I think I have just enough liquid courage now to do it."

My scalp prickles. Please god, don't let him be referring to that awful night when I told him how I felt about him. He may be buzzed enough to have this conversation, but I'm certainly not.

"It's okay," I say, desperate to stop him before he starts. "We don't need to talk about it."

"Yes, we do," Aiden says firmly. "Because I want you to understand why I reacted the way that I did when you told me—"

I hold up my hand. "Really. It's alright."

There's no need to revisit the most humiliating moment of my life. I certainly don't need him to spell out that he's not interested in me again.

"You were very clear about your feelings," I say. "And it's okay." He's entitled to not like me back.

"It's not okay," Aiden says. "And I definitely didn't make my feelings clear that night. If I had, then we would be in a very different place right now."

I swallow. What does that mean?

He's staring at me so intensely and I think…I think he wants to kiss me. But that can't be right, can it? I'm just reading him wrong. I always seem to get my signals crossed with him.

"I felt like such an idiot after you left," Aiden continues. "You caught me off guard and I just panicked. Telling you that I only wanted to be friends had nothing to do with me not wanting you—"

I blink. What? Did he just say that he wanted me?

"— but I was dating Madeline," he says. "And it was very awkward because you were working with her and I didn't know how that would go over with either of you."

My eyes widen. Well, that clears up my questions about their relationship timeline. He was dating Madeline when I confessed how I felt about him.

"It was so messed up and complicated with her being your boss," he says. "I didn't know how to tell you."

He's right. It would have been messy and complicated. And I'm not sure I could have continued working at the brokerage if I'd known about it then.

"And then I went ahead and made an even worse decision by signing your client a few days later," Aiden says. "Which, as we've already established, was a low-down dirty thing to do that I will be sorry about forever."

After I found out what he'd done, I sent Aiden a blistering text telling him I never wanted to speak to him again before blocking him and forwarding his emails straight to my junk folder. I didn't give him a chance to try and explain anything. I just completely wrote him out of my life.

He moves an inch closer to me. "What I'm trying to tell you is that I wanted you, Piper," he says, curling a strand of hair behind my ear. "I wanted you very badly then and I want you very badly now."

My heart is beating so hard I'm sure Aiden must hear it. His eyes have me pinned, I am powerless to look away from him, even if I wanted to. I give him the tiniest nod and he closes the last little bit of space between us and finally, he's kissing me. And we go from zero to a hundred: me crawling into his lap, his hands gripping my waist, my fingers threading through his hair, his mouth on my ear. A frenzy of need, of *oh my god* and *please*, of how fast can we get naked.

Years of wanting him, of dreaming about this, and it's so much better than anything I imagined. My dress is bunched around my thighs and I'm pulling at the buttons on his captain's uniform with shaking fingers. Aiden shrugs out of his shirt, groaning as I run my palms over his bare chest, then the black ink raven on his muscular arm.

He's hard and I'm rubbing against him, already halfway there. He slides the sleeves of my dress down, followed by my bra, and cups my breasts in his hands. I cry out as he brushes his thumbs over my straining nipples. I want him so much that I can barely stand it, but when he gently tugs on the end of my scarf I suddenly come crashing back down to reality.

What am I doing? I push his hands away, scramble off his lap and yank my dress down, already feeling the loss of him beneath me, but determined to listen to my head instead of my throbbing body parts.

"This is a mistake," I say, trying to catch my breath. "We can't do this."

If we have sex, then we can't ever take it back. Or I can't, anyway. I've just gotten used to not hating him and stepping over this line could mess up our friendship, not to mention damage our professional relationship. That's just not a risk I'm willing to take.

"Don't say that. We're not a mistake, P," Aiden says. He tries to reach for me, to bring me near him again, but I slide out of his grasp.

I shake my head. "We have to work together." This is the biggest listing of my career. Not only that, but we're competing to see which one of us will sell the house. I can't let my judgement be clouded any more than it already is. My future is at stake.

"Then we'll wait," Aiden says. "And we'll celebrate properly once we sell the house."

My pulse is still racing. I want to believe him, I want so much to believe that I could come out of this experience with a big fat commission check and a boyfriend, but the rational part of my brain is screaming that it would never work between us. For one thing, there's the bet—for one of us to win the other has to lose. And for another, it's a long shot that Aiden and I would even work out in the real world. He might want me in this moment, but he will eventually change his mind about me. Just like he did with Madeline and every other woman he's ever been with. He proven over and over again that he isn't the relationship type. There's only one realistic outcome to all of this and that's me ending up with a broken heart. Again. Only this time it would be so much worse.

But even if I'm wrong, even if Aiden doesn't change his mind about me, how would I ever explain him to Madeline? She's my boss. She and Aiden might not have been together long, but I'm pretty sure she wouldn't like me going out with her ex. And I don't want to hurt her.

Aiden rests his hand on my knee. "I can tell you're panicking, but it's okay, P. We'll figure this out."

I'm not sure that we will, though. And, more importantly, I'm not sure that we should. So I remove his hand and say the one thing that I know will slam the door on us—the same thing he said to me, all those years ago: "I think we should just be friends."

Aiden's eyes flash with hurt. I know he thinks I'm retaliating, trying to get back at him for saying those same words to me, which makes my heart ache. I should explain, but I'm not sure he would hear me right now—his expression has tightened, he's already started to shut me out.

He grabs his shirt, shoves his arms into the sleeves. "If that's what you want," he says coolly.

It isn't what I want. Not at all. But it is for the best. In time I hope he'll understand that. I hope we can move this past this and stay friends.

Right now, though, I just need some space from him. I get up off the couch, regretting that I had that White Russian because now I can't drive until the alcohol wears off. I guess I could call an uber to take me home, but that would mean waiting around for it to pick me up and at this point I'd rather just go upstairs and hole myself up in a guest room before I totally lose it in front of him.

"I should get some sleep," I say. Best case scenario we wake up tomorrow and pretend this never happened. Worse case we're right back to where we started.

"Goodnight," I say, but Aiden doesn't respond.

My stomach is in knots as I go upstairs and pick a room. A few minutes later, I hear him walk past the door and I hold my breath, part of me hoping that he'll knock, that he'll come inside and tell me I'm being ridiculous, that I shouldn't turn away from something that could be really great and that we can finish what we started downstairs. But he doesn't. And so I climb into bed alone and then I lie awake most of the night trying to convince myself that I made the right decision.

CHAPTER
SEVENTEEN

AIDEN'S ALREADY GONE by the time I get up the next morning. I'm partly relieved because I wasn't sure what to say to ease the tension between us, but I'm also kind of irritated that he took off without telling me. He could have at least sent me a text to let me know that he was leaving.

I'm still reeling that he wants to be with me. For so long I've believed that my feelings were one-sided, that he only ever saw me as a friend. Maybe everything would have been different if we'd both managed to get out of our own way back then. Or maybe nothing would be different—Aiden would have probably broken up with me the minute his head was turned by another woman.

I take a quick shower and change back into the dress from last night. I'm stuck here at the Davidsons house until the cleaning crew have erased all remaining signs of the party, so I carry my laptop into the kitchen so I can send some follow up emails. I've just made myself an espresso and I'm getting ready to settle in when Sita texts to ask if I'm still alive, her not-so-subtle way of pointing out that she hasn't heard from me in a while.

Guilt zips through me. I've been a lousy friend these past few weeks, putting her on the backburner while I try and get this house sold. I know she'll understand, but still. It's not cool that I've ignored her last few texts.

> **ME:** Sorry I've been MIA. This listing has taken over my life. We need to catch up! Coffee tomorrow?

> **SITA:** Can't. I'm around next weekend, though— want to come to the Salmon Festival with us on Sunday?

I check my calendar. Unless I land a showing then I should be able to make it.

> **ME:** 👍

I continue staring at my phone for a few more seconds, debating whether I should text Aiden. It's probably on me to break the ice, all things considered…only I still don't know what to say to him, so I set my phone down.

When I finally get home a few hours later, I find my sister watering Feyre, her spider plant. Leighton has given all her plants names from a fantasy series she loves and has been begging me to read for years. She also talks to her plants because she read somewhere that it helps them grow. And who knows, maybe it does.

"Hey," Leighton says, glancing at me. She's wearing denim overalls with a yellow and white striped t-shirt, her long blonde hair twisted into a milkmaid braid. "How'd the event go last night?"

"Pretty good, overall." A few realtors have already responded to my follow up emails. With any luck this house will sell quickly and I'll be able to tell my sister that I have the money to send her back to school. I can't wait.

"You'd better go and take your thyroid medication," Leighton says.

I sigh. I am supposed to take my medication at the same time every day but missing the window by a few hours isn't going to cause any major problems. If I skipped a few days, then yes, that would be bad, but that's never happened because I always remember to take it. I don't need my sister to remind me to do it. And yet she does. Every single day.

Still, I go into the kitchen to take the pill, along with the eight hundred supplements that Leighton has laid out for me. I've just swallowed the last vitamin when she bustles into the kitchen with her bright green, snail-shaped watering can. "Ryland's on his way over. We're going grocery shopping," she says, setting the can in the sink and turning on the tap. "Want to come with us?"

I shake my head. "I'm going on a walk with Tyler," I say. He'll be here any minute with Freddie and Maisie, in fact, so I should hurry up and change out of this dress.

Five minutes later, I'm lacing up my sneakers when my phone buzzes. I assume it's Tyler letting me know that he's downstairs, but instead it's Aiden's name I see on my screen. My heart thumps as I open his message.

> **AIDEN:** Got a showing lined up for Friday at ten. Can you make it?

Aiden asking me to come to his showing is a little odd considering we're still competing to sell the house—I would have thought he'd rather keep this client to himself, like he did the last time. It's what I would do. So maybe this is his way of telling me that everything's okay between us…or maybe he just wants to rub my nose in the fact that he has a potential buyer and I don't. Either way, I'm going to take him up on his offer.

ME: I'll be there.

AIDEN: Great.

And it is great. Or not great, maybe, but it is okay. I feel a lot better now that we've had contact, at least. My stomach flutters at the thought of seeing Aiden again, but I can handle a flutter. A flutter is no big deal.

I tuck my phone into the pocket of my hoodie, say goodbye to Leighton and go downstairs to meet Tyler. As soon as I push through the lobby door Maisie spots me and she goes crazy, barking and launching herself into the air.

"Aw, she remembers you," Tyler says as he passes me her leash. "That's true love."

"Don't get your hopes up. I still can't adopt her." I squat down so Maisie and I are at eye level. Her sweet little doggie face crushes me. She smiles as I stroke her fur and I can't help but wish the timing was better for us. I would have loved to have met Maisie a few years from now when I have a place of my own. She deserves a house with a yard that she can run around in, not a small, cramped apartment with an owner who isn't around enough.

"So," Tyler says as I straighten up and we start walking. "I heard what happened with Bowen."

I snort. Of course he heard about what happened. Everyone at the party did, thanks to Olivia's big mouth. At this point, I can only hope that word hasn't gotten back to Tim or Annabelle—I can't imagine either of them would be thrilled to know that Bowen was trying to get busy in their bed. And while it's not my fault that he's a pig, I'm the one who brought him into their house and I don't want them to blame me for my poor judgement. That would make it all too easy for them to fire me.

"Ugh," I say. "What is wrong with him? Who tries to have sex at a work event?"

"Apparently Bowen does," Tyler says. "He's just won himself a page in my burn book—Bowen Clarke is a fugly loser."

I laugh. Tyler is probably joking, but I wouldn't be that surprised if he does have a burn book kicking around somewhere.

"It's fine," I say. "I wasn't really that into him, anyway."

"Because you're into someone else," Tyler says, arching an eyebrow at me. "Come on. You can admit it. You love Aiden Miller."

I roll my eyes. "I don't love him." I'm wildly attracted to him, but I'm not in love with him.

I'm *not*.

"We did stay over at the Davidsons house last night, though," I add. I hadn't planned on telling Tyler about our impromptu sleepover, but I find myself wanting to talk about it.

Tyler's eyes practically pop out of his head. "Wait what? You had sex with Aiden?"

I shake my head. "No. It didn't get that far."

"You *almost* had sex with Aiden?"

I shrug.

"Oh my god, why on earth did you stop?" Tyler cries. "That man is so insanely hot. And honestly, Piper, you could use a really good—"

"Tyler," I say, smacking his arm.

"In all seriousness, when was the last time you actually had sex?" he asks. We've made it to the off-leash area, so we let the dogs roam free while we sit down on a bench facing the water and north shore mountains.

I flush. "It's been a while," I admit. Rob, my ex-boyfriend, is the last person I was with, and that was over a year ago. I could come up with a whole host of reasons why I've let so much time lapse, but what it really boils down to is this: I haven't met anyone that I like enough to do it with. Until Aiden came back into my life, that is.

"So you have this gorgeous guy who is clearly interested in you—I saw the way he was goggling at you last night—and you don't want to do it with him because…" Tyler trails off.

"I never said I don't want to do it with him," I say. If the situation were different, I would do it with Aiden all over the place. But it's not. So I can't. "But when has getting involved with a co-worker ever ended well? What's that saying? Don't shit where you eat?"

"Normally I would agree with you, but this is an exception," Tyler says. "You're working on a listing together but you're not working for the same brokerage. Big difference."

Okay, *technically* he's right. After we sell this house Aiden and I will no longer be working together—and he did offer to wait for me—so I guess that isn't a valid excuse.

"Yeah, but the whole Aiden-Madeline thing," I say. "I couldn't do that to her. It wouldn't be right."

Tyler shakes his head. "I'm all for girl code but she and Aiden went out on a few dates a million years ago. It barely counts as anything."

"Okay, but she's also my boss." And I saw the look on her face when Aiden walked into our office that first day. I think she might have some unresolved feelings.

"At least talk to Madeline about it," Tyler says. "Maybe it won't be a big deal."

Maybe he's right. Maybe she wouldn't care if I dated Aiden. But even if she gave me her blessing I still don't think I could do it. There are too many other insurmountable issues between us. But when I list them out Tyler knocks them down, one by one.

"Aiden stole my client," I say.

"He apologized for that," Tyler replies. "And he sent you presents. Next."

"His mother hates me." Maisie comes running up and rests her chin on my knee. I rub her ears.

"His mother hates everyone," Tyler says. "Grady Miller is scary, though. I'll give you that." He closes his eyes and turns his face up to the sun. "But it's still not a good enough reason to pass a guy like Aiden up."

"Okay, well how about this: he's a serial dater," I say. "He's never been in a long-term relationship. I think he's allergic to commitment."

Tyler opens his eyes and stares at me for a long moment. "Are you husband hunting?"

"What?" I laugh. "No."

"Then why not just have sex with him?" he asks. "This doesn't have to lead anywhere. You don't have to be in a relationship with him. You're in your prime, girl! Just get out there and get it on."

"I'm not wired for casual sex," I say. I don't have anything against it, I'm just not built for it myself. It would be a heck of a lot easier if I was. Then maybe I could relax and let myself enjoy Aiden and his incredible body without worrying about my heart getting involved.

"You are missing out, then," he says. "Mr. Right Now can be a super fun distraction while you're waiting around for Mr. Right."

I laugh. "You're a bad influence."

Tyler smirks. "I've been called worse." He takes a dog treat out of his pocket and gives it to Maisie. "You want to know what I really think?"

"No, but you're probably going to tell me anyway," I say as Maisie suddenly takes off, chasing after a squirrel.

"You're right, I am. Because that's what friends do. They tell each other the truth, even when it's hard." He reaches for my hand and squeezes my fingers. "I think you're throwing up all these roadblocks because you're scared."

"I'm not scared," I lie.

"You are," Tyler insists. "I've run from enough relationships myself to know what it looks like."

I grimace. "I just don't think it would work out between us in the long run." As I already pointed out, Aiden doesn't exactly have a great track record. And while I might not be 'husband hunting', as Tyler suggested, I am looking to be with one person.

To do that I'm going to have to let my guard down, no matter who the guy is. The thought makes my stomach lurch.

So there it is. The real reason I didn't let things go any further with Aiden last night—it had nothing to do with all these other excuses and everything to do with having to show him my scar. I can't tell Tyler that because he won't understand. He'd tell me to get over it, that Aiden would be way too busy staring at all my other naked body parts to be concerned with what's happening on my neck—and that's probably true. But showing all of myself to him would make me feel vulnerable. And I don't like feeling vulnerable.

"Are you psychic, Piper?" Tyler asks me.

"No."

"Then you don't know what's going to happen with you and Aiden," he says. "You're so focused on it ending when it hasn't even really started yet."

He's not wrong. But that doesn't mean I'll just magically be able to let go of my insecurities.

"Okay, I just heard myself and I sound like a total hypocrite," Tyler says with a long sigh. "I'm going to have to follow my own advice and call Nate, aren't I?"

Nate is the guy Tyler ghosted a few months ago for no apparent reason. Or at least not one that he's told me.

"Do you want him back?" I ask.

He nods. "I do. Do you think he'll forgive me if I beg?"

I mean I wouldn't. But I'm not Nate. "It can't hurt to try," I say.

"Maybe I should take a page out of Aiden's playbook and send him flowers," Tyler says. "Worked on you."

I smile. It was the little wooden sandpiper that worked on me, actually, but he doesn't need to know that. There is something else that I should confess to Tyler, though—if only because I'll need him on my side when Madeline discovers that I made a really stupid business decision. So I tell him about the bet.

"Excuse me, what?" Tyler asks, a horrified look on his face. "You bet your entire commission? What were you thinking?"

I wince. "I was thinking that I'd get a whole lot more money if I win," I say. "But it's not just pure greed. I want to send Leighton back to school. She's done a lot for me and I owe that to her."

Tyler shakes his head. "Oh, this is so much worse than going out with Madeline's ex," he says. "She could fire you for this."

I chew my thumbnail. The thought has occurred to me. I'm not completely delusional. "Do you think she will?" I ask.

"We're not going to find out because you're going to call this off."

"I can't."

"Yes, you can," Tyler insists. "You have to. Just tell Aiden you made a mistake. I'm sure he'll understand."

"I'm sure he won't," I say. "He'll think that I want to call it off because I know I'm going to lose."

"You *are* going to lose!"

I pinch his leg. "Gee, thanks for the vote of confidence."

"Piper, you cannot go up against someone like Aiden Miller and expect to have the slightest chance of winning," Tyler says. "It's not on an even playing field. You're not even in the same stadium!"

"That's a little harsh," I say. Okay, so telling him about the bet was definitely not the right move. I didn't expect him to be quite so freaked out about it.

Tyler rubs his forehead. "It's not a knock on you," he says. "Aiden's just been selling real estate longer than you have. He has more contacts, more resources."

It's nothing I haven't told myself a million times, but somehow hearing it from Tyler hits differently.

"He can't hold you to anything. I'm pretty sure it's not legal," he says. "Just tell him that you want out."

I swallow. He's right. I need to tell Aiden that I made a mistake before this stupid bet ends up costing me a lot more than my commission. Ugh, I hate the thought of having to admit that to him, though. I hate looking weak.

But what choice do I really have?

"Okay, fine," I say, sighing. "I'll back out of the bet." I'll just have to set my pride aside and settle for whatever commission split Aiden thinks is fair. Which will probably be a lot less than I deserve. Still, however we slice it I'm going to be earning a lot more money than I ever have before—enough to send Leighton back to university for a couple of terms anyway. I guess I can worry about coming up with the rest of her tuition later, once other listings start rolling in.

"Thank you baby Jesus," Tyler says, visibly relieved.

CHAPTER
EIGHTEEN

I KNOW I SHOULD tell Aiden the bet is off as soon as possible, but I'm not going to see him until Friday—while sending him a text would be vastly easier than talking to him person, but it seems kind of cowardly and I'm already feeling like enough of a loser. I want to be able to hold my head high and I can only do that if we're face to face.

The week passes in an anxious blur. Friday morning, I'm sitting in my car outside the Davidsons house, my stomach in knots as I wait for Aiden to arrive for the showing. When he pulls in beside me, I look over at him and my heart skips the way it always does whenever I lock eyes with him.

I smile and he smiles back, but he's got his realtor game face on. Maybe it's because he feels as awkward about the way things ended the other night as I do. Or maybe he's over it and, once again, I'm reading too much into everything.

I get out of my car. Aiden rolls down his window as I walk over to him.

"Hi," I say.

"Hi," he replies.

Yep, definitely awkward…

"I brought you some breakfast," I say, pulling a paper bag out of my tote. I pass the almond croissant I got for him through the window. The Aiden of old loved almond croissants, so this is a peace offering, my way of trying to melt the ice between us and get us back on solid ground. Which seems ridiculous now that I think about it. Like a baked good is somehow supposed to make everything okay.

"Oh," Aiden says, his eyebrows lifting in surprise. "That was nice of you. Thanks."

"You're welcome."

We're being so polite. So careful with each other. I can't stand it. I know the best way to get past what happened is to air everything out, but now is definitely not the time for that. I'm going to have to wait until after this meeting is over to talk to him.

Aiden wolfs down the croissant and then gets out of his car, brushing pastry crumbs from the front of his navy suit. The gesture draws my eyes to his chest, which makes me think of what's beneath that shirt—six pack abs and sprinkling of chest hair, warm, tan skin and a tiny mole just above his belly button. I flush as I'm hit with half-naked memories of the other night, of the way Aiden's big hands tightened on my waist, anchoring me in place on top of him. Feeling him tense beneath me as I kissed his neck. The growling sound he made when I touched him.

I shake my head. Tyler is right. I could definitely use a good—

"Should we go inside?" Aiden says, bringing me crashing back to reality. "They're going to be here soon."

I nod. The 'they' he's referring to is the other agent and whoever they're bringing with them to see the house.

"You told Annabelle we were coming?" Aiden asks as I follow him to the front door.

"Yes. She's away for the next few days visiting her sister on the island. She left last night."

"That makes things easier," he says. "I was worried she'd want to be here."

Me too, actually, even though I've gently explained to her that it's better for everyone if she and Tim aren't around when we're showing their house.

Just in case, Aiden knocks on the door and waits a few minutes before taking out his key. He opens the door, then stands back to let me go inside first.

We split apart, each of us taking a different floor, turning on lights and make sure everything looks perfect and nothing is out of place. Ten minutes later, we meet in the kitchen.

"All good?" Aiden asks as he shoves a pile of mail left on the counter into a drawer.

"All good," I reply.

But the words have no sooner left my mouth than a peal of laughter comes from the backyard. Aiden and I rush over to the window in time to see Tim doing a cannonball into the pool. Buck naked.

I gasp. Oh my god, I just saw Tim Davidsons penis!

Aiden and I exchange a shocked glance as a red-haired woman in a yellow one-piece strolls out of the pool house, jumps into the pool and swims over to Tim. They start making out. Like seriously going at it.

"Didn't you tell him we have a showing?" I ask Aiden, panicked. The clients are going to be arriving at any minute. This is going to be embarrassing for everyone involved, but especially for Tim.

"I definitely told him," Aiden replies, rubbing his jaw. "He must have forgotten."

"What are we going to do?"

He sighs. "We're going to have to interrupt Tim and his…friend."

"You mean you're going to have to interrupt them," I say. "He's your client." Mine is hundreds of miles away spending time with her sister, blissfully unaware that her soon-to-be-ex-husband is cavorting in their pool with another woman.

I grimace. Yuck. I can't believe that Tim brought a woman here. How could he do that to Annabelle? I mean, I know they're getting divorced, but still. This is their family home. The place they raised their daughter. It's completely disrespectful and gross. I'm so disappointed in him.

And just when I think it can't get worse, the woman peels off her bathing suit and tosses it onto a nearby chaise. So now they're both naked in the pool.

"Great," Aiden mutters. "Seniors gone wild." He takes a deep breath and slides open the patio door.

"Hey, Tim," he calls, purposefully not looking at them. At the sound of his voice, the woman squeals and ducks under the water. "Sorry to interrupt, but we have a showing. The client is going to be here any minute."

"Oh," Tim says, laughing a little. "Right, right. I guess I lost track of time. Sorry, we'll get out of your way." He swims to the edge of the pool. I turn away as he climbs out of the water because I don't need to see any of that again.

Aiden slides the door closed. He looks at me and we both just lose it, wracked with the kind of unstoppable breathless laughter that makes my sides ache.

"First time I've had to deal with naked clients," Aiden says, once he's gotten control of himself.

I wipe my eyes, relieved that the ice has finally been broken between us. I peek out the window again. Tim and his lady friend have disappeared into the pool house.

"You don't think they're going to hide out in there do you?" I ask. The clients are going to want to see it and it's not ideal if Tim and his girlfriend are lounging around in there. Or doing god knows what else.

"I hope not," Aiden says. But it turns out we don't have to worry because a few minutes later the two of them emerge fully dressed. Tim reaches for the woman's hand and they sneak around the side of the house. I don't relax until I hear one of his ridiculously expensive cars roar to life.

"Crap, that lady left her bathing suit on the chaise," Aiden adds, frowning. He goes outside and I start to laugh again as he grabs the long-handled pool skimmer, scoops up the discarded swimsuit with the net and then tosses it into the shed.

Aiden's just come back inside when the doorbell rings.

"That'll be my mom," he says.

I stiffen. His mom is the buyer's agent? He didn't mention that when he asked me to join him this morning. Probably because he knew I would find an excuse not to be here.

I trail after him into the foyer, my stomach churning. I'm not prepared to deal with his mother. Then again, I'm never really prepared to deal with her.

Aiden stops before he gets to the door. He takes a deep breath and runs a hand through his hair, which is when I realize that he's nervous, too. He's grown up in Grady Miller's shadow and impressing her is clearly important to him, but bearing the weight of her expectations has to be difficult—especially for someone like Aiden, who is a people pleaser at heart.

"Wait," I say, resting my hand on his arm. "Your tie is crooked." That will be the first thing Grady notices, I'm sure, because nothing ever gets past her. I'm suddenly protective of him and I don't want her to have anything to criticize him about.

As I reach over to straighten his tie, Aiden's blue/hazel eyes meet mine and there's that zip again. I can tell he feels it too, which reassures me a little. Maybe there's hope for us yet.

He smiles at me and his hand rests briefly on mine, light as a butterfly, before he turns and throws open the door. His mother is standing on the other side with a couple who look to be around my age.

"Welcome," Aiden says, letting them inside.

Grady gives me the once-over. "Piper," she says. "What a lovely surprise."

For both of us.

I paste on a smile. Aiden shoots me an apologetic look as his mother introduces us to her clients, John and Zoe. They're dressed down for people who can afford to buy a house like this. It makes me wonder if they have extremely well-paid careers or if they come from money.

As we tour them through the house, Aiden and I play easily off each other. Grady has a lot of questions and she aims most of them at me, which makes me feel like she's testing me or trying to trip me up. It's nerve wracking, but I answer every one of them without any fumbling.

It's hard to get a read on what John and Zoe think of the place because they don't say much. Until we get to the kitchen, that is.

"I hate white cabinets," Zoe says, wrinkling her nose. "They're so boring."

Most clients will find something about a house that they don't like—the color of the walls or the faucets in the bathroom or, in Zoe's case, the kitchen cabinets—but as we continue through the rest of the house I'm shocked at the sheer number of changes she claims she'd need to make in order to live here. This place is a palace, the kind of gorgeous turn-key property that could be featured in a magazine (and actually has been, several times). So either Zoe's already started negotiating and is priming us for a low-ball offer or she genuinely doesn't like this house.

We end the tour in the white room. I immediately flashback to the other night when I was sitting in Aiden's lap on that very comfortable couch. His shirt off, my hands in his hair, the feel of him growing hard underneath me.

Is it hot in here or is it just me?

"This is, uh, a great room for entertaining," Aiden says, the tips of his ears turning red. I bite the inside of my cheek to keep from smiling. Obviously I'm not the only one thinking about the last time we were in this room together.

Aiden hands John and Zoe the slick brochure his assistant created with more details about the house and then Grady asks us to give her a few minutes alone with her clients.

"Of course," Aiden says. "Take your time."

I follow him outside. As soon as the door closes behind us, he loosens his tie and shrugs off his suit jacket.

"Well that was a big fat waste of time," he says as we walk over to his car.

I nod. "You don't think they'll make an offer?"

"No. They definitely won't," I say. "I could tell ten seconds after they arrived."

If I was planning to stick to our bet I'd probably be happy about this—it would mean I still have a chance to win all of our commission—but I'm not, so it sucks.

I fiddle with my scarf. This seems like the perfect opportunity to tell Aiden that I want to back out, but I'm nervous at how he'll react. I don't want him to think less of me.

I'm trying to find the right words when Aiden says, "Do you think we should tell Annabelle there was a naked woman in her pool this morning?"

I snort. By 'we' he means 'me' because Annabelle is my client and, just like I made him confront Tim in the pool, I'll have to be the one to break the news to her.

"Are you kidding? Nothing good can come from telling her that," I say. Nothing good for me, anyway. Hasn't he ever heard of shooting the messenger? "It's really none of our business."

"Maybe not, but I'd want to know if my wife was having sex with someone else in our house," Aiden replies.

"Soon to be ex-wife," I correct him. "And we don't know that Tim is having sex with her."

Aiden rolls his eyes. "Oh, come on. They were naked. If I hadn't stopped them—"

He blinks and I know he's remembering that we were in almost the same position the other night. Only we weren't caught. And I was the one who stopped us from going any further.

My face is burning. "Okay, fine. They're probably doing it. But it's still not my place to tell Annabelle," I say. "Anyway, maybe she already knows. Tim didn't seem upset that we caught him with her." He certainly didn't act like he was worried that we'd pass on that tidbit of information to his wife.

Aiden nods. "Yeah, you're right. Maybe she already knows," he says. "I still feel bad for Annabelle, though. They've been together forever. It has to be weird for her that he's moving on so quickly."

"I'm sure it must be weird."

"Imagine spending decades of your life with someone, loving them, raising a kid with them, and having it just end? And then seeing them with someone else," he says. "It's heartbreaking."

I swallow. I don't remember Aiden being particularly sensitive. Or thoughtful. Or romantic. He's grown up a lot, that's obvious, but I still can't quite wrap my head around how much he's changed in the past few years. Or maybe he's always been this way and I just didn't know him quite as well as I thought I did.

Aiden crosses his arms. "I'm already so done with dating," he says. "I can't imagine having to do it when I'm their age."

Wait. Did he just say he's done with dating? Could Aiden Miller—the eternal bachelor—finally be ready to settle down and be in a committed relationship?

My chest tightens. I want to believe that he's in a place where he could be with one person (me!) but the sad reality is that I still don't fully trust him. There's no guarantee that it would work out between us and I'm so afraid to risk my heart on him again. I don't want to get hurt.

But Aiden is really, *really* hard to resist. Especially when he looks at me the way he's looking at me right now. Like he wishes he could kiss me. Like he wishes he could do more than just kiss me.

We're not even touching but I can feel him. My pulse starts to race. I want to give in, I want to drag him back into the house and finish what we started the other night, but this time I won't stop. No matter the consequences.

Maybe I can find somewhere dark, that way he won't see my scar. Why didn't I think of that before? Ooh, we could do it in the walk-in closet. He can lift me up on the island—it's the perfect height.

The corner of Aiden's mouth quirks up, like he can read my thoughts and he's fully on board with them. He inches closer and his arm brushes mine. It's an innocent enough gesture, but it doesn't feel innocent at all. I feel like I'm about to burst into flames.

The front door opens and we jump away from each other. Grady, John and Zoe walk out and we exchange goodbyes and thank yous before the three of them disappear in Grady's Range Rover.

And now Aiden and I are officially alone.

We need to go back into the house to close up and I'm sure that once we're inside we're not going to be able to keep our hands off each other. So I'm disappointed when Aiden says he has to get to another meeting.

"Would you mind locking up?" he asks me.

I nod. "Sure." I guess it's not super professional to have sex in a client's closet, anyway. We'll just have to wait for a better time.

It's not until he opens his car door that I remember I promised Tyler I'd call off the bet.

"Wait, before you go there's something I need to talk to you about," I say. "It's about our bet."

Aiden looks over at me and I almost lose my nerve.

I clear my throat. "I shouldn't have agreed to bet my commission," I say. "It was impulsive. I didn't really think it through."

"I was never going to hold you to that bet, P," Aiden says. "You think I'd really let you do all this work for nothing?" He smiles. "I always intended to split it with you, fifty-fifty."

I narrow my eyes. I know it's irrational—I should be thankful he's letting me off the hook—but instead I'm irritated. The arrogance! If Aiden had never planned on holding me to our bet then it's only because he never thought I'd win. He doesn't see me as competition. He never has.

So what did he think would happen if he won? That he'd ride in like a white knight and save the day and I'd be so grateful that I'd take his pity commission?

No. I'm my own white knight. I can save myself. Aiden might not believe in me, Tyler might not, either, but that doesn't matter. Because I know I can do this.

"Forget it," I snap. "The bet's still on." This might possibly be the stupidest decision I've ever made in my entire life, but I'm making it anyway. I'm not going to give up on myself. No matter what it might cost me.

Aiden's brow furrows. "Are you sure? You'd be giving up a whole lot of money."

I shake my head. He doesn't get it. He doesn't understand why I'm upset. He still assumes that I'm not a threat, that I don't have a ghost of a chance, and it *infuriates* me.

"I'm not giving anything up," I say, straightening my spine. "Because I'm going to win."

I turn on my heel, leaving him standing there muttering in confusion as I stalk towards the house. I'm going to prove to Aiden that he should never underestimate me.

I'm going to sell this house. Without his help.

CHAPTER
NINETEEN

I SPEND THE REST of the afternoon following up for the third time with every single realtor who attended the broker's open last weekend—with the exception of Bowen, who is dead to me. I also make some cold calls to a few clients in our database and send a last-ditch desperate email blast to all my family and friends, praying for a lead.

And it works! Because an hour later, Ryland, my sister's sometimes boyfriend, replies that his aunt has been searching for a house in the area—he's already forwarded her the listing and she'd like to see it as soon as possible. At first I'm suspicious because Ryland busks for extra cash and lives in a dumpy house with four roommates, so I'm not convinced that anyone in his sphere of influence can afford a multi-million-dollar property, but a quick Google search reveals that Susan is the CFO of a very successful tech company. After a quick chat in which she promises to send me proof of funds, I line up a showing for tomorrow evening.

Take that, Aiden.

I spin my chair towards Tyler and tell him the good news.

"Yay," he replies with a weak pump of his fists. He's not his usual sparkly self today—he's wearing jeans and a plain white sweatshirt, which is the most dressed down I've ever seen him. Something's clearly going on, but every time I ask him if he's alright he gives me a half-hearted shrug.

"I can't help you if I don't know what's wrong," I say, as Freddie crawls out from under Tyler's desk. He stands on his hind legs, begging to be picked up.

"I'm shame spiraling," Tyler says, grabbing his dog and settling him on his lap. "I did something ridiculous yesterday." He sighs wearily and I think he's going to leave me in suspense, but he adds, "I wanted to do something to show Nate just how sorry I am for ghosting him and maybe convince him to give me a second chance."

I nod, encouraging him to go on.

"But, you know, he's blocked me everywhere so I had no way to reach him," he says. "I had to get creative. So I sent a barbershop quartet to his law firm. Because who doesn't love a barbershop quartet?"

I wince. Me. I don't love them. I feel a spark of sympathy for Nate. I would die if someone sent me a singing telegram, especially at work.

"Nate's a Swiftie so I thought it would be cute if they performed *King of My Heart*," Tyler says. "But he definitely did not think it was cute. He unblocked me just long enough to tell me to fuck off and never contact him again." He gives me a rueful smile. "Needless to say, it appears that we are never, ever, ever getting back together."

I reach over and rest my hand on his arm. "I'm sorry."

Tyler shakes his head. "I should have just stuck with flowers," he says mournfully. "Not that it would have made any difference because apparently Nate's already moved on. Which I probably should have seen coming, but somehow I didn't."

"Well, at least now you don't have to go through life wondering what if," I say.

"That is a bright side," Tyler agrees. But he still looks so sad that I ask him if he wants to start the weekend early and go grab a drink.

He immediately pops out of his chair. "I'll just let Madeline know we're taking off," he says, tucking Freddie under his arm like a football and heading to her office.

While he's gone, I fire off a quick text to Annabelle to let her know that I'll be bringing a potential buyer through her house tomorrow evening. I give Aiden a heads up, too, asking him to pass the message on to Tim so I won't find him cannonballing naked into his pool again.

I don't invite Aiden to do the showing with me. I haven't heard from him since I told him the bet is still on earlier this morning and I don't really expect to hear back from him now. He knows I'm mad at him and who knows, maybe he's mad at me too. Not that I care.

Okay, I care. But I'm really trying hard not to.

"Maddy's coming," Tyler says, returning to his desk. "She just has to wrap something up so she'll meet us there."

I don't need to ask him where we're going because we always go to the same place, a cozy little pub down the street that has a dog-friendly patio and the best spicy blood orange margaritas in the city.

Tyler and I gather our things. He puts on his straw fedora, attaches Freddie to his leash and calls a hearty goodbye to "Sherry in the cherry pantsuit". I smile as we head out into the sunshine. I love this time of year. Vancouver really is at its best in the summer.

Happy hour means the bar is busy but luckily we manage to snag a table on the patio. Tyler ties Freddie's leash to the wrought iron table leg and then scans the menu, even though we both already know it by heart.

"So you've told Aiden that you want to cancel the bet, right?" Tyler asks just as the waiter appears with a bowl of water for Freddie. We order margaritas and Tyler gets a glass of rosé for Madeline, as well as mini corn dogs, an apple and gouda grilled cheese, and pulled pork dumplings.

"Might as well eat my feelings," he says once the waiter has left.

"I know it sucks but it just means that Nate isn't the one for you," I say. "Your other half is still out there."

I cringe. God, listen to me. I'm beginning to sound like my 'everything happens for a reason', 'rejection is just redirection' sister.

"Ugh, I don't want to talk about Nate anymore," Tyler says. "I want to talk about you. Don't think I didn't notice that you haven't answered my question about the bet."

My stomach tightens. I was hoping he wouldn't notice I was trying to steer him off topic.

I fidget with Leighton's crystal bracelet. "I told Aiden I wanted to call it off," I say. It's not a lie, exactly—I did tell him I wanted to call off the bet. Of course, I also took that back…but Tyler doesn't need to know that part.

"And? What did he say?" he asks.

I grimace. Of course he wants the full story.

"He said he wasn't planning to hold me to the bet anyway."

Tyler raises his eyebrows. "Because he assumed he'd win?"

"Yes."

"I don't love the arrogance, but really, who cares in the end, right?" Tyler says. "As long as you get your share of the commission."

I shift uneasily in my seat. "Right."

"Let's just thank god he let you off the hook," he says.

I take a sip of my water, avoiding his eyes.

Tyler stiffens. "Oh my god. You didn't call it off, did you?"

I give him a sheepish smile. "No," I admit.

"Piper!" he cries, loud enough to cause several heads to swivel in our direction. "You just told me that Aiden isn't going to hold you to anything."

"He's not."

"Then why aren't you taking him up on it?"

I shrug. When he puts it like that it sounds so easy, but it's not easy. Not for me, anyway.

Tyler throws his hands up in the air. "You have way too much pride. Who cares if Aiden doesn't think you can do it?"

I do, obviously.

I scowl at him. "He's not the only one who doesn't think I can sell this house."

That shuts him up. The waiter returns with our drinks and a plate of mini corn dogs, which Tyler immediately digs into.

"I hate that you think I don't believe in you," he says, once the waiter has departed again. "Because I do. But this is an impossible situation." He tears a corn dog into two small pieces and feeds one of them to Freddie underneath the table. "You're letting your ego get the best of you."

Maybe. Probably. But he still hasn't convinced me to back down.

"I can see I'm not getting through to you," Tyler says with a sigh. "Maybe Madeline can talk some sense into—"

"Do *not* say anything about this to her," I hiss at him. "I'll tell her myself once I've sold the house." I'll face the consequences then.

"Fine, fine," Tyler says. "But I wouldn't want to be in your shoes when you tell her."

My phone buzzes. I slide it out of my bag and glance at the screen.

> **AIDEN:** Hey. I've been thinking about it and I realized I owe you an apology (how many is that now? I've begun to lose count). I came across as

a condescending jerk this morning and that was definitely not my intention.

I swallow. Here I go, about to be drawn back in again…I have no willpower when it comes to Aiden Miller.

ME: Thanks.

AIDEN: Any plans tonight? If you're free, I'd like to make it up to you.

My breath quickens. Exactly how does he plan to make it up to me? Because I can think of a few interesting ways. None of which I should actually do.

I'm also surprised that he doesn't have plans. It's Friday night, after all.

AIDEN: I could make you dinner.

I didn't know he cooked. The Aiden of before couldn't even boil water.

ME: I can't. I'm with Tyler at the Crown and Anchor.

Why am I telling him where I am? Madeline is going to be here any minute and it would be very awkward if Aiden took that as an invitation and decided to show up. I wouldn't know how to handle that.

But thankfully Aiden responds that he knew it was short notice and we'll get together another night.

"Who are you texting so furiously?" Tyler asks, reaching for another corn dog. "Or do I even need to ask?"

"It's worked related."

"Right," he says with a knowing smirk.

"Stop it." I stick my phone back in my bag.

"I don't understand why you're fighting it so hard," Tyler says. "You should just go for it. It's not easy to find someone you really connect with."

Connecting with Aiden isn't the problem. It's everything else that makes it difficult.

"I don't know," I say.

"What are you two whispering about?" Madeline asks.

I jump. Tyler and I were so engrossed in our conversation that we never noticed her approaching the table. Oh my god, how much did she overhear?

"We were just talking about what we would do if a friend dated our ex," Tyler says breezily as Madeline sits down beside me.

I cut my eyes at him. What is he doing?

He smiles back at me.

"How recent is the ex?" Madeline asks, picking up her wineglass. "And how close is the friend?"

I'm kind of surprised that she's putting thought into the question and not just responding with disgusted outrage, like I would have.

"Not recent and pretty close," Tyler says. "I should add that it's not *really* an ex, but just a guy our fictional friend went on a few dates with."

My cheeks are burning. What does he think he's doing?

Madeline takes a sip of wine, thinking. "This is a purely hypothetical situation? Or are we actually talking about Aiden and Piper?"

My stomach drops. She knows about Aiden. My boss knows I have feelings for a guy she used to date.

I. Am. Mortified.

"You look like you're going to pass out," Madeline says to me, laughing a little. "It's okay. Aiden and I were barely a thing. But I appreciate that you've been taking my feelings into consideration."

"See? I told you she wouldn't care," Tyler says to me.

Madeline frowns at him. "Don't act so smug. That was kind of a dick move."

"What? I didn't tell you, you guessed," he says.

She rolls her eyes. "You said it without saying it. You knew exactly what you were doing."

"I was just trying to help," Tyler replies sheepishly. "Sometimes Piper needs a little push."

I'd like to push him right now. Off a cliff.

"Tyler," Madeline says sternly.

"Okay, okay. It was a favor disguised as a dick move," he says. "Sorry Piper."

"Can we change the subject, please?" I beg. It's great that Madeline is fine with the idea of me and Aiden, but it's still not something I'm really comfortable talking about with her. And I don't think I'll ever be.

"I just want to say one thing and then we'll move on," Madeline says. "Aiden is fun to spend time with, he's great in bed—"

Oh god.

"—but don't let yourself get too attached to him. I don't want to see you get hurt," she says. "Sooner or later his eye will wander."

My stomach tightens. "Nothing is even really happening," I say.

We discuss business for the next half an hour. The whole time, I'm praying that the three margaritas Tyler's downed won't loosen his lips any further—I really will push him off a cliff if he brings up the bet. Madeline might been cool about Aiden, but I don't think she'll be quite as understanding if she finds out I've gambled my commission.

Madeline leaves after she finishes her glass of wine, but Tyler and I hang around for another half hour. When the waiter comes by again to check if there's anything else we need, Tyler asks him for the bill.

The waiter shakes his head. "It's already been taken care of."

I assume Madeline must have picked up the tab on her way out—which is incredibly nice of her—but then the waiter adds, "Someone named Aiden called in and paid for you."

My heart flutters.

"I told you his love language is gifts!" Tyler crows.

I'm not sure love is the word that Aiden would use, but he's definitely got my attention, that's for sure.

Tyler won't shut up about it as we leave the pub. "That was so nice of Aiden," he says. "Nate would have never done something like that."

"Nate sucks," I say in solidarity.

Tyler's brow furrows. "I think I might be the one who sucked in that relationship but thank you for being on my side anyway."

"Always."

"Want to walk the dogs with me tomorrow?" he asks.

I nod. I'm showing the Davidsons house to Ryland's aunt in the afternoon, but otherwise I'm free.

"Great. I'll come by your place around ten." Tyler wraps me in a bear hug. I pat his back and then he's gone, disappearing into the night.

I've had a little too much to drink, so there's no way I'm driving home. I decide to leave my car at the office overnight and take an uber. I text Aiden while I'm waiting for my ride.

ME: Thank you from me, Tyler and Madeline.

AIDEN: You're welcome.

I chew my lip. I could go home, have a bath. Watch some Schitt's Creek. Read a book. Or I could listen to my heart instead of my head for once. I could put myself out there. Take a risk.

> **ME:** I'm free now. If you still want to get together.

> **AIDEN:** How soon can you get here?

CHAPTER
TWENTY

'VE BEEN STANDING in front of Aiden's door for several minutes, gathering up the courage to knock. I want to go inside—I think—but I'm still not quite over our argument this morning. Aiden might have apologized for acting like a condescending asshole, but I know he still doesn't believe I have any hope of winning our bet. So how sorry is he, really?

I shake it off. *Who cares if he doesn't think I'm a threat? Let him underestimate me. It will just make it that much more satisfying when I sell the house right out from under him.*

I take a deep breath and raise my hand to knock, but Aiden yanks open the door before I make contact.

"Exactly how long are you planning to stay out here, P?" he asks, smiling at me.

My heart starts to beat wildly. Aiden looks good. As usual. Worn-in jeans and a white t-shirt, his blonde hair predictably messy. But it's the glasses that really get me. It's the glasses that make me want to climb him like a tree.

I swallow. "I was just…thinking."

"That's your trouble," he says. "You think too much."

He's right, I do. I overthink *everything*—that's just how I'm programmed. And here I go again, my thoughts spinning with every possible scenario that could happen if I walk through his door. And most of them are very, *very* dirty.

Aiden takes a step back. "Do you want to come in?"

Yes.

No.

Yes. Definitely yes. But first…

"I don't want to be your friend," I say, fiddling with my scarf. "I don't know why I said that."

A lie. I know exactly why I said it —I was scared. We got so close so fast the other night that I completely panicked. I let my brain talk me into running away from him. But I'm not going to do that tonight. No, tonight I'm going to turn my brain off and let myself have what I really want: Him.

Aiden's smile widens. "That's good. Because I don't want to be your friend, either."

He holds out his hand. I take it and step inside the house…and into his arms. Aiden's hands slide into my hair. He lowers his mouth to mine and we're kissing and I'm suddenly desperately grasping the hem of his t-shirt, ready to tear it off him, right here in the doorway for all his neighbors to see. But we can't slow down or I will probably chicken out again—then again, I don't think we could do this slowly, anyway. We're a struck match, already burning.

Aiden stops kissing me just long enough to remove his glasses. He tosses them on a console table near the door, then lifts me up. I wrap my legs around his waist and he nudges the door closed with his foot. Still kissing, he walks us down the hall to his bedroom and gently deposits me on his bed. A proper bed, not the musty futon I once glimpsed at his old apartment.

Aiden off takes his shirt in one smooth movement, then unbuckles his belt and shucks his pants. In nothing but black boxer-briefs, he stares down at me from the foot of the bed, his blue/hazel eyes heavy with desire. I let my gaze roam all him, pecs and stomach and tree-trunk thighs. Hard in all the right places.

My breath quickens. I reach for him, anxious to have his weight on top of me. He obliges, aligning his body with mine—leg to hip to chest—so that I can feel every inch of him. And he feels amazing. With one hand, he pushes my dress up, his fingers trailing along my bare leg. Up and up and up until he hits the edge of my underwear. I gasp as his thumb skates over the middle of the silky material. He starts to move in small circles and I close my eyes, lost in the swirl of his fingers.

I am so close, but I don't want it to end like this. I want more. I want him inside me. Right. Now.

I slide my hands onto his ass and pull him even closer to me. Aiden groans. He pauses to quickly shed his boxer-briefs and grab a condom from a drawer in his nightstand. I'm half out of my mind as I watch him roll it on, desperate to be close to him again.

Instead, he kneels over me, tugging the top of my dress down, along with my bra. I let out a small cry as he bends and draws my nipple into his mouth. He licks and sucks and teases until I can't take it anymore. I push my underwear off to the side, grab him and guide him into me, feeling him stretching me and oh my god…

"Like that?" Aiden asks, pinning my hands above my head.

"*Yes*. Exactly like that."

Our eyes lock together as we begin moving in rhythm. I'm so turned on that it doesn't take long before I'm coming apart. Aiden soon follows, collapsing on top of me, his breath in my ear.

After a moment, he gives me a kiss and rolls off of me. We're side-by-side, staring up at the ceiling, trying to catch our breath. "That was…"

"Yeah," I say. "It was."

Aiden laughs. And *oh*, I love the sound of his laugh. He squeezes my hand and gets out of bed. I watch his perfectly sculpted naked backside until he disappears into the bathroom.

I smile. That was so much better than I expected. In my experience, first time sex with someone new has always been fumbling and awkward—it eventually gets better with time as we learn each other's bodies. But this first time was different. Aiden and I fit together in a way I've only read about in books.

I'd like to bask in this feeling for a while, but now that my body is satisfied my brain has found its voice again—it wants to know if this was just a one-time thing. Now that we've done it, maybe the flame has been extinguished. Maybe, despite what he said about being tired of dating, Aiden isn't interested in anything but a quick roll in the hay.

Stop. It.

Miraculously, I manage to push all the bad thoughts away.

A moment later, Aiden's back. He picks his boxer-briefs up off the floor and puts them on. Which is a shame.

"Hungry?" he asks.

I smile. "Starving." I only picked at the food Tyler ordered at the bar.

"I was making tikka masala just before you got here," he says. "I should have been watching it, but I got a little distracted." He gives me another one of his devastating smiles. "Hopefully it's not burned."

My heart glows. Aiden was cooking dinner for me. I'm worrying for nothing.

"Sounds great," I say.

Aiden tosses me his white t-shirt. "Meet you in the kitchen."

Once he's gone, I climb out of bed and get naked, then slip the shirt over my head. It smells like him and I kind of love that now it will smell like me, too. Like us. I briefly debate taking off my scarf, but I'm not quite there yet—Aiden may have seen my boobs, he may have been inside me, but I'm not sure I'm ready to reveal that part of me to him. Then again, I don't know if I'll ever be ready.

I walk down the hall, taking in all the details of his house that I missed in our haste to get to his bedroom. His place is small and spare, a work-in-progress, but he's made some effort, which is a far cry from his last apartment. The walls are freshly painted a creamy white and the hardwood floors are polished to a shine. He has grown-up furniture in his living room—a sectional couch and a maple coffee table, a bookshelf and a big screen TV. No sign of the ugly black leather recliner I used to tease him about.

I follow the smell of spices to the kitchen at the back of the house. Aiden's standing with his back to me at the stove, stirring the tiki masala in a pot. I glance around the kitchen, impressed. The cabinets are painted a deep, dark green and the counters are covered in veined white marble. Rough wooden shelves are mounted above the stainless-steel farmhouse sink, but aside from a couple of cookbooks and a black and white photo of his dad—which makes my heart catch—they're bare.

"Wow. This is gorgeous," I say.

"Thanks," Aiden replies, glancing at me over his shoulder. "You should have seen it when I bought it. It was a total mess. Needed a gut renovation."

"You did a great job." It isn't really a surprise—Aiden has an eye for design. I'm sure it's part of what draws him to real estate. It's what drew me, anyway. I'm all about the house porn.

"I did a lot of the work myself," he says and I hear a note of pride in his voice. "I installed the cabinets and the countertops, which is harder than you might think."

A ripple runs through me. Aiden cooks, he's handy and he's great in bed? I might have found myself a unicorn.

Don't get carried away and make this into something more than it is, I tell myself. I've done that too many times before. *Just stay in the moment and enjoy being with him now. Don't think about what happens next.*

Aiden sighs and turns around to face me. "So bad news," he says. "Dinner's totally burned. I don't think it can be saved. It's stuck to the bottom of the pot. Plus I think I used way too much seasoning."

I smile, secretly delighted that I managed to make him forget all about the food cooking on his stove. "Totally worth it."

He smiles back. "Yeah. It totally was."

He sets the pot in the sink and goes to the cupboard. "Mac and cheese?" he asks.

I nod. "My favorite."

Aiden takes out a blue box and fills another pot with water. While he's doing that, I open the door that goes out into his backyard. It's rained since I was last outside and the night air smells fresh. His yard is postage-stamp sized but the lawn is mowed and there's a hydrangea bush in the corner. The windows of the surrounding houses look directly onto his property and since I'm in nothing but a t-shirt, I close the door.

After we've eaten our mac and cheese—standing up in the kitchen because Aiden doesn't have a table yet—we're ready for round two. He leads me back to his room. Once we're in bed, I reach to turn out the lamp, but he stops me.

"I want to see you," he says. "All of you."

My heart drops. He wants me to be completely naked, but completely naked means taking off my scarf. It means showing him my scar.

"You have to trust me, P," Aiden says gently. "Or this is never going to work."

My stomach flips. Is this his way of telling me he wants us to be more than just friends with benefits? I think it is. And he's right—if we're going to be together then I have to trust him.

And so I close my eyes and I take off my scarf with shaking fingers. My cheeks burn. I can feel Aiden looking at me, studying my scar. I flinch as he gently traces the tip of his finger over the slightly raised crescent-shape.

"This is what you've been so worried about?" he says. He leans forward and presses his lips to my neck. "This is nothing, P."

It's not nothing—he's just trying to make me feel better—but I relax a little. The hard part is over. And I'm proud of myself for letting down my guard. For letting him see me.

I open my eyes.

"You're so beautiful," Aiden murmurs. He strokes my hair, then leans over to kiss me, his hand sliding underneath my t-shirt and cupping my breast.

Over the next few hours, we find a few different ways to use the scarf.

CHAPTER
TWENTY-ONE

I WAKE UP EARLY the next morning to the smell of coffee. I'm curled in a ball in Aiden's bed, alone. I can hear him moving around in the kitchen. Whistling.

I smile as I sit up, feeling pleasantly sore and completely satisfied as I reach for my phone on the nightstand. I fully intended to go home last night, but Aiden talked me into staying over. I sent Leighton a message so she wouldn't worry, but worry is her default setting, at least when it comes to me, so I'm not surprised that I have a bunch of missed texts and even a few phone calls from her.

I scroll to her last message, sent ten minutes ago.

LEIGHTON: Where are you?

Yeah, so I might have left that part out on purpose… Not because I thought my sister would care that I had a sleepover with Aiden, but because I didn't want her to make a huge deal out of it. I'm trying to stay cool and not blow up whatever's happening between Aiden and me into something bigger than it is, but if I tell Leighton she'll probably start planning our wedding.

I let myself dream about that for a moment. Maybe everything will work out for once. Maybe Aiden and I will get married and buy a house together and have two point five kids and a dog and open our own brokerage. Maybe we'll live happily ever after.

I shake my head. Or maybe I'm getting way, way ahead of myself.

ME: I crashed at Tyler's.

I hate lying to my sister, but I don't see a way around it. Anyway, she doesn't need to know every detail about my life. She just thinks she does.

LEIGHTON: Are you going to be home soon?

I chew my lip. Shit. My thyroid medication. She's worried I'm going to miss another dose. I really should keep it in my bag.

ME: Not sure. But don't worry, I'll take my meds as soon as I get back.

Aiden comes into the bedroom with two mugs. My heart skips. His chest is bare and he's in grey jogging pants, his blonde hair sticking up all over the place. I set my phone in my lap as he hands one of the mugs to me.

"Thanks," I say as he climbs back into bed beside me. I take a sip of coffee, smiling at the taste of maple. He is a maestro at re-membering the little things. I'm not used to being with someone who is so attentive.

Unicorn, I think.

"So. I'm free today," Aiden says. "What do you have planned?"

"I'm going on a walk with Tyler in a few hours," I say. "Do you want to come?"

I might not be ready to bring him around my sister yet, but Tyler can be my test run—I'd like to see how Aiden fits in with my friends. Plus I want to spend more time with him today.

"I'd love to," Aiden says, leaning over and planting a kiss on my shoulder.

I text Tyler to let him know that I'm bringing Aiden and that we'll meet him at the shelter instead of at my apartment—that way we won't accidently run into Leighton.

I sigh. Yeah, so it's probably a mistake bringing Aiden around him.

> **ME:** If you behave yourself I'll give you all the details later. If you don't, then I'll never tell.

> **TYLER:** You can count on me!

I'm not sure about that—he might not be able to help himself.

Aiden and I finish our coffee and take a shower together, which leads to more sex, and we end up running dangerously close to being late to meet Tyler. He's waiting for us outside the shelter with Freddie and Maisie and he grins as we get out of Aiden's car. Maisie starts to dance around as she spots me.

"Well, well, well," Tyler says. "Hi, Aiden. Nice to see you again."

"Good to see you too, man."

Aiden and Tyler shake hands while I give Maisie some attention. Aiden bends down beside me and vigorously pets both dogs.

He laughs when Maisie licks his cheek and I am officially a goner. Apparently Aiden loves dogs just as much as I do, which is just one more reason to love him.

Not that I love him, I hastily correct myself. Although I'm dangerously close to losing my heart to him, I can't let myself go there yet. Not until I'm certain that Aiden feels the same way about me. I have to protect myself in case I'm in deeper than he is.

Aiden and Tyler chat all the way to the dog park. Aiden glances over at me questioningly a few times and I can tell he's wondering why I'm so quiet, but it's because I'm happy. And nervous. And terrified. All rolled into one.

"WANT TO GRAB some lunch?" Aiden asks me after we say goodbye to Tyler and the dogs. "I was thinking we could go to Granville Island."

I smile. "Sounds perfect."

On the way, we stop by my apartment and Aiden waits in the car while I run upstairs to change and take my medication. Fortunately Leighton isn't home so I don't have to lie to her face about where I'm going and who I'm going with. I'm not ready for my worlds to collide, not until I've figured out if what's happening with Aiden is more than just a fling.

Parking is always next to impossible on Granville Island, but after we circle a few times Aiden finds a spot. He reaches for my hand as we walk into the market and I'm so happy my heart feels like it might burst.

We grab bagels and iced coffee, which we eat outside by the water, laughing as we shoo away the seagulls. Afterwards, we wander around the market, checking out the booths—artisanal cheeses, handmade soaps, hammered silver jewellery. I'm looking at a tiny crocheted toad, wondering if I should get it for my sister, when Aiden stiffens beside me.

I glance over at him. His face is tense and the tips of his ears are starting to turn bright red.

"What is it?" I ask, alarmed. "What's wrong?"

"I think we're about to have a very awkward run-in with my ex-girlfriend," he says warily.

My stomach drops. I turn around. A stunning blonde woman in head-to-toe workout gear is glaring at us from the vegetable stand across the hall. She sets a red apple back on the pile and stalks over to us.

"Aiden," she says.

He clears his throat. "Emily. Hi. Good to see you."

"Is it?" she asks, cocking her head. "I have to say, I'm a little surprised to see you. I thought you were still traveling."

"I actually got back a few months ago," Aiden says.

"Interesting." She gives him a tight smile before her gaze flicks to me.

He rests his hand on my lower back. "Piper, this is Emily. Emily, Piper."

"Hi," I say, smiling at her to try and ease some of the tension. I've run into an ex when he's with someone else and it's not an awesome feeling. Especially if he dumped me, which I'm guessing is what happened here. Emily wouldn't be so irritated with him otherwise.

She nods. "Sorry. I don't mean to make this weird for you," she says to me. "It's just that Aiden told me he'd call me when he got back from Thailand. And like an idiot I believed him."

"Oh," I say, because I don't know what else to say. The worst part is I understand exactly how she must feel. Because I've been there.

Aiden grimaces. "Emily, I think I was pretty clear when I left—"

"You said you'd call me," she insists. "So no, I guess you weren't clear."

"Maybe I should let you two talk," I say.

"No, that's okay." Emily holds up her hand. "I've heard enough. I don't need to talk to him anymore. Or ever again." She shakes her head. "Good luck, Piper. I think you're probably going to need it."

She storms off and Aiden lets out a long breath. "Well that went a whole lot worse than I expected it to," he says, rubbing the back of his neck.

I swallow. "It didn't go well, that's for sure."

I know there are two sides to every story, but it's pretty clear that Aiden is the villain in Emily's. I wish I could shrug this off, but that's hard to do when I have my own complicated history with him.

I've been squeezing the crocheted frog for the past few minutes and now it's a little mangled. As I go over to the cashier to pay for it, Emily's warning reverberates in my head: *Good luck, Piper. I think you're probably going to need it.*

Maybe I should listen to her. Breaking hearts does seem to be a pattern with Aiden—he dumped Emily, he dumped Madeline, he'll dump me next. It's what he does.

I chew the inside of my cheek. What's that old saying? A leopard never changes its spots.

"You're spiraling," Aiden says, when I walk back over to him with my mangled frog. "I can tell."

"Did you tell Emily that you'd call her when you got back?" I ask. It's important that I know if he deliberately led her on or just mishandled the situation.

"It's a bit more complicated than that," he says, which is not at all the answer I want to hear. "Look, let's go sit down somewhere and I'll tell you the whole story."

My stomach is churning as I follow Aiden out of the market to the same wooden bench we happily ate our bagels on earlier.

I sit down beside him. Aiden leans forward, resting his elbows on his knees.

"Emily and I started dating about a year before my dad passed away," he says. "She's a great person and I liked her a lot but I was in a terrible place emotionally. I was not a very good boyfriend to her."

I frown. Okay, so this story is not off to a great start.

"After my dad died, I broke things off with her." Aiden stares out at the water instead of looking at me. "I'd decided to go travelling. I told her that I wasn't in the right headspace to be with anyone, which was true. I felt awful about hurting her." He lets out a sigh. "I'm not sure how we got our wires crossed, because I *never* said that I'd call her. I told her I had no idea when I'd be coming back and that I didn't expect her to stick around and wait for me."

Ah. He may have thought he was being perfectly clear, but all Emily heard was 'wait for me'. I know because I've fallen into the same trap myself before. Some men have a way of twisting words, of trying to let you down gently. And some women—me, Emily— aren't able to read between the lines.

"Obviously I didn't handle my breakup with Emily in the best way that I could have," Aiden says, glancing over at me. "I've made mistakes. A lot of them. But I want to be a better person for you, P. I *can* be better for you."

My breath catches. He sounds like he believes that, but do I?

I want to. Very badly. But I'm not sure that I do.

"At some point you have to trust me, Piper," Aiden says, reaching for my hand. "You have to or this is never going to work."

He's right, but I don't know how to let go of my fear. I can't help thinking that the best predictor of future behaviour is past behavior. Aiden's already fooled me once. Am I really going to let that happen again?

My heart sinks as I stare down at our intertwined fingers. I need some time to myself to think this all through. Being around him clouds my judgement. I could so easily forget about Emily and every other woman Aiden's let down and just lose myself in him. Pretend that I'm different. That I'm the one who can change him.

But what are the odds of that?

I let go of his hand and stand up. "I should probably get ready for my showing," I say. It's a lie—I still have a few hours before I'm due to meet Ryland's aunt at the house—and Aiden knows it.

"Fine," he says tightly.

It's a short, silent ride to my office, where I left my car last night. I spend most of it wishing we'd never gone to the market—if we'd just stayed in bed, we never would have run into Emily and I wouldn't be questioning everything now. I would still be in his arms, not worrying that we're already over before we've even really begun.

"Let me know how the showing goes," Aiden says as he pulls up beside my car. I wonder if it bothers him that I haven't invited him along. It would probably be a good way to ease some of this awful tension, but I don't want him to come with me. Because despite everything that's happened between us I'm still caught up in winning our bet.

I'm not sure what that says about me.

"I will."

I lean over and give Aiden a kiss on the cheek—I can't help myself—and he gives me such a sad smile that I almost crack. But while giving in might feel good right now, it wouldn't help me in the long run. I have to work through my trust issues if we're ever going to have something real.

I get out of the car. "I'll see you later?"

"Yeah. See you later."

I watch Aiden drive off.

I don't cry until he's turned the corner and disappeared from sight.

CHAPTER
TWENTY-TWO

TO: Aiden Miller <aiden.miller@avenuerealty.ca>
FROM: Piper Anderson <piperanderson@pinnacle-realty.ca>
RE: Offer!

Following up on my text and forwarding you the details of the offer from Susan Williams. I think it's a great starting point! Are you free to present to the Davidsons with me tomorrow afternoon? Apparently Tim's out of town until then.

P.

PS – Happy Canada Day!

TO: Piper Anderson <piperanderson@pinnaclerealty.ca>
FROM: Aiden Miller <aiden.miller@avenuerealty.ca>
RE: **RE**: Offer!

Looks good. And yes, I'll meet you there.

A.

PS – Congratulations.

FROWN AT MY laptop. Ugh, Aiden put a period at the end of 'congratulations' and not an exclamation mark, which can only mean he's annoyed that he's about to lose our bet. To be fair, I wouldn't have given him an exclamation mark if he was about to win. I might not even have congratulated him.

I'm suddenly glad I followed my instincts and texted him the news this morning instead of calling him—there's no way I'd have been able to keep the excitement out of my voice and Aiden would have assumed I was gloating. And he would have been right. I wouldn't have been able to resist.

I sigh and sink back against the couch. Winning is awesome, obviously, but at the same time it also feels like one more brick in the wall that's being built up between Aiden and me, which isn't so awesome. A big part of me wants to ignore Emily's warning and make things better between us by asking Aiden what he's up to today—maybe he'd want to tag along with me to Sita's. Meet some more of my friends, have some barbecue and a beer or two. Go back to his house later and have some leisurely holiday sex…

I shake my head. That feels too couple-y and I really do need to take some space to figure out if couplehood is the direction I want to go in with him. Yesterday, I would have said yes, no question, but running into Aiden's ex-girlfriend at the market has set me way back. It was an awful reminder of who he used to be—an insensitive, thoughtless womanizer, someone who can't be trusted. I know that he's changed a lot since then, I know that if we're ever going to have a chance I need to forget about the past, but god that's so much easier said than done.

The door to my apartment suddenly flies opens. Leighton comes inside carrying a canvas tote bag full of groceries and a six back of beer. She's having Ryland and a few other friends over, which means our apartment will stink like weed for days afterwards.

"What are you still doing here, Pips?" Leighton asks, kicking the door closed behind her. Mr. Tumnus darts from underneath the couch to greet her. "I thought you were supposed to leave for Sita's an hour ago?"

I nod. "I was but something came up."

My sister shakes her head. "Something's always coming up."

"Yeah, well, that's real estate for you." It's a drop everything and do it right now, all-encompassing career. But I love it.

Leighton walks into the kitchen to put away the groceries, Mr. Tumnus trotting behind her. I want to tell her that I might have just sold my first luxury listing, but I won't because it's not official yet—the Davidsons still need to accept the offer and then, after the papers are signed, there's securing financing and home inspections. The house could fall out of escrow and the deal could fall apart—I've seen it happen before—but I'm going to take a page out of Leighton's book and believe that the universe has my back and everything will work out this time.

I close my laptop as my sister comes back into the room with her snail watering can. "Do you need some help cleaning up?" I ask her. I haven't touched the dishes in the sink and the carpet could stand to have a vacuum run over it.

"Nah, don't worry. I've got it," Leighton says.

Freed from responsibility, I get off the couch and go into my room to change out of my pajamas and into something equally comfortable to wear to the Salmon Festival. I settle on a navy-blue sundress and white converse, along with the vintage scarf Aiden gave me. I slather on SPF 50—the sun is really sunning today—and head over to Sita's.

Thirty minutes later, I park in front of her townhouse in Steveston. Cars are lined up and down the block already—the Salmon Festival is a popular event and crowds of people are already walking towards the village.

"Hey you," Sita says as she flings opens her front door. She's in a bright red t-shirt printed with a white maple-leaf and capri jeans, her long, dark hair drawn back into a ponytail. "I've missed you."

"I've missed you, too," I reply, giving her a hug. Normally the two of us get together every few weeks or so but I've been working so much lately that I haven't seen her since the night we crashed the gala. Which feels like forever ago.

Thinking about that night reminds me of Aiden. Then again, everything reminds me of Aiden. Absolutely everything.

I wonder what he's doing today. Maybe I should have invited him. Then again, Aiden could have asked me what I'm up to and he didn't, which probably means he already has plans. My stomach tightens. I don't want to think about who he might be celebrating the holiday with.

Sita takes a step back and looks me over, her eyes running critically over my outfit. "Piper! It's Canada Day," she says, frowning. "Why aren't you wearing any red?"

Whoops. "I didn't know that was a rule," I say.

"It is in our house," her husband Raj says as I step inside the house. He and Ishan, their adorable two-year-old son, are wearing matching maple leaf t-shirts.

"Don't worry. I have an extra t-shirt upstairs you can borrow," Sita says.

Of course she does. That's the mom in her—she's always prepared.

While we wait for Sita to fetch the shirt, Raj tries to wrestle his son into his stroller but Ishan is wailing and arching his back, determined not to be strapped in. I have to say, the kid's strength of will is impressive.

"Buddy, you need to relax," Raj says in a soothing voice.

"He wants to walk," Sita says, sighing as she comes back downstairs. "But that's just not going to happen. He'd run into the crowd and we'd never see him again."

"Maybe this will help." I suddenly remember the Batman bubble wand I brought for Ishan. I dig it out of my bag and hand it to him and he stop mid-cry, the distraction buying Raj just enough time to buckle him into the stroller.

"You're a life saver," Sita says as she hands me the t-shirt.

"Thanks." I pull the shirt over my head. It's so big that it hangs almost to my knees, a dress over my dress. Sita decides I can't go out in public this way and she goes back upstairs to get me a belt.

Once she's finished fussing with my outfit, we walk to the village, trailing bubbles behind us. The park is set up with a bunch of food and craft booths and the air is heavy with the smoky smell of barbequed fish. A band is playing classic rock and kids are crawling all over the playground and splashing around in the water park.

We hover around a family cleaning up a picnic table. As soon as they get up to leave, Sita pounces.

"Why don't you take Ish to get his face painted?" she asks her husband as she takes a plastic tablecloth out from the bottom of the stroller and spreads it over the scarred wooden tabletop.

Raj's eyebrows lift. "Have you seen the line?"

"Yes."

He sighs. "Fine. We'll meet you back here." He frees a joyous Ishan from his stroller and takes his son's hand, leading him over to the booth.

Sita and I sit down on opposite sides of the picnic table. She opens two bottles of ginger ale and slides one over to me.

"So fill me in," she says. "What's new with you?"

Where to start...

"Well," I say. "I got an offer on my listing."

Sita beams. "That's amazing!"

I smile. "It's just the first step—Aiden and I have to present the offer to the sellers tomorrow, but I'm hopeful we can reach a deal." Susan came in very close to the asking price and the contingencies she's requested are all common practice, so with a bit of back and forth, I can't imagine that Tim and Annabelle won't accept. I am *so close* to winning this bet and, more importantly, having a little financial freedom for the first time in my life. Not to mention how selling this listing will help me grow my client list.

Sita opens a Ziplock bag of goldfish crackers and places them on the table between us. "What's it been like working with Aiden?" she asks me.

"Better than I expected," I reply. I thought he'd be a lot more combative and competitive with me—especially after we made the bet—but he's actually been pretty easy to work with.

And play with.

I blush, thinking of our night together, and Sita of course notices.

"You little minx! You slept with him," she says.

"I slept with him a few times," I admit, grabbing a handful of goldfish crackers. "I'm not sure it's going to happen again, but it was nice while it lasted." Very nice. So incredibly nice.

"Why can't it happen again?" she asks.

I shrug. "He's not interested in a real relationship."

"He told you that?"

I make a face. "I mean…not in so many words." What Aiden did tell me was that he's tired of dating, but I'm not going to interpret that to mean he wants anything more from me than (fantastic) sex. He's good with words—it's his actions that are the problem. In his past relationships, anyway.

"If he didn't tell you that, then where did you get the idea that this isn't something real?" Sita asks.

I fill her in on how we ran into Emily at the market yesterday.

"She basically warned me not to get involved with him," I say, reaching for more goldfish. God, these things are addictive.

"Why? Did he cheat on her?" Sita asks.

I think back to my very one-sided conversation with Emily. "No," I say. "From her perspective, Aiden didn't make it clear that he wanted to break up. He was going traveling and I guess he let her believe there was a chance they'd get back together when he returned home."

Sita studies me with narrowed eyes. "So he led her on?"

"I don't think he meant to," I say. "But somehow the fact that he was breaking up with her for good got a little lost in translation."

"Aiden probably thought he was doing her a favor by letting her down easy, when he should have just spelled it out." Sita shakes her head. "I hate it when men do that."

Me too. Either they don't want to be the bad guy and have a hard conversation or they mistakenly believe they're being kind, either way it's bullshit. I would a million times prefer brutal honesty, even if it hurts.

"Aiden should have been clear with her," Sita continues. "But maybe it's not all on him. Maybe Emily purposefully didn't hear him because she didn't want to believe that it was over. I've been guilty of that in past relationships."

"If it was just Emily then I'd agree with you," I say, telling her about Madeline.

Sita nods thoughtfully. "Okay, so I think he's off the hook for not being a great communicator," she says. "It sounds like he was upfront with her that it was over."

"He was," I agree. At least, Madeline hasn't complained otherwise. "But my point is that Aiden seems to have left a trail of unhappy ex-girlfriends in his wake."

"And you don't want to end up on that list."

"Exactly."

Sita raises one perfectly sculpted eyebrow. "You can't blame Aiden for having a past, Piper," she says. "Everybody has a history. Even you."

I shrug. True, but mine isn't anything that he needs to worry about. I don't have ex-boyfriends coming out of the woodwork to tell him that I'm not trustworthy. Most of my breakups have been fairly drama-free, mutual decisions to amicably part ways. I haven't cheated on anyone or done them dirty. Can Aiden really say the same?

"Do you think you might just be looking for reasons why you shouldn't be with him?" Sita adds.

She sounds like Tyler.

"No. Why would I do that?"

"Because you're scared," she says. "And you don't trust yourself. Or your decisions."

I bristle. "Yes, I do."

"No, you don't." Sita reaches across the table and takes my hand. "I say this with love: you, Piper Anderson, are the queen of second guessing everything."

Okay, yes, maybe I do second guess myself sometimes. Maybe I waffle and worry and spend way too much time wondering if I should have done A instead of doing B. Which I realize causes me a whole lot of unnecessary stress. But it's how I've been since I was a kid—I don't know how to not be that way.

"You're letting Emily and Madeline make this decision for you, instead of making up your own mind," Sita says. "Their feelings about Aiden are *their* feelings. I could be wrong but it doesn't seem like he purposefully set out to hurt them. It doesn't sound like he was being a disrespectful asshole—I think he was just trying to extricate himself from a relationship that wasn't working. Maybe he didn't do that as gracefully as he could have, but it's kind of hard to fault him for that. There really is no good way to break up with someone."

I pick at the label on my ginger ale, gathering my thoughts. She makes it sounds so easy, but it's not. I can't just forget Emily and Madeline's warnings. Because what if they're right? What if I give in and let myself completely fall for Aiden and then he dumps me as soon as another woman turns his head?

I frown. "Why are you riding so hard for him?" I ask her. She's only met Aiden once.

"I'm not," Sita says. "I just want you to be happy. At some point you're going to have to let someone in. Whoever that is, whether it's Aiden or some other guy, you're going to need to trust that everything will work out. And if it doesn't, then you have to trust that you will be okay. Because you will be." She gestures at my scarf. "You've been through much worse than a broken heart."

She's right. My cancer diagnosis was the hardest thing I've ever gone through—a breakup, even with Aiden, wouldn't come close to touching that. That experience left scars on me, the kind that are visible to the eye and the kind that aren't. I know I've given fear a whole lot of power over me. I've let it stop me from really living, at least when it comes to relationships.

"Isn't it more terrible not to take a chance at all?" Sita presses. "Do you really want to live your life wondering what would have happened with Aiden if you'd just gone for it?"

At that moment, Raj and Ishan return. Ishan's beaming, his face painted to look like Spiderman. Sita pulls him into her lap and gives him a big hug and my eyes sting.

I could have this. If I let myself, I could have the same thing—love and a family, people who would be my home.

Sita settles Ishan into his stroller. We spend the rest of the afternoon eating BBQ salmon and making our way through a huge bag of salt-water taffy. Sita buys a lovely painting of the Japanese Canadian Culture Centre from a local artist and I buy a pair of hammered silver hoop earrings. I almost buy a new scarf, too—green silk printed with koi fish—but at the last second I decide that maybe I need to retire the scarves. I've been hiding behind them for long enough.

Ishan falls asleep in the stroller as we walk back to the townhouse. Sita invites me to hang out at her place until the fireworks, but I've decided that I want to spend what remains of the holiday with Aiden. Because she's right—I don't want to ever want to look back with regret. I need to take a chance.

And so, after I hug Sita and Raj and Ishan goodbye, I sit in my car and send him a message.

> **ME:** Happy Canada Day! What are you up to right now? I thought maybe we could get a drink.

What I'd really like is to skip the drink and go right to sex, but I'm too nervous to be that forward over text. I'd rather use body language to spell it out for him when I see him.

> **AIDEN:** Can't—I have some friends over right now. Why don't you come by?

I swallow. He wants me to meet his friends. That's a good sign, right? He wouldn't want to introduce me to his inner circle if I was just a casual hookup. At least, I don't think he would.

Then again, he didn't mention anything about a party to me earlier. Which means I wasn't on the guest list. I'm starting to second guess texting him when I remember that I told him I had Canada Day plans, so maybe that's why he didn't say anything.

I take a deep breath. I can get in my head about this or I can just assume that the reason he didn't ask me was because he thought I was busy.

I take a deep breath.

> **ME:** Okay. See you soon.

> **AIDEN:** 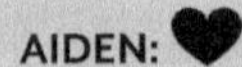

A heart emoji. He sent me a heart emoji! My own heart starts to beat faster. And before I can overthink what I'm doing or question myself, I send him one back.

CHAPTER
TWENTY-THREE

THE SUN IS already beginning to set as I follow the sound of laughter and the smell of smoked meat around the side of Aiden's house and into his backyard. There are quite a lot of people here—more than I expected—but I spot Aiden immediately, sitting in an Adirondack chair, his head tipped back in laughter.

My heart squeezes as he catches my eye and smiles. He's wearing the captains hat again, the one from the broker's open that made me hot all over. I wonder if I can convince him to keep it on later…

Aiden sets down his beer, gets out of his chair and hurries over to me.

"Hi, P," he says, enfolding me in his arms. He nuzzles my neck and I wish there wasn't a backyard full of people staring at us right now. As curious as I am about his friends, I'd still much rather have him all to myself.

"I'm so glad you're here," Aiden says. He kisses me like no one is watching, so okay, I guess we're doing this. We are announcing to the world—or everyone at this party, at least—that we are officially a thing.

"Everyone, this is Piper," he bellows.

I blush at the chorus of cheers, the beer cans raised into the air. Aiden takes my hand and, after grabbing me a hard lemonade from the cooler, parades me around to formally introduce me to each of his friends. It's a little overwhelming and I hope no one quizzes me on names, but they're all perfectly nice and welcoming.

Aiden leads me over to the last couple, a tall, striking blonde and her equally tall and striking partner who is busy devouring a hamburger.

"This is Gavin," Aiden says. "He's a former client turned good friend."

Gavin is mid-chew, so he just nods at me.

"And this is his lovely girlfriend, Lacey."

"Fiancée," Lacey corrects him, holding up her hand to show off the enormous rock on her finger.

"Right. Fiancée." Aiden glances at me. "They got engaged last week."

I smile at Lacey. "Congratulations," I say. "Your ring is gorgeous."

"Thank you," she says, flipping her hand around to admire her ridiculously huge diamond. "He did a great job, didn't he?"

"Pretty hard to mess it up when I was sent a thousand very specific photos," Gavin says before taking another bite of hamburger.

Lacey shrugs. "How else would you have known what I wanted?" She looks at me and shakes her head. "I'm the one who has to wear this ring for the rest of my life. Is it so wrong that I wanted it to be perfect?"

"Not at all," I say, mostly because I know that's the answer she's looking for. First impression: Lacey is an alpha and she likes things her way. She's also flashy and obviously has very expensive taste—I saw the bright green Alaïa minidress she's wearing on Rent the Runway a few weeks ago, although I'm sure that her dress isn't borrowed. I can't help feeling like a mouse next to her in my boring navy sundress, but I guess it could be worse—I could still be wearing the red maple leaf t-shirt Sita lent me.

"So how did you two meet?" Lacey asks.

"Through work," Aiden says, sliding his arm around my waist. "Piper's a realtor, too. We're working on a listing together." There's a note of pride in his voice that makes me very glad I took Sita's advice to ignore all the outside noise. He's done his best to prove to me over and over again over the past few weeks that I'm the one he wants and that's what I need to focus on. Not what any of his ex's might have to say.

Gavin wipes his fingers on a napkin. "Lacey and I met at a BC lions game," he says. "She was a professional cheerleader. I took one look at her out there on the field and I just had to meet her."

Lacey rolls her eyes. "That was a while ago. I'm in PR now," she says to me. "Although I think I'll probably quit working to focus on the wedding. There's just so much to do."

From the expression on Gavin's face this is news to him, but he seems more amused than rattled.

"Maybe I'll get into real estate after we're married," Lacey adds. "I've been thinking about making a career change anyway. And I do love looking at houses."

"I think there's probably a lot more to the job than that," Gavin says.

"There is, but I'm happy to sit down with you sometime and give you an idea of what to expect if you're serious about it," Aiden offers her.

"That would be great," she says. "Thank you."

"Are you still thinking about getting out of the business?" Gavin asks Aiden.

The smile freezes on my face. Aiden's never mentioned anything to me about leaving the industry before. I would have assumed that if he was thinking about quitting the subject would have come up at some point. My brain start to whir. Why would he keep something like this from me? Was it intentional or did he just forget?

"I'm not sure. I'm still mulling it over," Aiden says. He squeezes my hand, a signal that he knows I'm spiraling and that we'll talk about this later, which makes me feel a little better.

Gavin decides he wants another hamburger, so he walks over to the BBQ. A moment later, someone—I can't remember his name— calls out to Aiden. He gives me a questioning look, silently asking if I'll be okay if he leaves me with Lacey, and I nod. I appreciate that he's protective, but I can handle myself with her. Or anyone else, for that matter.

"So," Lacey says, once he's out of earshot. "I can't remember the last time Aiden brought a girlfriend around. How long have you been seeing each other?"

"Not very long," I say.

"Well, you got yourself a good one," she says, tugging down the hem of her minidress. "I can't stand most of Gavin's friends, but Aiden is a keeper."

I smile, delighted to be getting a positive review about him for once. And from someone who knows him well.

"I like your scarf," she says. "Hermés?"

I nod. And then, instead of just thanking her for the compliment, I do something I've never done with a virtual stranger before—I tell her why I'm wearing it.

"It covers my scar," I say. "I had thyroid cancer."

Lacey gives me the face, the one that always comes when some-one hears about my diagnosis. A combination of compassion and sadness, and, yes, pity.

"It's okay," I say. "I'm alright now."

"Thank goodness," she says, squeezing my arm.

And then we move onto another topic. Lacey asks me for the scoop on what it's really like working in real estate. I give her an honest assessment of the pros and cons, even though I don't think many of the cons would apply to her. Honestly, she's already primed for success in this industry—she's outgoing and confident and, most importantly, she has built-in VIP connections through Gavin. Apparently her fiancé is a high-powered lawyer and he comes from a wealthy family, something I'd already figured out long before she told me.

It's hard not to feel a little resentful that Lacey will automatically start her career in a better place than I did, but despite that, I find myself cheering for her. She's asked me some insightful questions and while she might have a big personality, she's hard not to like. So when she asks me if she can take me to lunch next week so we can talk about it some more, I agree and we exchange contact information.

Gavin returns with his hamburger. He murmurs something under his breath to Lacey and she laughs and rests her hand on his arm. I glance around, looking for Aiden, and find him smiling in our direction. When our eyes meet, an electric current zips through me that's so strong that it forces me to finally admit to the truth to myself. Which is: I love him. Against my better judgement and despite trying my very best not to, I have fallen deeply and totally in love with Aiden Miller. He is more than a friend, more than a fling. More than any other guy I've been with. He is everything.

I want to kick everyone out of the party right now. I want to touch him, I want him to touch me, I want to be naked in his bed. I want him on top of me and inside of me and *oh my god*, why are all these people still here?

Aiden's grin widens and I know he's read my mind. And that he's thinking the same thing.

IT'S ALMOST MIDNIGHT before the last guest finally leaves. Aiden and I have spent hours exchanging longing glances, anxiously waiting for the party to end so we can be alone. At one point I consider dragging him off to the bathroom to have my way with him, but this is the first time meeting his friends so perhaps that wouldn't leave the best impression.

The minute Aiden waves to his old high school buddy and closes the door, I pounce on him. All that waiting was pure torture, but it was also kind of hot, and both of us are more than ready. We do it on his couch, too impatient to make it all the way down the hall to his bedroom, and the sex is crazy-good. There's a fire between us that I've never experienced before. Maybe because I've never felt so connected, so completely on the same page with someone.

I love you, I think as we lay half-dressed on the couch, catching our breath. Aiden is the big spoon and I'm curled in his arms. I'd like to stay here with him forever but I'm in danger of falling asleep and my sister is expecting me home tonight.

"I should go," I murmur.

Aiden tightens his arms around me, pinning me in place.

"You're staying," he whispers in my ear. "I like sleeping beside you."

"I like sleeping beside you, too," I say, smiling. "And okay. I'll stay over. I just have to let Leighton know, otherwise she'll worry."

I reluctantly untangle myself from Aiden's arms and get up to grab my phone from the side table. While he sits up and stretches, I chew my lip, thinking about how to tell my sister that I'm seeing Aiden. It's happy news, I know she's going to be excited—she's been not-so-subtly pushing me towards him—but still. I'm nervous. I guess because Aiden and I haven't defined our relationship yet. He may have introduced me to his friends, but he didn't use the word 'girlfriend'. Should I be reading into that?

No. I'm not going to let myself spiral over this. Aiden and I are still early days, but I feel like we're definitely heading in the right direction. I know I'm not alone in my feelings, anyway. So there's no need to keep him a secret from my sister any longer.

I take a deep breath and start typing.

> **ME:** I'm staying over at Aiden's tonight.

> **LEIGHTON:** WHAT??!!!!!!

I smile.

> **ME:** I'll tell you everything tomorrow. Promise.

> **LEIGHTON:** You're end game! I knew it!

I turn my phone around so Aiden won't accidently read my screen. My sister's enthusiasm is sweet but also a bit premature and I don't want to send him running for the hills.

"Ready for bed?" he asks, yawning.

I nod. I set my phone down, take his outstretched hand and follow him into his bedroom.

CHAPTER
TWENTY-FOUR

T ISN'T UNTIL I wake up the next morning that I remember what Gavin said last night about Aiden wanting to quit real estate.

"Hey," I say, poking him in the ribs.

Aiden opens one eye and looks at me, smiling lazily. "Hey yourself," he says, rolling over and pulling me into his arms. He has morning breath—I'm sure mine is just as bad—but when he starts kissing my neck I don't even care. I don't care about anything but being close to him.

Of course all that touching leads to sex, but once we're finished and my brain starts working again I'm back to wondering about Aiden leaving the industry.

We're lying on our backs, side-by-side, staring up at the ceiling. "Are you really going to quit real estate?" I ask him. *And why am I hearing about it from someone else?*

"Maybe," Aiden says. "Nothing's for sure, yet. I've just been tossing the idea around lately." He turns his head to look at me. His eyes, those interesting blue-hazel eyes, draw me in. "I wasn't planning on giving it up, but something you said at the yacht party really stuck with me. Got me thinking."

I blink. Something I said made him want to give up being a realtor?

He smiles. "You really don't remember?"

"No." In my memory, that night was about Aiden looking unbearably hot in a captains uniform. It was White Russians and lobster shaped cookies and grinding on top of him on the Davidsons couch. Freaking out and telling him I just wanted to be friends. Spending the night alone in a guest bedroom, wishing I'd kept my mouth shut. I don't recall saying anything to him about changing careers.

"Is this about the bet?" Maybe he's sour because I'm going to win. I quickly realize that can't be it—Aiden isn't a sore loser (unlike me) and besides, he wouldn't give up his career just because he lost a bet.

He laughs. "No," he says, curling a strand of hair behind my ear. "You told me I didn't have to work for my parents brokerage if I didn't want to. And I realized that you're right. I don't have to."

I frown. The conversation is coming back to me now, although I think Aiden might have misinterpreted what I was actually saying—I wasn't advising him to walk away from real estate altogether, I was simply pointing out that he could strike out on his own if he wanted to.

"You told me your mom would never get over it if you quit," I say, my stomach churning. His parents built a kingdom for him and now he wants to give up the crown? I know I mentioned he could start his own brokerage, but I never thought he'd actually do it. Oh god, if his mother finds out I'm behind this, she's really going to hate me.

"My mom will definitely be upset," Aiden agrees. "And I don't like letting her down. But is that reason enough for me to stay in a job that I hate?"

I sit up, pulling the sheet around me. "You *hate* being a realtor?"

"Well, maybe hate is too strong of a word," he says. "But I don't love it. Not the way you seem to."

I do love it, he's right. Despite the fact that this job can be hard and stressful and frustrating I love it. There's nothing else I'd rather be doing. Which is surprising, I guess, for a girl who craves stability as much as I do.

"But you're so good at it," I say. Aiden is one of the top earning brokers in the country. The entire country! And yes, he's had a hand up in getting there, but he works hard. He's earned it. How can he just give all that up?

"And I'll be good at something else," he says. "Something I actually enjoy. Something that feels more meaningful to me."

Okay, so this doesn't sound like Aiden is just thinking about quitting real estate—it sounds like he's already made up his mind.

I swallow. "What would you do instead?" *Please don't say you're going to travel around the world again, maybe open a bar on a beach somewhere.*

"I'm not sure. Maybe I'll go back to school," he says. He laughs and reaches up to gently smooth out the wrinkle between my eyebrows with the tip of his finger. "Don't look so worried. We'll figure it out."

We. He's including me in his plans—that's a good sign. Except that it's not enough to reassure me. Aiden might believe that it's all going to work out, but I'm not so sure that it will. Obviously I don't want him to be stuck in a job he doesn't like, but going to school is a years-long commitment, depending on what path he decides to pursue. It's going to put pressure on our relationship.

Of course, going back to school is exactly what I want for my sister, but she's in her early twenties and that is what your twenties are for—figuring out what you want to do with the rest of your life. Aiden is a full decade older than Leighton is. He should already know what he wants by now. And it scares me that he doesn't.

"P," Aiden says, sitting up. He leans forward and rests his forehead against mine. "No matter what I decide to do, I promise that it's all going to be alright."

Here's where we are different: Aiden trusts that everything will be okay because, for the most part, everything has always worked out for him. Me, I am always waiting for the other shoe to drop.

I let out a deep breath. Some people might come out of a health scare with profound gratitude and a newfound appreciation for life, and I *am* grateful and appreciative, but I'm also traumatized. Life changed for me in an instant and I live in near-constant fear that it will change again just as quickly. Because bad things happen. Out of nowhere, all the time, to people who don't deserve it.

But good things happen, too. Like falling in love. Or finding a client their dream home. Or having a sister who would drop anything to make sure I'm okay.

"We'll figure it out," I say, leaning over to kiss Aiden. In the end, it doesn't really matter to me what he wants to do with his life, it just matters that I'm in it.

A FEW HOURS later, I dash home to change into something more presentable for our meeting with the Davidsons. I have half an hour before Aiden comes by to pick me up so we can drive to their house together.

I'm expecting Leighton to jump on me the minute I walk inside our apartment, but instead I find her on the couch, a blanket pulled up to her chin. That's the first sign something is wrong—unlike me, my sister doesn't usually enjoy lying around like a sloth.

The second sign is the bunch of crumpled up tissues on the coffee table.

"What's wrong?" I ask. "Are you sick?" I don't walk any closer to her, just in case.

Leighton's lip quivers. "Ryland broke up with me." She sounds stuffed-up, like she's been crying for a long time.

I scowl. I might not get why my sister sees in Ryland, but she seems to really love him, so I want to nut-punch him for hurting her. I'll have to wait on that, though, until after the Davidsons house is officially sold—word could get back to his aunt and I can't risk losing this offer.

"When did this happen?" I ask as Mr. Tumnus wanders out of Leighton's bedroom. He walks past me like I'm not even here and heads over to his water dish.

Leighton reaches for the box of Kleenex on the coffee table. "Last night," she says, blowing her nose. "After everyone else left."

Right. She had a few people over. Now that she's mentioned it, I can smell traces of weed and patchouli in the air.

I walk over to the couch and Leighton moves her legs so I can sit down beside her. "Was this before or after I texted you?" I ask.

"Before."

I shake my head. "Why didn't you tell me? I would have come home."

"I didn't want to ruin your night," she says.

Scenes of what I was up to with Aiden while my sister was getting her heart broken flash through my mind. As amazing as last night was, I would have immediately come home if Leighton needed me.

"You're more important than anything else," I say.

She gives me a weak smile.

Through sobs, she gives me the whole story and it's the same one I've heard a few times before—Ryland needs his freedom, he doesn't want to be tied down, having to be accountable for his whereabouts is a drag, blah blah blah. He's an idiot, but I'm careful not to curse him out too much—that backfired on me when they got back together a few months ago.

"He's not the one for you," I say.

She nods. "I know. Still stinks though."

Breakups do stink, but I really hope this one sticks. I want so much more for my sister than the scraps of attention Ryland gives her. She deserves someone who feels lucky to have her in his life.

"Rejection is protection," I say, parroting one of her positive affirmations back at her.

Leighton gives me a true smile. She sits up on her elbows. "You're right. This is probably the universe clearing my path for someone better."

My sister isn't someone who stays down for long and I'm relieved that she's already starting to come around. Then again, she's also a big believer in second/third/fourth chances so it's possible that Ryland will worm his way back in.

I pat her leg. "Why don't I make you some peppermint tea?"

"That would be great," she says. "Thanks."

I'm about to get off the couch when her face lights up.

"Pips, you're not wearing anything to cover your scar," she says. "I can't believe I didn't notice."

My hand flies to my neck. I forgot to put my scarf on as I was leaving Aiden's house. This is the first time my sister has seen my bare neck in ages.

Leighton reaches over and moves my hand away. "It's really not that bad," she says. "I bet once it's faded a little more you'll hardly be able to see it at all."

I'm not sure that's true—the scar isn't going to magically disappear—but it's definitely a lot better than it was in the beginning. After my surgery, I could barely look at myself in the mirror—my skin was angry and swollen and the black stitches made me feel like Frankenstein. It was also much longer than I was expecting it to be, almost half the width of my neck. My scar is still pink, still slightly raised.

But, I realize, it's part of my story. This scar is a part of me. I need to stop hiding behind a scarf and try and put the whole experience behind me. And I think I'm ready to do that. I think that I'm ready to let it go and move on with my life.

Finally.

CHAPTER
TWENTY-FIVE

"AW, NO. THAT sucks," Aiden says after I tell him that Leighton got dumped. "Is she okay?"

"She will be," I say, glancing over at him from the passenger seat. At least, she will be as long as she stays strong and doesn't take Ryland back when he starts sniffing around again. Which, if their history is anything to go by, will be sooner rather than later. He's like a reoccurring fungal infection.

I offered to stay home—Aiden could have presented the offer to the Davidsons on his own—but Leighton wouldn't hear of it. I promised that we'd order Thai and marathon bad 90s movies tonight, a tradition when one of us is going through a breakup.

Speaking of breakups…

"I'm so glad that Tim and Annabelle have agreed to sit down together for this meeting," I say as we pull into the Davidsons driveway. "I was fully expecting that we'd have to present the offer to them separately."

"Yeah, me too," Aiden replies, parking behind Annabelle's Lexus. "Ready?"

I nod. "Ready."

I grab my tote bag, inside of which is the initial offer from Susan's realtor. I'm always nervous before presenting to a client, but there's an extra layer of stress today because this is multi-million-dollar deal. A career-making deal.

Before I can get out of the car, Aiden picks up my hand and kisses my palm. "We make a great team. I've really loved working with you," he says.

My heart flutters. *Love.*

"I've really loved working with you too," I say.

I'm not just saying this because I'm about to win, but to hell with this stupid bet. Aiden deserves half of the commission. He's earned it. But also, being in a situation where one of us has to lose so the other can win isn't exactly the healthiest foundation for a relationship. Plus he's going to need the money if he plans on quitting his job.

"Alright. Let's do this," he says.

We get out of the car. Aiden does the button up on his suit jacket and adjusts his cuffs while I smooth down the front of my yellow shirt dress. My rattan Jimmy Choo wedges—bought at an end of summer sale last year on a deep discount—put me almost level with his chin. I reach to straight my scarf, forgetting for a moment that I'm not wearing one. I guess it's going to take a while to break that habit.

Aiden and I walk up to the house. He knocks on the door and a moment later, Annabelle opens it—although it takes me a moment to register that it's her, because she looks so different. Her beautiful silver hair is now dyed a deep red.

A bunch of thoughts whirl through my head at once: Annabelle's hair is red—the woman we caught with Tim had red hair—Tim doesn't have a mistress—Annabelle is the naked redhead in the pool.

Oh my god.

Aiden stiffens up beside me, so he's obviously arrived at the same conclusion.

"Wow, your hair looks great," he says.

"Thank you," Annabelle replies. "It felt like it was time to shake things up a little."

Well, she's definitely shaken me up. More than a little. I mean, it's great that she and Tim are on such good terms—getting divorced after so many years of marriage is awful and sad and it would be amazing if they managed to work things out—*however*, I'm now very worried about what this means in terms of selling their house.

My palms are sweating as Annabelle stands aside and opens the door wider, inviting us inside.

"I'm sorry about the other day," she says. "Tim and I got carried away and lost track of time. I'm so embarrassed that you discovered us like that."

"No need to be embarrassed," Aiden says smoothly. "We didn't see anything."

Not true. I saw it all. Tim's penis as he ran across the cement, his ass as he cannonballed into the pool. Annabelle's boobs floating like buoys on the water. That's all going to live rent-free in my mind forever.

"Tim, honey, Aiden and Piper are here," Annabelle calls up the stairs.

Honey. I sneak a look at her hand and yup, there's a golf-ball sized diamond solitaire on her ring finger. So their pool sexcapade wasn't just one last hurrah—they're definitely back together.

My chest feels tight but I keep smiling as Tim joins us in the foyer, the picture of relaxed and casual in jeans and a grey t-shirt, his feet bare.

"Hi guys," he says. "Good to see you both. Thanks for coming by."

I slowly let out a breath. It's possible that I'm panicking over nothing—Tim is a businessman, after all, and we're bringing him a strong offer. Surely he'll want to consider it.

Maybe they'll still want to downsize, I think. Annabelle seemed really excited about several of the listings I sent her last week. I've already made appointments to view a few of them with her.

Annabelle asks if we'd like some water or coffee, but Aiden and I both decline. We follow her and Tim into the white room. I sit down beside Aiden, pushing away memories of how I straddled him on this very couch a few weeks ago, as the newly reunited couple sits across from us.

Aiden gestures at their entwined hands. "So, this is good news," he says, smiling at them.

"Isn't it?" Annabelle's face lights up and she inches a little closer to her husband. "Thank goodness we came to our senses before it was too late."

"True love wins," Aiden says. "We're happy for you."

I nod, but I notice that Annabelle is avoiding my eyes. My stomach twists. I think this deal is about to circle the drain, taking all my dreams with it.

And sure enough, Tim clears his throat. "I know you came here to present us with an offer, but we've decided to take the house off the market," he says.

My smile freezes. I feel like I'm going to be sick.

"Are you sure?" Aiden asks. "As you know it's a seller's market and this is a really great offer. The buyer has come in just under full ask, but I think we could get her to come up a little."

Annabelle shakes her head. "It doesn't matter how much she's offered, we've made up our minds," she says. "This is our family home. We just aren't ready to give it up yet."

"We'll reconsider it in few years," Tim says.

I don't know what to say so I don't say anything. On the one hand, I'm happy for them—they're lovely people and I'm glad they've worked past their issues and are able to keep their family together—but on the other, I am devastated. Because I am screwed.

Annabelle spins her ring around on her finger. "I know this must be disappointing, especially after how much work you've both put into trying to sell our house," she says.

We *have* put a lot of work into this listing. And money. So much money. We're not going to get a dime of that back and oh god, I never should have agreed to take such a big risk. I should have put all my time and energy into drumming up other clients, focused on the little fish instead of trying to catch the big one.

"It's okay," Aiden says to her. "That's how it goes in this business sometimes. We know that."

He glances at me with thinly veiled concern. And he's right to be concerned—I'm barely keeping a lid on my emotions, in danger of totally melting down. There's a few more minutes of polite chat, which I don't really participate in, before Aiden stands up.

"We should get going," he says.

Annabelle and Tim seem relieved.

"Thanks again for understanding," she says as they lead us back into the foyer. "I really was very impressed. Especially with you, Piper."

I smile weakly at her. I can tell that Annabelle genuinely feels bad.

"Thank you for the opportunity," I reply. This may not have turned out how I hoped it would, but I do appreciate that she took a chance on me.

The knife twists a little when Tim reminds Aiden of a business meeting later in the week. Apparently they're working together on a new condo development in Point Grey. Something else that Aiden forgot to mention to me. I don't know if he does it on purpose or if he genuinely forgets because he isn't used to sharing his work life with someone. Either way, it's annoying.

As soon as the Davidsons close the door, my smile drops. Aiden and I are silent as we get in the car. Silent as he turns out of the driveway. Silent as he drives down the street.

It's not until he stops at a traffic light that he lets out a long sigh. "Well, that meeting went very differently than I expected it to."

I nod.

Aiden reaches over and takes my hand, squeezes my fingers. "I know it's disappointing, P, but there will be other listings."

I shake my head. He doesn't get it. What's merely a disappointment to him is catastrophic to me. This listing was my big break, my chance to get into the luxury market and change my life, but I'm right back where I started now. Actually, that's not true—I'm worse-off than when I started because this listing has *cost* me money. Money that I don't even have.

I pull my hand away from his. It would have been better if Aiden had won the bet and collected all our commission. At least that way I wouldn't be on the hook for half of our expenses because that money would have come off the top. But now that there is no commission, I'm going to have to pay tens of thousands of dollars that the agency fronted me out of my own pocket. Unlike Aiden, I don't have a condo building all lined up to sell. I don't have any prospective clients, I don't have money to market myself and I certainly don't have enough to send Leighton back to school.

I don't have anything.

I roll down the window to let in some air.

"I'll bring you in on another listing," Aiden says. "We'll find something else to work on together."

A dark voice whispers in my ear that the only reason he's even suggesting that we co-list again is because he still doesn't think I can do this on my own. He wants to help me but he doesn't believe in me. But I guess I can't blame him for that because I'm no longer sure I believe in myself.

"Thought you were quitting," I mutter. It's childish—pathetic, even—but instead of feeling thankful that he's willing to give me another shot, I am simmering with resentment. Aiden has plenty of opportunities. He was given everything he needed to succeed right from the beginning, which means has no clue what it's like to have to fight for what you want. He's never had to knock on strangers doors, hoping to get a lead. He's never had to hustle, not in the way that I have. Everything has just landed in his lap, been handed to him on a silver platter. And yet he wants to give all that up. He's living my dream and he wants to throw it away and do something else.

"I can hang on for a while," he says.

I shake my head. I don't want to ride his coattails and that's exactly what it would look like if I was tagged onto more of his listings.

I swallow the lump in my throat. Maybe I'm the one who should throw in the towel. Maybe this is a sign to give up. I'm sure I could convince Leighton to leave the city behind and move somewhere more affordable. She could teach yoga and I could get an office job, which I'll probably hate, but hey, at least I'll have a steady paycheck. At least I'll be off this rollercoaster.

"We'll figure this out," Aiden says, but I've already started putting the wall back up between us, brick by brick. None of what happened today is his fault but it suddenly seems like just another obstacle in a relationship that's already hit its fair share of roadblocks. That might not be reasonable or fair, but it's how I feel.

When I notice Aiden heading in the direction of his house, I ask if he would mind dropping me at my apartment instead. I need some time to clear my head. Figure out my next steps. I can't do that if we go back to his place. I'll just end up in bed with him again.

"Okay," Aiden says. He keeps casting worried looks at me, but I pretend not to notice.

The car has barely rolled to a stop in front of my building before I jump out—I don't want to give him the chance to kiss me and change my mind.

"We'll talk later," I say, closing the door. Even though I'm pretty sure there isn't anything left to talk about.

TWENTY-SIX

"WHAT'S WRONG?" LEIGHTON asks as I kick off my shoes and drop my tote bag on the floor. She's sitting cross-legged on the couch, a thick book folded face-down in her lap, her blonde hair hanging in two long damp braids.

"Headache," I say, rubbing my temples as I walk into my bedroom. "Can't talk. Need to lie down."

I climb into bed fully clothed and yank the duvet over my head. A minute later, I feel the mattress sag as Leighton sits down beside me.

"I brought you some peppermint essential oil." Her hand slips under the covers and she passes me the tiny amber roll-on bottle.

"Thanks," I mumble.

"You're probably dehydrated," she tsks. "You don't drink nearly enough water." She gets up to fetch me a glass, along with some magnesium, which she claims is more effective than aspirin, when I throw back the covers and sit up. I feel guilty letting her fuss over me when I'm totally lying to her.

"No. It's okay," I say. "I don't need anything. I don't actually have a headache."

Leighton blinks at me, confused. "Oh."

"My listing fell through." My chin quivers. Normally I wouldn't dump my problems on my sister, but I can't keep this in. I've been tamping down my emotions for far too long. I have to let them out or I'll give myself an ulcer.

She sits back down on the bed. "That sucks, Pips. I'm sorry," she says. "But there will be other listings, right?"

It's almost word for word what Aiden said to me in the car. I don't understand how the two of them always mange to look on the bright side of everything. I wish that kind of optimism came so easily to me, but it just doesn't.

"Not like this one," I say miserably. "I think it's time to find a different job."

Leighton's eyebrows rise. "You can't give up, Pips. You love your job."

"Yeah, well, clearly it doesn't love me back," I say, tears stinging my eyes. It's been forever since I last sold a property, months and months since I've had any money coming in. I've been working my ass off for the past few years and I don't really have anything to show for it. I live in a tiny apartment with my sister, I lease a vehicle I can't afford, I have a closet full of clothes that I don't even own. I'm fairly certain the universe is telling me it's time to give up the dream.

"Please don't quit yet," Leighton says. "Just give it a little longer. I have enough saved up to carry us for a while."

I stare at her. What is she talking about? She works at a bar. She teaches the occasional yoga class. Neither of those things bring in enough to support two people. Not in this city, anyway.

Still, it's sweet of her to offer. Once again, she's trying to look out for me.

"I couldn't let you do that," I say. "You've already given up so much to take care of —"

Leighton pinches my arm. "Stop it," she says. "You're my sister. That's what family is for."

"Tell that to Mom," I say, scowling at her as I rub my arm. Our mother couldn't even be bothered to send a care package, much less get on a plane to come and see me when I was sick. She's only texted me a handful of times in the past year and yet she remains confused about why I'm not particularly interested in having a relationship with her. But narcissists are gonna narcissist, I guess.

"We might not be able to count on Mom, but we can count on each other," Leighton says. "And I know you would have dropped everything if I'd been the one who got sick."

That's true, I would have. In a heartbeat.

"And I didn't give anything up," she adds.

"You dropped out of school," I point out.

She shrugs. "I was planning to do that anyway."

"What?"

"I'd already figured out that naturopathic medicine wasn't the direction I was meant to go in before you got sick," she says. "So it was an easy decision to leave school. And it was the right one because I ended up finding my true calling a few months later."

"Your true calling," I repeat. *Yoga instructor? Reiki master? Life coach?*

Leighton smiles. "ASMR."

I narrow my eyes, thinking. "Those whisper-y videos where people tap on things?"

"Yes," she says. "I started a channel on YouTube last year. ElftasticASMR. I have over three hundred thousand subscribers."

She slides her phone out of her pocket, searches for something and hands the phone to me.

I gape at a video of Leighton in prosthetic elf ears and a flower crown, drumming her nails against a wooden coaster. I guess the mystery of why she has so many pairs of press-on nails has just been solved. "Why have you never mentioned this?" I ask.

"I don't know," she says. "I guess I assumed you'd think it was weird."

I frown. "God, am I really that judgy?"

"I mean, yeah. You kind of are sometimes." But she smiles to take the sting out of her words. "But you're not the only one. Ryland doesn't get it at all."

Ugh, apparently Ryland and I have something in common—we're both judgy assholes.

I lean back against my pillow. "How did I not notice you have a whole new career?" Am I that self-involved, that unplugged from my sister's life?

"I only record when you're at work," she says. "And I do most of it my room."

"So what does ASMR stand for?" I don't really know much about it, but I want to learn. All that matters to me is that Leighton is happy. If this is what she's meant to do, then I am fully behind her. I need her to know that.

"Autonomous sensory meridian response," she says as I scroll to another video. In this one, she's wearing a bright blue wig and pretending to give the viewer a scalp massage. "It's really better if you use headphones. That way you can hear the layered sounds."

Real-life Leighton's cheeks flush as on-camera Leighton makes a bunch of clicky mouth sounds. "I know it seems silly—"

"It doesn't," I say quickly. I might not get it, but I don't have to. I just have to support her.

"I like to help people relax, ease their stress and anxiety," she says. "And I'm really good at it."

"I'm not surprised." I can personally attest to my sister's ability to make people feel better. "But I am amazed. I'm really proud of you."

"Yeah?"

I nod.

My bedroom door squeaks open and Mr. Tumnus saunters in. He jumps on my bed and kneads my duvet before curling into a ball beside me.

"Aw, see? He loves you," Leighton says as he starts to loudly purr.

I smile. The deal with the Davidsons may have fallen through, my future as a realtor—and in general—may be in question, I may not know what is going to happen with Aiden, but I have finally won over this cat.

I'll take that as a victory.

MY STOMACH IS in knots as I sit down at my desk the next morning. The thought of telling Madeline that the Davidsons pulled out makes me light-headed—she's invested tens of thousands of dollars of the agency's money in this listing with the expectation that I'd be able to pay it back when the house sold. And I have no idea how I'm going to do that now.

I'm the first one in, so the office is quiet. I turn on my laptop, my heart skipping as my phone chimes with a text. I don't want to check my messages because I'm scared it's Aiden again and I still don't know what to say to him. I know it's wrong, I know he doesn't understand why I'm so upset, but I don't want to respond to him until I've figured out exactly what I'm going to do. Talking to him will only cloud my judgement.

I sigh and rub my eyes. I should never have pretended that I had money to sink into our marketing plan. My stupid ego kept me from admitting to Aiden that I couldn't afford it. If I confess now I'll look like a total fool. Knowing Aiden, he'll want to solve this for me somehow, but I can't let him dig me out of this hole. If I want to save any of my self-respect I have to do it myself.

"Hello, hello," Tyler calls out. I glance up to see him breezing towards me, Freddie tucked under one arm.

"Good morning," I say.

Tyler places Freddie on the dog bed underneath his desk, then sits down in his chair.

"Here," he says, handing me a pastry bag. "I brought you a cruffin."

"Thanks." Cruffins are my favorite.

Tyler shrugs. "I figured you'd need the sugar to drown your sorrows in when I tell you the bad news."

I frown at him. Oh god, I don't think I can handle any more bad news…

"Maisie was adopted," he says. "I went by the shelter last night and they told me someone snapped her up yesterday."

My heart sinks. I knew this was coming, of course, but that doesn't mean I'm not crushed. Mr. Tumnus is finally warming up to me, which is great, but I still think Leighton and I could have made room for Maisie, too. I should have tried harder to convince her.

"I hope she found a good home," I say, taking a bite of my sympathy cruffin. Hopefully whoever adopted her loves her as much as I do. That dog deserves everything.

"Me too," Tyler says. His eyes skate over my bare neck, taking in my scar. He smiles and I give him a small smile back, our silent conversation speaking volumes.

I'm really going to miss working with him.

I'm not sure what I'm going to do with the rest of my life, but I've resolved to start job hunting when I get home from work tonight. There has to be something else I'm qualified to do, something that will pay me real cash money—and quickly. Leighton is still trying to talk me into sticking with real estate, letting her ASMR career support us until I get on my feet, but I think it's time to admit that some mountains are just too high to climb.

I'm halfway through my cruffin when the front door opens and Madeline walks in. My heart drops. She usually comes into the office much later. I was hoping for a bit more time to prepare myself before I had to talk to her.

"Morning," Madeline says as she passes by our cubicles.

"Morning," we chorus back.

"Tyler," I whisper as soon as she's disappeared into her office.

"Yes," he whispers back.

I scoot my chair closer to his desk. "The Davidsons pulled out," I say. "They've cancelled the listing."

His eyes widen. "Oh shit."

"Yeah."

"What are you going to do?"

"What can I do?" I say. The deal is dead. That's all there is to it.

"Maybe you can help the buyer find something else," Tyler suggests.

I shake my head. "She already has an agent."

Suddenly I can sympathize with the pressure Aiden was under when he poached my client. Different circumstances, sure, but the temptation to get ahead in any manner possible is in me, too. I'm just better at resisting it. Although to be fair, I don't believe that he'd make that same choice again. I think he's learned his lesson.

"You should ask Aiden if he has another luxury listing you can piggyback on," Tyler says. "I bet he'd bring you on."

"He offered but I declined."

His jaw drops. "Why on earth would you do that?"

"Because he doesn't believe I can do it on my own."

Tyler shakes his head. "Seems to me like you're the one who doesn't believe in you," he says.

"That's not true." Is it?

"This man is trying to give you a leg up," he says. "This should be the easiest yes ever. And yet you're turning him down because…?"

"Because I don't feel like I deserve it."

Wow. There it is. The real reason I didn't take Aiden up on his suggestion that we co-list another property.

"Faith, trust and pixie dust," Tyler says. "That's the key."

"You sound like my sister," I say.

He smiles. "She's a smart girl."

But there is one other reason I didn't immediately jump on Aiden's offer. "Don't you think that people would talk?" I ask Tyler. Word will eventually get out that Aiden and I are involved. So how is that going to look? Like I'm sleeping my way up the ladder.

"I know what you're thinking and stop it," Tyler says. "I don't see why you can't mix business with pleasure. Who cares what other people think?"

I mean, I do. I wish I didn't, but I do.

"The people who know and love you will know the truth," he says. "And *everybody* uses their connections to get ahead, Piper. And if they don't, then they really should."

I sigh. He's right—this business is built on connections. I have to find a way to put my insecurities aside and let Aiden help me. I have so much to lose if I don't.

Tyler can obviously tell I'm softening because he says, "Get over yourself and call Aiden. Tell him you changed your mind."

"I will," I say. But this is really a conversation I should have with him in person. I need to apologize for overreacting yesterday. And for ignoring his messages. And for shutting him out again.

And if he forgives me for all of that, then I'll ask him if he'd still be willing to co-list with me. That's assuming, of course, that he hasn't already changed his mind about working with me. Or quit his job.

And if he has, well, we'll find a way through it. Because real estate isn't my only dream—somewhere along the way Aiden became a dream, too.

My inbox chimes. I'm feeling a little big lighter as I slide my chair back over to my desk and glance at my computer.

TO: Piper Anderson <piperanderson@pinnaclerealty.ca>
FROM: Andrew Lamont <DrewLamont768@gmail.com>
RE: Recommendation

Hi Piper,

My sister, Annabelle, passed your contact information on to me. My wife and I are looking for a house in West Van in the six-to-seven-million-dollar range and she recommended I get in touch with you...

I grin as I scan the rest of the email. Leighton would say that this is the universe conspiring to help me, dropping a client into my lap just when I need one the most. Fate, luck, serendipity—whatever you want to call it, I'm finally ready to surrender and trust that things will work out. I'm going to stop waiting for the other shoe to drop.

Faith, trust and pixie dust, I think as I hit reply.

CHAPTER
TWENTY-SEVEN

MADELINE TOOK THE news about the Davidsons surprisingly well—of course, landing another VIP client definitely softened the blow. Annabelle's brother and his wife have already fallen in love with the photos of a property I sent them and we're going to tour it tomorrow. There are no guarantees, obviously, but I'm hopeful that they'll put in an offer.

Madeline also let me off the hook for the cost of marketing the Davidsons property, chalking it up to the cost of doing business. Thank goodness because I was terrified I'd be buried under that debt for a long, long time. Bonus: Tyler promised to keep the story of me betting my commission in the vault, so Madeline doesn't need to know just how big of a fool I was.

It's mid-afternoon when I turn onto Aiden's street. His car is parked in front of his house. I pull in behind him, then get out of my car and walk up to his door, my stomach in knots. I've pushed him away so many times already that I'm afraid that this time I might have pushed him away for good.

I take a deep breath and knock on the door. A minute passes, then two, but Aiden doesn't answer. I knock a little harder, second guessing my decision to just show up at his house unannounced. I probably should have texted him, asked if it was okay to come by, but I didn't want to give him the chance to turn me down.

I've just pulled out my phone to send him a message when I hear music coming from the backyard. I slide my phone into my pocket and walk around the side of the house, Jimmy Buffett becoming louder with each step.

My heart skips when I spot Aiden sitting in an Adirondack chair, a straw fedora tipped over his eyes. He's in cargo shorts, his chest bare, that sexy raven tattoo on display. I want him, more than I've ever wanted anyone else. He is my great love. My person.

"Hi," I say.

Aiden opens his eyes and glances over at me. "Hey," he replies.

He doesn't make a move to get up, so I walk across the grass towards him. His hurt is obvious in the tense line of his shoulders, the way his fingers tighten on the arms of his chair. I used to think that nothing ever got to him, that he cruised through life without taking anything too seriously. But now that I've seen below the surface, I know just how deeply he feels things.

"I owe you an apology," I say. "For yesterday. And for all the other times I shut you out. I'm sorry."

Aiden shrugs. "You don't trust me, Piper," he says. "And that's my fault. We wouldn't be in this position if I hadn't stolen your client." He lets out a long breath. "I wish I could take that back, but I can't. And I don't know where we go from here."

My stomach lurches at the thought that he might be giving up on us. He's right, we might not be in this position if he hadn't betrayed me, but then again, we each wouldn't be who we are today if we hadn't gone through that. I think we've both grown and changed in the past two years. We're not the same people we were back then.

"We're both going to continue to make mistakes," I say. "Neither of us is perfect."

"But we're perfect for each other?" Aiden says, holding back a smile.

I nod. It's cheesy, maybe, but it's true.

Hope floods through me as he stands up and reaches for my hand.

"We're in this together, then. Deal?" he asks.

I smile, light-headed with relief. Everything is going to be okay. "Deal," I say.

We shake on it and then Aiden pulls me into his arms. I loop my hands around his neck, waiting for him to kiss me when I hear a dog bark behind me. I turn around and there, standing in the open doorway of Aiden's house, is Maisie.

"Oh my god," I cry as she bounds towards us. I bend down to pet her and she turns in excited circles. "Maisie, what are you doing here?"

Aiden crouches down beside me. "I'd been thinking about adopting a dog for a while," he says. "I couldn't stop thinking about her after we took her out for that walk so I went back to the shelter yesterday and lucky for me she was still there."

"I'm so glad," I repeat, glowing with happiness for Maisie and for me. Aiden's going to be the best dog dad. And I can help him take care of her.

"It was very easy to fall in love with her," he says. His blue-hazel eyes meet mine and a charge of electricity shoots through me. I don't think he's talking about Maisie. I do think he's nervous about telling me he loves me outright in case he scares me off again.

But that's not going to happen. Not today, not tomorrow. Not ever. I'm as sure of that as I've ever been of anything.

"It was easy to fall in love with you, too," I say.

Aiden grins. He helps me stand and then we're kissing and then he's leading me towards the house, towards his bedroom, towards our new life together. Wherever it takes us.

ACKNOWLEDGEMENTS

Thank you to Sandy Hall, Randi Hirte, Michelle Zink and Stephanie Anderson at Alt 19 Creative for their help bringing this book to life.

Thank you to my friends and family for their unwavering support and encouragement, especially: Julia Adamson, Carla Cassone, Erin Cassone, Dallas DePaige, Dawn Dingman, Michelle Gillett, Leiko Greaves, Joy Honeybourn, Claire Kann, Pam Morrison, Stacie Palivos, Shani Petroff, Justyna Pyzowska, and Missy Robinson, Kiandra Rodgers, Taylor Silva, Elizabeth Terlicher, Kylie Wasser and Kelly Watt.

And thank you, always, to Tony and Lila.

ABOUT THE AUTHOR

Amelia Hall loves beach sunsets, traveling and being swept away by a good book. When she's not writing, you can find her reading, watching a romantic comedy or hanging out with family and friends.

She is the author of several young adult books (under a different name) that have been positively reviewed by NPR and School Library Journal. One of her books received a starred review from Publisher's Weekly, while another was chosen as a Junior Library Guild gold standard selection. She is also a recipient of a Canada Council for the Arts Grant.

Originally from Vancouver, BC, Amelia now lives in a quaint town in southwestern Ontario that could definitely be the backdrop of a Hallmark movie.

KEEP UP WITH AMELIA:

NEWSLETTER: ameliahallauthor.com
INSTAGRAM: @ameliahallauthor
TIKTOK: @ameliahallauthor
FACEBOOK: Amelia Hall author